MURDER IN GRASSE

THE MAGGIE NEWBERRY MYSTERIES BOOK 22

SUSAN KIERNAN-LEWIS

Murder in Grasse. Book 22 of the Maggie Newberry Mysteries.

Copyright © 2023 by Susan Kiernan-Lewis

All rights reserved.

BOOKS BY SUSAN KIERNAN-LEWIS

The Maggie Newberry Mysteries
Murder in the South of France
Murder à la Carte
Murder in Provence
Murder in Paris
Murder in Aix
Murder in Nice
Murder in the Latin Quarter
Murder in the Abbey
Murder in the Bistro
Murder in Cannes
Murder in Grenoble
Murder in the Vineyard
Murder in Arles
Murder in Marseille
Murder in St-Rémy
Murder à la Mode
Murder in Avignon
Murder in the Lavender
Murder in Mont St-Michel

Murder in the Village
Murder in St-Tropez
Murder in Grasse
Murder in Monaco
A Provençal Christmas: A Short Story
A Thanksgiving in Provence
Laurent's Kitchen

The Claire Baskerville Mysteries
Déjà Dead
Death by Cliché
Dying to be French
Ménage à Murder
Killing it in Paris
Murder Flambé
Deadly Faux Pas
Toujours Dead
Murder in the Christmas Market
Deadly Adieu
Murdering Madeleine
Death à la Drumstick

The Stranded in Provence Mysteries
Parlez-Vous Murder?
Crime and Croissants
Accent on Murder
A Bad Éclair Day
Croak, Monsieur!
Death du Jour
Murder Très Gauche
Wined and Died
A French Country Christmas

The Irish End Games

Free Falling
Going Gone
Heading Home
Blind Sided
Rising Tides
Cold Comfort
Never Never
Wit's End
Dead On
White Out
Black Out
End Game

The Mia Kazmaroff Mysteries
Reckless
Shameless
Breathless
Heartless
Clueless
Ruthless

Ella Out of Time
Swept Away
Carried Away
Stolen Away

The French Women's Diet

1

The glittering blue slice of the Mediterranean sparkled in Maggie's rear view mirror. She smiled as she turned to look at Grace in the passenger's seat as they drove out of Cannes where they'd just had lunch and picked up their rental car.

Grace was wearing a stunning white poplin shirt dress by Alexander McQueen. She looked as fresh as the blanket of spring flowers that surrounded them.

"Excited?" Maggie asked her.

Grace adjusted her sunglasses, looking every bit the picture of the iconic style maker, Grace Kelly, whom she was named after.

"Seriously?" she said. "I've been wanting to go to Grasse practically since I moved to France."

"Knowing your obsession with perfume," Maggie said with a smile, "I'm shocked you haven't gone before now."

Maggie and Grace lived within ten kilometers of each other now in Provence and had been best friends for over twenty years—with a few breaks in between.

"Well, I'm going now," Grace said. "And that's what matters.

Did I mention I'm going to have them help me create a signature fragrance for *Dormir*?"

"Only a few times," Maggie said teasingly.

Dormir was the *mas* in Provence that had once belonged to their dear friend Danielle and her first husband. When Eduard died in prison, Danielle sold the property to Laurent who immediately took the adjoining vineyards, added them to his own holdings, and renovated the property, making it into a bed and breakfast which Grace managed for him.

"I've just heard from so many social media influencers," Grace said, her face puckering into a frown of seriousness, "that something like a signature scent can make all the difference in attracting new guests."

"I'm sure it will be very helpful."

"I know you think it's silly," Grace said as she turned to admire the scenery along the winding road out of town. "But I don't care."

"I don't think it's silly," Maggie said.

The hill leading into Grasse seemed to showcase the dozens of wealthy private homes, multi-level hotels and brilliant omnipresent fields of jasmine, and lavender visible on every side of the rocky hillside road.

Maggie took in a breath of the sweet spring air, imagining that she could already detect the heady fragrances of Grasse.

Known as the perfume capital of the world, Grasse although nestled in the hills of the Alpes-Maritimes department of France was removed from the glitter of the Côte d'Azure—ten miles northwest of Cannes—so it had kept its provincial charm intact.

It was Maggie's husband Laurent who had suggested she and Grace go to Grasse and enjoy a girls-only weekend. Maggie and Laurent were raising his four-year-old granddaughter and while Maggie was only too delighted to do it, she had to admit that childcare was more exhausting than she remembered.

"I'm glad Laurent and Amelie are staying with Danielle at *Dormir* while we're away," Grace said. "She's been acting downright weird lately."

"Weird how?" Maggie asked.

"Secretive and jumpy."

"That does not sound like Danielle."

"I know, right? I asked her about it but you know how the French are. She was nearly insulted that I would point out the obvious about her behavior."

"Danielle's a dear," Maggie said.

"Of course she is! She's helped me raise Zouzou *and* Philippe plus I don't know what I'd do without her to help me run *Dormir*."

Danielle had moved to *Dormir* to help Grace after the death of her second husband Jean-Luc.

Maggie turned a sharp corner and faced a dramatic presentation of ochre and ivory-colored homes stacked in stairstep fashion one on top of the other.

"Is it strange that I'm expecting to smell the perfumes as we drive in?" Grace said.

Maggie laughed. "I was thinking the same thing!"

"You don't realize until you leave home how much you needed the break," Grace said softly.

Maggie turned to glance at her. She wanted to ask if everything was okay between her and her ex-husband Windsor who'd moved in with Grace last year. Windsor was in Atlanta for the next couple of weeks visiting his young daughter by his second wife. Maggie knew that Grace would talk about it when she was ready.

"I was shocked you were willing to leave, what with Jemmy and Luc coming home," Grace said.

Years earlier, when the two older boys had left for college Maggie had struggled with empty nest syndrome which only intensified last year when her youngest Mila left home. All three children had chosen universities in the States where they all, except for Luc, had dual citizenship.

Having little Amelie at home had helped immensely in Maggie's feeling of loss over the older children leaving, but Grace was right. In no other time could Maggie have imagined leaving Domaine-St-Buvard for some "me time" knowing her two boys were coming home.

"They'll be there when I get home," she said.

"Is everything okay with them?" Grace asked.

Maggie smiled ruefully. She wasn't the only one who could pick up on emotional undercurrents and unspoken subtext. She hadn't even had a single night before leaving for Grasse to see Luc—he was due to come in today—but in that brief time, she'd found herself uneasy, not only about him, but also about Jemmy. She'd been careful not to mention it to Laurent since he scoffed at her intuitions. She wasn't in the mood to have her fears dismissed out of hand.

"I think so," she said. "I'm half sorry Luc is coming so soon. If Laurent had more time alone with Jemmy, he'd probably be able to worm out of him if something really *is* going on with him."

"Oh?" Grace said. "Is something going on with Jemmy?"

"That's just it. I don't know. He's had this great job at Delmont's Designs in Atlanta for the past year and all of a sudden he's taking the summer off to come home to France. You don't think that's odd?"

Jem had graduated from Georgia Tech two years earlier and immediately settled in Atlanta. While Maggie was from Atlanta —and her mother and brother still lived there, not to mention Jem's cousin Nicole—she was disappointed that he hadn't opted to come back to France.

"Good question," Grace said. "Did you ask him?"

"I did. He said it's not unusual since the pandemic for employees to take time off."

"So he didn't quit?"

"He says he's still employed there."

"But you don't believe it?"

Maggie laughed. "I don't know what to believe. But trust me, I'll get to the bottom of it. Or Laurent will."

"I'd ask you how Mila is doing," Grace said, "but since she's with Zouzou, I pretty much know."

Mila was spending the summer in Atlanta with her maternal grandmother after her first year at the University of Florida. Grace's youngest daughter Zouzou was visiting her from Paris where she worked as a junior *patisserie* chef.

"What about Laurent?" Grace asked. "Will he try to convince the boys to stay, do you think?"

As the owner of a three-hundred-hectare vineyard, Laurent was busy nearly all the time in every season. He hired seasonal help of course, but there was always more work to be done. Jem and Luc's involvement in the vineyard would be a monumental help. But not likely.

Even Luc, who was French, had stayed in California after graduating from college there.

"Time will tell, I suppose," Maggie said with a deep sigh, but when she said the words, she felt a queasy twist deep in her stomach, a feeling that didn't at all match earlier expectation of a relaxing weekend.

2

The gardens of *Dormir* were slowly coming to life. Meandering gravel paths intersected careful flower beds and wove past patches of bright color with the marigolds, daylilies and nasturtiums that Danielle had planted.

Laurent was feeding small sticks into his wood grill which sat on a stack of cinderblocks. The scent of aromatic burning wood filled the air.

Amelie ran squealing past Danielle where she stood, flower basket in one hand, trying to decide which blooms to cut for tonight's table. Philippe's dog Kip and the two terriers from Domaine St-Buvard were fast on the child's heels.

"Don't let her get too close to the grill, Laurent!" Danielle said as she turned to peer at him from under her straw hat.

"Don't worry," he said, glancing at his four-year-old granddaughter who had stopped to pet each of the three dogs. "She's fine."

The child turned and ran again with the dogs, coming to the perimeter stone wall that encircled the *Dormir* property and hesitated. She put her hands on the wall and Laurent could see her brain working. She knew that everything past the wall was out of bounds for her. She turned her head to glance back at him. The sun shone on her head of brown curls. She was a pretty child with blue eyes and an elfin shape to her face. Laurent turned his eyes back to the grill. If she was going to decide to disobey him, he wouldn't make it easy for her.

He picked up a handful of dried grape vines that he'd had Amelie collect the week before at Domaine St-Buvard and tucked them on top of the burning wood on the grill.

When he turned back to look at Amelie, he saw that she had made her choice. She was gathering the wild lavender that grew along the stone path leading back to the main house. He nodded with satisfaction.

Maggie often accused him of being too lenient with the child and he supposed that might be true. He remembered being much stricter with Jem and Mila when they were small.

He thought of Amelie's mother, Elodie, his eldest child—the one he'd never known existed until two years ago. He thought of how Elodie had never gotten the benefit of anyone caring enough to be strict with her. His heart flinched as he remembered that terrible night in St-Tropez—during a wedding anniversary trip with Maggie. The night he'd found the body of his daughter, his first child.

The pain in his heart had not healed, not at the loss of her or from the stark realization that he would never get a chance to make it up to her or get to know her.

"*Opa?*" Amelie said.

Laurent was surprised to see she was suddenly at his hip and much too close to the grill. Tempted to pull her away from it, he hesitated. Maggie was right. He was too indulgent with Amelie. And that would not serve her well as she got older.

"The grill is hot, *chérie*," he said, hoping his warning would be enough.

He watched her eye the grill, fascinated. She wasn't willful but neither was she as compliant as Mila and Jemmy had been as children.

As Maggie often said, Amelie was a whole new ballgame.

"Laurent! Don't let her touch that!" Danielle called out, a thread of hysteria in her voice.

"I'm not, *Mámère!*" Amelie called back to Danielle, almost indignantly.

It was then that Laurent realized that Amelie had in fact been about to touch the grill to see for herself. It would have been a painful but necessary life lesson, but he found himself grateful to Danielle.

"Go wash up," he said to Amelie. "Dinner is nearly ready."

"My hands aren't dirty," she said, holding them up where anyone could see evidence of dirt and grass stains.

"Go now or lose dessert," Laurent said, annoyed that she'd made him threaten her instead of just accepting his word—again, as the older children would have.

Amelie sighed heavily and ran her hand through her short dark hair before turning to make her way back to the house. Laurent saw Danielle drop her gardening trowel in the basket at her feet in order to follow her. There was much inside the house where a child could hurt herself. Things to burn her, cut her, poison her. He sighed. Always there would be a threat and danger. Knowing it didn't mean he could accept it. He might not be as bad as Danielle in showing it, but the need to protect the girl was every bit as powerful.

Amelie was their precious foundling. The one they'd rescued less than nine months ago. The one who belonged to them by blood and primogeniture —but in other ways never would.

Laurent wondered if he would ever forgive himself for the life Amelie had led before coming to Domaine St-Buvard.

His phone rang and he felt for it inside his jeans pocket. A glance at the screen told him it was Frère Jean. He hesitated before answering.

Normally at this time of year, Laurent was busy running the vineyard and managing the series of mini homes he'd built for the constant influx of refugees to the area—all of whom were initially sheltered and fed by the nearby monastery, *l'Abbaye de Sainte-Trinité*, which was run by Frère Jean. Laurent employed the young people who showed up at the monastery to work in his vineyard—especially during harvest time. Those that showed an affinity for the work were offered more or less permanent accommodations in one of his little houses.

"*Allo, mon frère,*" he said, answering the phone.

"*Allo,* Laurent," Frère Jean said. "How are you on this fine day?"

"I am well, *mon frère.* How can I help you?"

Laurent glanced at the plate of seasoned Pollock fillets before him. If it wasn't an emergency, he should be able to at least grill them before he had to leave.

"A family has come needing a place for the night," Frère Jean said. "Perhaps the week. I was hoping you might have something?"

Not an emergency, then.

"I have a vacancy," Laurent said. "Have they eaten?"

"They are in the process, *mon vieux.*"

"*Bon.* Do they have transportation?"

"I'm afraid not."

"*D'accord.* I will come within the hour."

"*Merci*, Laurent," Frère Jean said.

As he disconnected with the monk, Laurent heard the sound of a car driving up the *Dormir* driveway, gravel crunching loudly under its tires. He dipped his fingers into a glass of water on the table beside him and scattered the droplets onto the fire. It hissed. He carefully laid the fillets on the grill, then glanced back at the house where he saw his two sons Jemmy and Luc with a young woman walk up the path toward the house.

He glanced back at the grill, the fragrance of the dried grape vines wafting up and around his head like an aromatic cloud. He wiped his hands on a towel hanging from a handle on the grill. He could already hear Amelie's squeals of joy as she greeted the newcomers—her brother Jem, although technically her nephew, and Luc her adopted brother, although technically her first cousin.

Laurent smiled. Maggie was right about that too.

No matter how complicated it looks on paper, it only matters how it works in real life.

He turned to join his family, his heart light and happily expectant. At least for the moment.

3

The weekend house rental would do nicely, Maggie decided as she wheeled her luggage into the single bedroom with its two single beds. Grace chose the bed nearest the ensuite bathroom and Maggie took the other one.

Grace immediately examined the soaps—hand milled in Arles—that had been placed on their beds along with hand towels.

"You already have soaps at *Dormir*, don't you?" Maggie asked as she unpacked her sundresses and walking sandals. She expected to do a lot of walking this weekend.

"Yes, but not personalized," Grace said. "I should have the *Dormir* logo imprinted on ours."

"Is that very expensive to do?"

Maggie's voice was light, and she hated that Grace turned to look at her when she said it. *Dormir* was owned by Laurent and managed by Grace. While Grace had made the bed and breakfast successful not only with her natural acuity on social media but by her genius at shopping for just the right furnishings to make each of the three little cottages of *Dormir* exquisite and quintessentially French, the fact was that the bills would come to Laurent.

"Not particularly," Grace said with an arched eyebrow.

Maggie was determined not to make another comment the whole weekend long that might appear to criticize Grace over her spending. Laurent had told her over and over again that the *gîte* was doing fine and that Grace—regardless of her excesses in the past—was not spending out of bounds.

Maggie held up a linen sundress.

"What do you think? Too summery for dinner tonight?"

Grace smiled, clearly aware of Maggie's artless attempt to reroute the conversation topic.

"It's perfect," she said. "Did you bring a shawl? The temperatures might drop."

Maggie pulled out a pale pink pashmina from her suitcase.

"That'll work," Grace said. "Could you *believe* all those pink umbrellas hanging over the street when we drove into town?"

Brightly colored canvas umbrellas had fluttered in the gentle breeze, making a dramatic show against the ochre-colored houses—most with laundry hanging from balconies down each tiny, labyrinthine street.

"I heard they do that every spring in honor of the Grasse May rose," Maggie said. "Supposedly, it only blooms in May."

"Very romantic," Grace said absentmindedly.

Maggie finished unpacking, reminded once more that Grace seemed to have something on her mind this weekend—and it wasn't Maggie's earlier tactless comment about her spending habits.

After a lovely stroll from their rented cottage down rue Jean Ossola to the historic section they stopped at a café for coffees. Grasse appeared to be a collection of large squares, sprouting narrow alleys and steep staircases, with medieval ruins scattered among the cafés and shops. Leafy plane trees shaded the town squares and café tables.

The café they chose, Café Constant, was popular but not too crowded. Lights bobbed on a wire overhead and a simple blue and white striped awning stretched the full length of the café. Maggie and Grace sat on the terrace so as not to miss a moment of the street life they had come to Grasse to enjoy.

As she sipped her coffee, Maggie noticed a handsome young man watching her. He sat loose-limbed and relaxed, as if he owned the café, his lips full and smirking. When he saw that she'd caught him looking, he curled his lip in a sneer and looked away.

"Did you see that?" Maggie said indignantly to Grace.

"Good-looking men often don't feel the need to be charming, too," Grace noted. "They can get by on the bare minimum in the behavior department."

"Even so, it's pretty bad when you can tell he's a jerk before he even opens his mouth," Maggie commented with annoyance.

After finishing their coffees and soaking up the weak sun—it was supposed to rain later—they walked down the street to the Musée International de la Parfumerie. The museum was away from the main section of the village where most tourists seemed to be drawn, and Maggie was glad to have an hour to wander through the building and read about the heritage of perfumes from this area.

As soon as they stepped back outside, it began to lightly sprinkle which spurred them to scurry beneath the nearest overhanging eaves as they made their way back to their rental apartment. They'd decided that, in spite of their recent coffees, an afternoon nap sounded just the thing.

"I'm going to totally relax while I'm here," Grace said as she kicked off her shoes next to her bed.

"Me, too," Maggie said as she texted Laurent that they'd arrived safely and asked how things were at *Dormir*.

<All is well, chérie. We will survive but barely.>

Haha. *Funny guy*, Maggie thought wryly before putting a heart on his text and kicking off her own shoes. She noticed that Grace had just put her own phone down. Maggie imagined she'd been trying to call Windsor.

As Maggie closed her eyes, she smiled again at Laurent's text. She knew he wanted her to enjoy this weekend and her time away from child duties. With everything else on his plate, she couldn't help but feel her heart squeeze with gratitude and love for him that even after twenty-six years of marriage and three children, he always did his best to look out for her.

For dinner that evening, Maggie chose her pale blue sundress with matching pashmina and opted for plain sandals. She had long since stopped trying to compete with Grace in the fashion department—Grace, who could wear a garbage bag and look chic. They walked down to La Petite Table, a restaurant they'd seen earlier that day and had called in a reservation.

Maggie instantly registered that La Petite Table was the kind of homey, friendly restaurant that Laurent loved. It was a place where you were sure to get a stellar *coq au vin* or some other home-cooked meal prepared and served to perfection. The dining room gave glimpses of the kitchen which featured open cabinetry with upholstered banquette seating which gave the interior an organized but cozy look. She and Grace both ordered bowls of Cassoulet.

"How's Windsor doing in Atlanta?" Maggie asked.

Grace made a face and reached for her glass of Sancerre.

"I can't say," she said, "since I haven't heard from him."

Maggie frowned. Windsor had been gone for three days. He'd taken their grandson Philippe with him so that he might get to know Peoria, Windsor's daughter by his second wife and the main reason for Windsor's trip.

"Seriously?" Maggie said. "What's going on?"

Grace sighed.

"I know he's busy there. He's feels guilty as hell for dropping out of Peoria's life."

Guilty or not, Maggie thought, he can at least send a text to Grace letting her know how things are going.

"I'm sure Susie doesn't make it easy," Maggie prompted.

She knew Windsor's relationship with his ex-wife wasn't a harmonious one, especially after Windsor came back to France to reunite with Grace, his first wife.

"She doesn't," Grace agreed. "She badmouths Windsor to Peoria all the time."

"That's terrible. It's such a burden on the child when parents do that. Where's he staying while he's in town?"

"With Susie."

Maggie's eyes widened. Windsor had lived in Atlanta for nearly eight years. Not only was he perfectly able to afford a top tier hotel for the time he was visiting, he had plenty of friends there.

"So things are *less* acrimonious than I thought," she said.

"Oh, don't start, darling," Grace said with a sigh. "They are still plenty acrimonious. It's just that Susie made the offer—probably so she could slip into Windsor's room at night and garrote him—and Windsor said yes because, well, you know."

"Because it gave him constant access to Peoria," Maggie said. She looked at Grace with surprise. "Surely you're not worried about Windsor and his ex-wife?"

"I don't know what I am, darling. Honestly, he's been acting a little distant for a few weeks leading up to the trip."

"He probably had lots on his mind."

"On my bad days I imagine that maybe all that crap he tells me about Susie is a lie."

"Oh, Grace, don't be silly. You trust Windsor."

"Do I? I guess so."

Maggie's eyebrows drew together in concern. This wasn't at all like Grace. She was used to being the most desired woman in the room. And from what Maggie had always seen of Windsor's behavior, he adored her. On the other hand, Grace wasn't a fool. If she thought she was picking up on strange behavior from Windsor, Maggie wouldn't discount the idea.

Surely, Windsor wouldn't be so mad to let her go a second time!

The cassoulets came served in individual and colorfully glazed *cassoles*. The bowls of meat and bean stew were crusted on top with breadcrumbs, the exquisite aroma nearly lifting Maggie out of her chair in rapture. Their server brought a basket of fresh baguette chunks and a small dish of cornichons.

"Enough about me, dearest," Grace said as she picked up her fork. "Tell me about your book."

Maggie had been writing a cozy mystery for the past two years and had been struggling to finish it.

"Oh, you know," she said evasively. "It's coming along."

"You don't have to talk about it if you don't want to."

"It's not that. It's just that I've sort of convinced myself that if it's this much of a challenge, perhaps it's not something I should be doing. That's one of the reasons I chose to come to Grasse when Laurent suggested a weekend away. I think I'd like to write an article on Grasse and its place as the perfume capital of the world."

"Good idea, darling. Because *that's* never been done before," Grace said wryly.

"Laugh if you want," Maggie said. "But I've learned to jump on those things that stir a visceral interest in me. So I'm jumping."

"Fair enough. What publication are you writing it for?"

"I'll worry about that later."

"Great strategy, Miss Scarlett."

After that Grace seemed happy enough to let the topic go and focus on her meal. Maggie turned her attention to her own cassoulet and found it as good as she'd ever had. Its hearty mixture of white beans, pork and duck confit warmed her up on the cool night and gave her a sense of luxury and pampering.

She glanced around at the other diners and saw so many smiling and engaging in intimate conversations and found herself forgetting for a moment whatever Grace was keeping to herself as she experienced a fleeting sense of the contentment she'd felt earlier in the day.

4

The dinner table had been set in the garden with mismatched faience that Danielle and Grace had found in various flea markets around Provence. Laurent had strung lights on poles over the garden terrace a few years back and tonight the lights bobbed in the evening breeze, giving a swaying, relaxing atmosphere to the table setting.

Amelie sat next to Danielle with all three dogs by her chair. Jem and his American girlfriend Natalie sat beside each other and Luc sat opposite Danielle.

Danielle smiled at the children and felt how each of them —Luc, Jem, and Amelie—was so very special to her. While she'd never had children of her own, she had spent the last twenty years of her life as a part of this family, helping to raise five grandchildren who weren't hers by blood but who she had no doubt loved her as if she were.

Jemmy was tall and dark, like his father, but his eyes were blue like Maggie's and tonight his handsome face was more serious than Danielle was accustomed to seeing. He fiddled with his wine glass but had drunk little. Laurent had left moments after plating the meal of perfectly grilled fish with potatoes Dauphinoise—one of her specialties—and cherry tomatoes from the garden. It was not unusual for Laurent to be called away to the monastery where the needs of the homeless and the lost were many and constant.

"I can't believe Dad had to leave," Luc said as he gazed at Jem's American friend Natalie. "You'd love him, Nat. He's a total force of nature."

Luc, also a Dernier by blood but the son of Laurent's brother Gerard, was also tall but wiry. He had the Dernier brown eyes, eyes that were always searching. His eyes told you all you needed to know about the first fifteen years of his life.

Amelie had jumped up to sit in Luc's lap, squirming and obviously uncomfortable but not willing to surrender his lap to sit in her own chair no matter how many admonishing glances Danielle gave her.

The American girl Natalie leaned across the table and tapped Luc's hand in a suggestive manner, her eyes large and seductive.

There is no other word for it.

"If he's anything like you, I can only imagine," she said.

Danielle was surprised at the show of coquetry since she was sure Natalie was Jemmy's girlfriend. There was something about her that unsettled Danielle. She decided that it might be a good thing Laurent wasn't here this evening. Not because he would be uncomfortable seeing this brazen American girl flirt with both his sons, but because Danielle was sure the girl would flirt with Laurent as well.

Laurent *was* a force of nature, of that nobody could deny. He was also tall and handsome. Danielle knew for a fact that there had been many times when Maggie had been uncomfortable with the female attention Laurent couldn't help but attract.

As if she ever had anything to worry about.

"This potato dish is amazing, Danielle," Natalie said, turning her gaze to Danielle.

Danielle was familiar if not at all accustomed to the younger generation calling her by her first name. She realized she would never get used to it. In her world, it was a sign of disrespect to speak to your elders as if they were your equals. She wondered if Jem had told Natalie ahead of time to call her *Madame Alexandre*? She glanced at Jem who was glowering into his plate and decided that of course he'd told her.

"So what is it you do, Natalie?" Danielle asked politely.

"Me? Well, just about anyone who's willing, really," Natalie said with a giggle as she looked from Luc to Jem.

"Natalie is a student," Jem said hurriedly. "At Georgia State in Atlanta. She's studying social media."

"I see," Danielle said. "How interesting."

"Oh, it totally is," Natalie said. "I'm posting every minute of this whole week, all about the life of a working vineyard deep in southwest France. The *likes* I get will be in the thousands, maybe hundreds of thousands."

Danielle wondered if the girl truly did not know where she was since they were certainly not in southwest France. She smiled without comment.

"*Mámère*, can I watch TV, please?" Amelie asked, clearly bored.

Danielle shook her head.

"You may stay with the grownups if you behave," Danielle said. "Or you may go to bed."

"I hate bed!" Amelie said, smacking her little fist on the table.

"Not me!" Natalie said with another giggle. "I love it. Don't I, Jemmy?"

Danielle blushed and looked at Jem who at least had the good grace to refuse to look at her.

"I'll watch TV with you, Amelie," Luc said, standing up with the child in his arms. "Is that okay, Danielle?"

It would have to be, Danielle thought as Amelie gave her an impishly gloating look.

"That would be fine, Luc," Danielle said, standing and picking up her dish.

Instantly, Jem jumped up from his seat and reached for dishes too. Luc put Amelie down and started to help clear the table.

"Come on, Amelie," he said. "Can you carry something?"

"Do I have to?" she whined.

"Only if you want to watch TV with me."

Amelie picked up a dish from the table and turned to walk toward the house, followed by Jem and Luc. Natalie remained where she was and pulled out a cigarette.

"You sure got a great gig here," she said, lighting her cigarette and blowing the smoke out into the night air. "And they're not even really related to you, are they? I think that's what Jem said?"

Danielle felt a hard pinch of sorrow at the girl's words. She very much hoped that Jem *hadn't* said anything of the sort but then how did Natalie know she wasn't blood-related to them? She forced herself not to think of it, nor allow the girl to get to her.

"I'm sure Jemmy will be out in a moment," Danielle said as she smiled woodenly at the girl before carefully making her way over the uneven ground of the garden.

The glow of the house beckoned her and she found herself wishing that Laurent would hurry back, even though dinner was over, and even though she was sure Natalie would aggravate him severely.

But when she saw the comforting light from the main house spill out onto the slate walkway, she was reminded of how happy she was here at *Dormir*. And how she had something important to tell Laurent.

A shudder of unease settled across her shoulders.

Because while she thought she knew how Laurent would react to her news—one never *really* knew. And right at the moment, not knowing was about as uncomfortable a feeling as Danielle could ever remember having.

5

A light rain had fallen during the night, but the streets of Grasse were dry by the time Maggie and Grace walked to the nearest café for their breakfast. Le Café de l'Espérance was much less grand than its name implied but the baskets of fresh hot croissants along with espresso and pots of jam made up for it. From where they sat enjoying their breakfast, they could see the line of pink umbrellas that marked every half block up and down both sides of the street.

The tourists hadn't slept in this morning either, Maggie noted as she looked up from the map she was studying of the village along with a print-out itinerary of a number of perfume factories they were hoping to see today. She and Grace had reserved spots in two of the factory tours but the one they were both keen to see—Parfums Galimard—had been booked up for the weekend and their only hope was to snag a couple of stand-by spots.

"Okay, so which one are we doing first?" Grace asked as she reapplied her lipstick after her coffee.

"There's this smaller family-run factory called La Nuit Est

Belle," Maggie said. "It's gotten some press recently because it created a fragrance that some French actress endorsed."

"What's the name of the fragrance?"

"No clue."

"Honestly, Maggie," Grace said with mild exasperation.

"You will have all your questions answered after the two-hour tour," Maggie said, gathering up her papers from the table. "Ready?"

The factory at La Nuit Est Belle was unimpressive in its blandness, Maggie thought—merely a large, corrugated metal building before which the tour group had gathered.

She noticed that the group she and Grace had joined was comprised mostly of Americans with a sprinkling of Europeans. All spoke English, as did their factory tour guide, a petite redhead named Vivienne who had an engaging smile and a voice that carried easily to the back of the crowd.

"Good morning, all," Vivienne said as she stood in front of the crowd with the stair-step display of more than one hundred filled fragrance bottles behind her. "We are so glad you could join us at La Nuit Est Belle as we are always delighted to share our amazing products with you."

A woman next to Maggie—dressed in an oversized t-shirt that read *I'd rather be in Disney World*—raised her hand.

"Will we be able to buy the perfume that Brigitte Bardot wears?" she said in an American accent.

Maggie frowned and inched away from her, but the tour guide only smiled.

"Of course, Madame," she said. "Although Mademoiselle Bardot wears many fragrances, I think you are perhaps referring to Anais Dellacroix?"

Maggie turned to Grace and whispered to her.

"That's the name of the actress I was telling you about."

Grace nodded and turned back to focus on the docent.

"How many of you have visited the Museé International de la Parfumerie in the village?" Vivienne asked.

A few people raised their hands along with Grace and Maggie.

"Very good," Vivienne said. "For those who have not been, the museum chronicles over three thousand years of perfume history. Plus, on a fine day like today, you may also visit the flower garden. Today I will tell you the history of perfume making as well as the historical and current techniques for producing these high-end fragrances, ending with a visit to the La Nuit Est Belle gift shop where you may purchase any of our fine products."

She turned and sought out the American woman next to Maggie who had not stopped talking to her husband since the moment she'd raised her hand.

"And also, Madame, I believe you are referring to the new fragrance by our competitor. It is called *Mon Sang*."

"Yeah, that's the one!" the American woman said loudly. "Does it really mean *my blood*?"

Maggie thought she saw something flinch in the tour guide's face, but her composure never slipped.

"In English, I suppose it could be translated like that," she said evenly. "But I believe in my language—the language that the fragrance was created in—it refers to *my passion* or *my heart*."

"Then why not just say that?" The American turned to the man by her side and laughed abrasively as if she had just been terribly witty.

Maggie glanced at the woman's husband—a quiet man with kind eyes whose ears had gone quite pink—and smiled at him.

"Shall we begin?" Vivienne said before turning and leading the group into the building.

Maggie let the obnoxious American woman go on ahead,

hoping she didn't intend to walk right behind the tour guide and badger her the whole time.

A few minutes later, after giving a brief overview of the history of perfume in Grasse, Vivienne signaled to someone in the crowd and a tall man wearing a white lab coat emerged and joined her at the front of the group.

"I would like to introduce you to who many people believe is the most important person in any fragrance operation," Vivienne said. "This is Monsieur Tremblay, and he is *le nez* for La Nuit Est Belle. And yes, Madame," she said, turning to the abrasive American woman who had indeed positioned herself in the front of the group, "before you ask, *le nez* is French for the nose."

"The nose?" the American woman said with a braying laugh.

"*Oui*, Madame," Vivienne said. "In this industry, *le nez* is essential to a successful fragrance business." She waved to the unsmiling man in the lab coat. "Monsieur Tremblay is one of a rare and incomparable group of specialists who study and train as long as one would to achieve a medical degree. It is true."

Vivienne picked up a bottle of murky amber fluid and handed it to the man.

"*Le nez* must be able to identify individual scents as well as scents when they are mingled with one another," she said, smiling at the group. "To do so, Monsieur Tremblay must refrain from any activity such as drinking alcohol, smoking, and eating spicy food, that might interfere with his olfactory abilities. Can you imagine such self-restraint in France of all places where our food and wine is second to none?"

"What *else* does he have to refrain from?" the loud American woman, said with a guffaw.

Monsieur Tremblay clearly understood enough English to get the gist of what the American woman had said, and his face hardened as he turned on his heel and left the stage.

"Excuse me, Ma'am," Grace said to the American woman. "Would you mind letting the rest of us enjoy the tour without your constant input?"

Maggie heard the woman's husband groan in humiliation as the woman turned to look at Grace.

Grace Van Sant was the physical height of most fashion models and every bit as regal. Maggie could only imagine how this coarse American loudmouth might feel being publicly corrected by such a paragon of elegance and style.

The woman blushed and stepped back into the crowd, her husband's arm around her. For a moment, Maggie felt sorry for her. She wasn't being obnoxious on purpose. She was probably just generally curious and insensitive to how she was coming off. She'd probably looked forward to this trip for months if not years.

Now that Grace had put her in her place, Maggie found herself sorry they hadn't both been more tolerant with her.

6

After "the nose" had stormed off stage, Vivienne carried on as if nothing had happened. Maggie imagined that unwanted audience input must be a regular part of the job for her. She was well aware that, for her, the key irritant in today's disturbance was the fact that the one who'd been causing the disturbance was her own countrywoman.

Vivienne led them further into the factory where they saw a display of bottles arranged on stair-stepping shelves like a massive pipe organ of glass bottles. The group murmured in awe at the towering display.

"Yes, it looks like a musical organ, does it not?" Vivienne said as she stood before the impressive arrangement and swept her hand to indicate the bottles behind her. "It is called the perfumer's organ for this very reason. Here are one hundred and thirty base fragrance notes. These are the vials of raw scent arranged on different levels at different strengths, each of which may be mixed with another to create a unique aroma. You can see how composing a new perfume can be compared to composing music, *non*?"

"It's really quite extraordinary," Grace murmured, clearly fascinated.

One of the Canadian couples timidly raised her hand.

"Yes, Madame?" Vivienne said. "You have a question?"

"All these vials are made from flowers from around here?"

"A very good question, Madame," Vivienne said. "Some are from around here. Our local flowers are roses, jasmine, violets, mimosa and of course lavender. These are the flowers that have made Grasse famous the world over."

Another woman raised her hand.

"I'm from South Carolina. Is your jasmine like our Confederate Jasmine?"

Vivienne smiled broadly.

"Yes, and no, Madame. Just as the jasmine grown in Egypt or Morocco is different from the jasmine grown in Grasse, so your American South jasmine will produce a totally different fragrance." She turned to address the crowd, clearly passionate about the topic.

"Did you know that jasmine is so delicate that we still pick it by hand? And quickly since it must be done before the tiny flowers can wilt. Then they must be transported to a factory like this one at La Nuit Est Belle, close by, where the pure flower scent is extracted. It takes about a ton of flowers to extract a single kilo of what we call *jasmine absolute*."

"How does that measure out money wise?" a woman asked.

"Each kilo is worth over fifty thousand euros," Vivienne said. "Or about sixty thousand US dollars."

An appreciative gasp escaped her audience and Vivienne nodded at their appreciation.

"Chanel No 5 is made with jasmine, isn't it?" Grace asked.

Vivienne turned to her and smiled.

"It is. But it can only be made with the jasmine grown in Grasse. Because of the *terroir*. You know this term?"

Maggie, of course, was very familiar with the term since she and Laurent owned and lived on a vineyard. She raised her hand.

"It means the specific characteristics of the place that helps to create a unique agricultural product," Maggie said.

"*Exactement*, Madame. *Merci*. The soil, the sun, the geographic location—all of it will create a different product whether flower or wine. Just like wine, you can have the same type of grape but you will not have the same wine. And now allow me to show you the gift shop."

"I'm impressed," Grace said as they followed the small group out of the main showroom down a hallway. "Especially for such a small operation."

Maggie spotted the abrasive American, now walking demurely behind the crowd, holding her husband's hand. Maggie hated to think of how she'd been publicly chastised. Yes, she was obnoxious, but she hadn't deserved to be publicly scolded.

"Fragrance is a big business," Grace said.

"This is news to you?" Maggie said tartly. She realized that she felt a flinch of irritation with Grace for how she'd admonished the loud American.

Grace glanced at Maggie and then moved over to where the American and her husband were edging toward the door, clearly opting to skip the gift shop.

"Excuse me," Grace said.

The two turned to look at her and the husband instantly started blushing, probably assuming, Maggie thought, that someone was coming after his wife again. The poor soul. He probably should be used to it by now.

"I just wanted to apologize for speaking to you like that," Grace said. "I hope you'll forgive me."

The woman's face opened into an expression of surprise and relief. She stuck out her hand.

"Karen Dixon," she said. "This is my hubs DJ. We're from Winter Park, Florida."

"Grace Van Sant," Grace said, shaking her hand. "And this is Maggie Dernier."

"I don't know why I get going like that," Karen said, glancing guiltily at her husband who smiled indulgently at her. "I guess I don't get out enough." She laughed loudly and then covered her mouth. "Oops."

Grace laughed. "Is this your first visit to France?"

"How did you know?" Karen laughed again. "But I just love perfume. Perfume of all kinds, really. Don't I, DJ? The ladies in my book club have all been to the factories here in Grasse and I just couldn't be the only one left out."

Grace smiled. "Where are you staying?"

"At the *Sunflower*. Do you know it?"

Maggie remembered seeing the hotel on her map. It was close to the center of Grasse.

"Why not meet us for an *apéro* later this evening?" Grace said.

"A pair of *what*?"

"Drinks, darling. Before dinner?"

"Oh my gosh I would love that!" Karen said exuberantly as she turned to look at her husband who was looking at Grace with gratitude.

"Then it's a date. Say six o'clock? At *L'Océan*? That's behind the cathedral."

"We'll find it," Karen said eagerly, her eyes glittering as she smiled at both Grace and Maggie and then turned with her husband in tow to head toward the gift shop after all.

"That was sweet of you, Grace," Maggie said, wryly. "In fact, maybe even over and above the call of duty."

Grace laughed. "You are never satisfied, darling. Anyone ever tell you that?"

As they moved down the hall toward the now packed gift

shop, Maggie spotted Vivienne standing at the end of the hall. She was facing a man who had his hand on her arm. Vivienne's head was down, her eyes on the ground. Maggie could see the man was speaking harshly to her. He tugged on her arm as if emphasizing his words.

Maggie was about to turn away, scolding herself that it was none of her business, when she realized that the man with Vivienne was the same man she'd seen earlier. He was the handsome young man who had sneered at her.

7

They decided on lunch at the Le Lion d'Or on rue de Cannes, a restaurant Grace had read about in Travelocity that said the Lyonnaise salad there was not to be missed. After they were seated on the terrace to people watch, she and Maggie both ordered the salad along with a bottle of Sancerre Sauvignon. It wasn't raining but the flat white sky looked threatening, as did the bite in the breeze since the morning.

Maggie texted Laurent for a general check-in and got her usual generic response from him.

Domaine St-Buvard could have burned to the ground, and he would still text: <*all good and we are missing you*>

She glanced at Grace, but her friend's phone stayed firmly in her purse, not on the table as it would have if she was expecting a call from Windsor. Either Grace had given up on hearing from him or she had heard from him and now didn't expect to any further. Maggie wondered why Grace wasn't sharing what was going on.

Unless it's something bad in which case sharing almost always makes it more real.

"So do you think that was Vivienne's boyfriend she was arguing with?" Grace asked as she reached for her wine.

"I hope not," Maggie said. "It certainly felt intimate. But in a bad way."

"She seems so sweet. I hate to think she might be in an abusive relationship."

"I know. Is she leading the second half of the La Nuit Est Belle tour this afternoon, do you know?"

"I don't know who else would," Grace said. "I understand it is a very small operation."

"Vivienne is certainly passionate about her job," Maggie said.

"It's obvious she loves what she does." Grace glanced at her watch. "Darling, we need to hurry, or we'll be stuck at the back of the group. Oh! I've got a time slot for the Fragonard fragrance workshop after our tour. Are you sure you don't want to come too? You could make a one-of-a-kind fragrance to drive Laurent wild."

Maggie laughed. "He likes my own scent."

"You're not telling me you don't wear perfume?" Grace looked aghast.

"No, I do. But I like the basics. You know, Ma Griffe, Joy and Coco. No, you go ahead. I think I'll just walk around the village and find a café to just sit and watch the world go by."

"Well, suit yourself, darling. I have to say that this perfume class is positively the highlight of the whole weekend for me."

The afternoon tour once more began in the square in front of the La Nuit Est Belle factory. Vivienne stood, smiling and waiting patiently for the group to assemble and then quieten. There was no sign that she was upset over the altercation with the handsome jerk that Maggie had witnessed.

Maggie and Grace waved to Karen and her husband who seemed to have become friendly with the Canadian couple.

Maggie assumed they must have gone to lunch together. She was glad they'd connected.

Even obnoxious people deserve friends.

"We are all here and ready to go, *n'est-ce pas?*" Vivienne said brightly. "Let us begin."

She led them into the building and through a stylish lobby filled with shelves displaying many kinds of bottles and flagons holding various colored liquids.

"After our tour this morning—for those of you who attended—you will not be surprised to know that Grasse is the center of a twenty-billion-euro perfume industry. There are roughly thirty perfume factories in Grasse as well as museums, shops and even a school. Unlike most of the Côte d'Azur, Grasse makes most of its revenue from the perfume sector—not from tourism."

Maggie found her mind wandering back to the altercation she'd witnessed between Vivienne and her boyfriend and wondered what had been going on there. But as soon as she did, she heard Laurent's voice in her head reminding her that whatever was going on was none of her business.

"Which perfumes are made with whale vomit?" a familiar voice called out.

Maggie turned to see Karen once more at the front of the crowd, her husband cringing beside her.

But Vivienne smiled, unflustered.

"Hello again, Madame Dixon," she said. "You are referring to ambergris, I believe." She turned to the crowd. "Ambergris is an intestinal slurry that comes from sperm whales. And, yes, it is a highly coveted perfume ingredient. In fact, it can sell for thousands or even millions of euros."

"Gross!" Karen said and looked around, waiting for the small ripple of laughter which inevitably came from her contingency of fellow tourists.

"It is for that very reason," Vivienne continued, "that it is used less and less. More authentic means have been discovered that are much cheaper to harvest." She grinned good-naturedly. "As I'm sure you can imagine. Shall we move on?"

The rest of the tour was much like the morning, full of interesting facts and history of Grasse and the perfume industry. At the end of the hour, Vivienne brought the group to a window where they were able to watch two men in lab coats working with clear and colored vials in a laboratory setting.

A few people were sitting at benches with laptops. Maggie had read somewhere that they were translating formulas into production processes. Others seemed to be examining the quality of flowers and other raw materials with scales, meters and calibrating equipment.

"These are our chemists," Vivienne said proudly. "As you can see, one of them is Monsieur Tremblay who we met this morning, and the other gentleman is Monsieur Florent Monet who is the owner of La Nuit Est Belle and who himself possesses an amazing and singular nose."

Unfortunately, because Florent Monet's actual nose was quite prominent, Vivienne's comment prompted a wave of tittering in the group, American and non-American alike. Florent Monet turned and waved at the group through the window, but Tremblay never looked up from the scale of rose blossoms he was weighing.

8

Later, after the tour ended, Grace left to go to her create-a-fragrance workshop at Fragonard. The rain was still holding off for which Maggie was grateful since she didn't want to have to go back to the apartment to get her rain shoes.

She walked down Place du Petit Puy past the city hall, or *Hôtel de Ville de Grasse*, noting the Saracen tower as she did. There was so much to see, so many beautiful architectural hallmarks, that before she knew it she was nearly to the *Jardins de la Princesse Pauline*, a stunning city garden with views overlooking Grasse's Old Town and its surrounding hills.

Maggie walked through the garden, passing a children's playground that made her think of Amelie. She smiled, wondering what the child was up to today. Rounding the square, she came upon a stone bench on a small abutment overlooking yet another a garden in full riotous bloom. She was tempted to pull out her phone to capture the colorful botanic cacophony but forced herself to sit instead and enjoy the view without recording it—or God forbid posting it somewhere on social media.

There was something timeless and perennial about sitting here, no sounds of traffic or conversation reaching her from the village streets. It was peaceful, and the panoply of flowers moving with the breeze and their faint fragrance drifting up to her was exquisite.

Laurent had sent a photo of Amelie and Danielle in the kitchen at *Dormir* making *pain beurre* for breakfast. Amelie was particularly fond of Danielle, whom she called *Mamère* as did all of Maggie and Grace's children. But for Amelie, Danielle was something special, since it was Danielle who had come to St-Tropez and spirted her away back to Domaine St-Buvard—away from poverty and slaps and always being hungry to a life of hugs and kisses and warm beds, puppies, good food and love.

In a way, Maggie knew that Amelie would always see Danielle as her rescuer, not just the grandmother she'd never had, but her fairy godmother.

Even after the nine months she'd spent at Domaine St-Buvard, the child was reserved and watchful—not surprising considering the first four years of her life when she lived in a slum with four other children watched over by two disinterested and occasionally abusive caretakers.

Now that Amelie was living at Domaine St-Buvard, Maggie and Laurent were doing everything in their power to erase the memory of those first four years.

Looking around the garden, Maggie saw peonies, poppies, full shrubs of lavender and the omnipresent jasmine. She tried to identify the different strains of fragrances. She could see rose bushes, along with violets and mimosa. She smiled to herself thinking she would never make it as a Nose. It all smelled lovely, but she couldn't pick out any separate floral fragrances. She would love to bring Mila here some day and, when she was old enough to appreciate it, Amelie too.

"Bonjour, Madame," a voice said from behind her. "Am I interrupting you?"

Maggie turned and was surprised to see the docent Vivienne coming down the steep walkway, an umbrella in her hand and the wrappings of what must have been her lunch in the other.

"Not at all," Maggie said. "Join me, please. It's the loveliest view."

"I know," Vivienne said as she seated herself on the bench next to Maggie. "I often come here."

"I so enjoyed the tour you led today," Maggie said. "You really made the information come alive."

"I am glad you enjoyed it." Vivienne smiled and Maggie caught a glint of gold in the girl's otherwise burnished red hair.

Once more, Maggie found herself searching for any overt signs of distress from the argument she'd witnessed that morning between Vivienne and the young man, but there were none. Or at least, nothing she could put her finger on. Like with the tour guide's presentation, there did seem to be something wistful right under the surface. Something that Maggie detected but couldn't identify.

"You're from Grasse?" she asked.

"My family has been here for three generations," Vivienne said almost sadly. "The perfume business in Grasse has always been a family business."

"Is your family no longer in the area?"

"My parents are dead. My grandparents long gone. They worked as growers for decades."

"So the perfume business really is in your blood," Maggie said.

"I suppose so, yes. But it is changing."

"For the good?"

"I suppose that depends. It is for the good as far as the consumer is concerned if prices of the perfumes drop."

"Is that what's happening?" Maggie looked around the garden. "I would hate to see all of this go away."

"Oh, no, Madame, I think as long as there are tourists in the south of France this will not go away."

"But this isn't really the perfume business," Maggie gestured toward the garden. "Is it?"

Vivienne sighed.

"The perfume industry in Grasse cannot compete against the large chemical multinationals, and most customers cannot tell the difference between a fragrance created in a lab and one that required the advantage of generations of knowledge of the flowers themselves."

"I suppose all things must change and move with the times," Maggie said. "But surely there will always be small-batch operations like La Nuit Est Belle to uphold the old traditions?"

"But how long can they do that if nobody is willing to pay the higher prices?" Vivienne asked.

Maggie had to admit she had a point.

"Besides," Vivienne said, "the product you dab on your wrist today is less about quality than celebrity endorsements and branding launched globally with no personal engagement or connection between the woman and her fragrance."

"That's rather beautifully put," Maggie said. "If incredibly sad."

"You see that shed?" Vivienne pointed to a small terracotta-roofed shack at the base of the garden about sixty yards away. It was covered with vines and Maggie hadn't noticed it until Vivienne pointed it out.

"Not long ago, that is where the pickers cooked and slept and lived so that they would be able to pick the fields at dawn. Such dedication and devotion to quality! Who is there to do that now? The refugees from Iran or Syria? They want food and shelter for their families—perhaps a wide screen TV—not satisfaction in handpicking jasmine. Can you blame them?"

"It's the way of the world and progress, I guess," Maggie said.

"Except so much is lost with progress," Vivienne said as she stared out over the garden, her eyes suddenly filling with tears.

9

Later, after returning to the Airbnb, Maggie found Grace already dressing for dinner. Maggie took a quick shower and then laid down for a brief twenty-minute nap.

She'd enjoyed her afternoon of wandering around Grasse and felt like she finally understood the town's unique characteristics which distinguished it from so many other French villages in the south. She enjoyed the fact that, as Vivienne had said, Grasse didn't rely on tourists—no matter how many fragrance tours it hosted for its visitors. As the fragrance capital of the world, Grasse had a center that held firm without the steady influx of tourists and their limitless American Express cards.

As she changed into a pair of linen slacks and a light cashmere sweater to meet up with Grace, Maggie reflected back on her conversation with Vivienne. When the girl had spoken of the old ways of perfume-making and the future of the fragrance business in Grasse, Maggie had been surprised at Vivienne's sudden show of emotion. It reminded Maggie of the flicker of true feeling she had detected in the girl earlier in the day.

Grace had gone on ahead, so Maggie took a moment to refresh her makeup before locking the apartment and walking down avenue Guy de Maupassant to where they were meeting up with Karen and her husband.

L'Océan looked as if it had seen better days and, for a moment, Maggie could imagine it in the sixties crammed with celebrities and the universal and certain belief that Grasse was the epicenter of the fragrance world.

Karen was already seated with Grace at one of the terrace tables when Maggie arrived. The woman was talking a mile a minute—and loudly—as she stuffed *gougères,* one right after the other, into her mouth. Grace looked up at Maggie with a look of exasperation and gratefulness.

"Hello, you two," Maggie said as she sat down. "Where's your husband, Karen?"

"He wanted to come," Karen said. "But there was this ballgame that he discovered he could get on his iPad so I told him to take the afternoon off and we'd make it a hen party tonight."

Maggie signaled to the waiter.

"All the husbands on the tour seem pretty long-suffering, I must say," Grace said.

"I know, right?" Karen said with a grin. "Although in my defense, I did promise him we'd go to the BMW factory in Munich after this, or maybe do some hiking or hunting, although just between us girls, we're booked for Paris next. There's this amazing exhibition there I want to see."

The waiter came and took Maggie's order for a Kir Royale. When he did, Karen insisted he bring her one too.

"So what did you think of the tour today?" Grace asked.

"Oh, my gosh! Didn't you love it? Although honestly, I'd done my research before I came. I could've given the tour myself and half of what she said was wrong."

"Really?" Maggie said, raising an eyebrow at Grace.

"All that stuff about hand-picking the jasmine? I saw a

YouTube video that shows them doing it with a machine so that was all BS. But I wasn't going to say so in front of everyone."

"That was kind," Grace said.

"Yeah, well, I know she's trying to make a living, you know? But it ticks me off when the French try to take advantage of the tourists, you know? I mean, let's don't forget who saved their bacon in World War Two, am I right? Oh! Can you ask the waiter to bring more of those cheese puffs? There was hardly enough for two let alone three people!"

Maggie took in a breath and kept an eye out for the waiter when she spotted a woman gliding into the café with all the presence and panache of a film star who expected to be recognized. She had blonde hair framed against a complexion of bone china perfection and dark eyes.

Several of the waiters scurried to find her a table and as much as French waiters can, appeared to be giving her homage. Maggie tilted her head and frowned.

"Who are you looking at?" Karen said loudly, twisting her head around.

"Nobody," Maggie said quickly, suddenly afraid Karen was going to cause a scene.

"Oh, my gosh! That's Capuccine Dix!" Karen said in a loud voice as she craned her neck to see better. "I saw pictures of her in the brochures for the tour at Dix Fleurs. DJ and I are taking that tomorrow. Dix Fleurs is, like, twice the size of the one we went to today. I think she's totally the real deal, you know? I mean just look at her. Still gorgeous and she has to be, what, sixty? She's probably had work, but still. Oh!"

Just then, Karen looked down at her phone which had dinged and then looked at Grace and Maggie as the waiter brought their drinks.

"DJ said he found a burger joint in Grasse!" She burst out laughing. "He was so afraid he was going to have to eat frog food while we were here. Oops!" She looked at the waiter and tittered, "Sorry!"

"He doesn't speak English," Grace said smoothly, not at all sure he didn't.

"Anyway, you guys want to have burgers with us?"

"We would love to," Maggie said. "But we can't. We're meeting some people."

"Oh, that's rotten luck!" Karen said, making an exaggerated frown. "Why don't you ask them if they want to come too? Are there any men in the group you're meeting? I think DJ's getting tired of the all-female revue."

"Sorry, darling," Grace said. "All gals, and none that speak English."

"Well, they won't get far not speaking English," Karen said as she downed her drink quickly and stood up. "Maybe next time. Catch you later!"

"I guess she'll pay her own drinks tab next time, too," Grace said as she watched the woman hurry off down the street.

"I'd say you've definitely done your good deed for the year," Maggie said with a smile as she sipped her Kir.

At that moment Maggie saw a man approach Madame Dix at her table where she sat alone. From the look on her face, she was not happy to see him. Their conversation was brief. When he turned away, his face flushed and pinched, Maggie recognized him as the man she'd seen in the last tour—Florent Monet, the owner of La Nuit Est Belle.

"Don't look now," Maggie said under her breath to Grace, "but the owner of La Nuit Est Belle just got the heave-ho from the owner of Dix Fleurs."

Grace turned to scan the room just as Florent Monet spotted them and walked over. He held out his hand and shook Grace's hand.

"We meet again, Madame Van Sant."

Maggie registered surprise. When had Grace met the owner of La Nuit Est Belle?

"Maggie, you remember Monsieur Monet?" Grace said to her.

"Yes, of course," Maggie said. "Please join us."

"*Merci*, Madame," Florent said. His curly brown hair was cropped short which accented his sharp cheekbones and dark eyes behind thick lashes. "I hope you are enjoying your visit to Grasse?"

"Very much so," Grace said. She turned to Maggie. "Monsieur Monet and I met this afternoon when I was shopping for a souvenir for Philippe while you were out walking."

Florent turned his eyes on Grace—clearly infatuated with her as most men were.

"I was hoping to offer my services later for a private tour of Grasse," he said. "Do you have dinner plans?"

"We have reservations at Le Trésor," Grace said evenly, her eyes bright.

Maggie realized that Grace was mildly flirting with him and she found herself wondering if she would be doing that if everything was totally fine with Windsor.

"*Quel dommage*," Florent said, his eyes holding Grace's for several seconds longer than necessary.

"We've been enjoying your tour guide Vivienne Curie," Maggie said, hoping to break the spell. "You're so lucky to have her."

"Vivienne is a jewel," he said, finally turning to look at Maggie. "Her family name alone holds a cache that is difficult to find in this business."

"Her family were growers, right?" Maggie said.

"*Exactement*. For generations. I myself am a virtual newcomer compared to Vivienne and her family. I do not know what I'd do without her. But alas, I'm afraid I must go." He stood up, his eyes on Grace once more. "I have a prior engagement I have just remembered but I hope you will enjoy the festival later. You are familiar with it?"

Maggie had read about the festival which was an annual *fête* in honor of the flowers of Grasse and their importance to the village's livelihood. The parade route was to go right by their restaurant table. They'd specifically asked for a terrace table for that reason.

"We're looking forward to it," Grace said, extending her hand to him and without doubt making it sound like her words meant more than they did on the face of them.

10

The *Dormir* kitchen was always a peaceful place to be, Danielle thought. It never ceased to surprise her to remember that this kitchen had been the one her husband had taken her to when she was first married. In it, she'd baked and cooked and did everything she could to be a good wife to Eduard.

She ran a sponge down the counters, collecting crumbs from their breakfast. The aroma of bacon and baked croissant hung in the ground.

Yes, she had lived at *Dormir* years ago when it went by another name.

And she had never been more miserable.

She glanced at the three dogs who sat waiting patiently, hoping for a dropped crust of anything. She'd not been allowed to have an animal in those days. When she thought of how much comfort and pleasure she got from these three, she wished she'd had at least one back then. It would have helped so much.

"What will we do today, *Mémère*?" Amelie asked from where

she sat at the kitchen table, dawdling over her breakfast. "Can we give the dogs baths?"

Danielle nearly laughed at the awfulness of that suggestion and then, for Amelie's sake, affected to be considering it. She wished Luc and Jem had stayed. When she had first heard they were coming home she assumed they would help out with the child—at least more than they had. Not that she'd want to rope them in as babysitters, but they could help a bit more, it seemed to her.

Laurent was once again at the monastery. He had come home last night too late for her to have a word with him. And of course, the boys had gone back to Domaine St-Buvard with their American friend. Danielle made a face as she scrubbed at a particularly stubborn piece of baked-on food remnant on the stove.

In her day, such a thing would be unthinkable. Two young men and a woman alone in a house with no chaperone? And while Danielle knew those days were long gone, it was still an unseemly situation in her mind. She tried to imagine how she would feel if it was Zouzou—Grace's daughter and the girl Danielle had lovingly raised for the last fifteen years—alone in a house with two men.

No, she wasn't wrong. The state of affairs was not at all proper.

She set a plate of strawberries on the table by Amelie who had pushed her breakfast plate away and was now flipping through a Babar comic book. All three dogs shifted their stations to set up beside Amelie's chair. When the child peeled off three pieces of her *pain beurre* for them, Danielle pretended not to see.

The girl had spent her life not having enough food. It must feel like a beguiling luxury to be able to feed the begging dogs.

"Can we play in the garden?" Amelie asked.

Danielle glanced out the kitchen window where the rain

was coming down in sheets and briefly envisioned the muddy mess that *that* enterprise would generate. She quailed at the thought.

"How about a movie day?" Danielle said. "And we can bake a yoghurt cake."

"Oh! You will teach me to make it?" Amelie asked, jumping out of her chair and bouncing from foot to foot in her excitement.

"Yes, *chérie*. We will surprise your *Opa* when he comes back to a fresh baked *gâteau*."

Amelie clapped her hands in delight and began singing "*gâteau-gâteau!*"

Danielle smiled fondly at the child, feeling her heart torn once more between worry and joy in the girl's happiness.

There were so many instances at dinner last night that Danielle knew would have enraged Laurent. On the one hand it would have been nice to have had the support of another sensible adult at the table. But on the other, she knew how it would have upset him. Just the tense interplay between Jem and Luc was worrisome—never mind the rude things the girl had said—but because Laurent hadn't seen it for himself, he would think Danielle was overthinking it or being a worrywart.

That doesn't mean there's not something to worry about.

Danielle sipped her coffee and then fed pieces of waffle to the waiting dogs herself. In the end, she'd gotten through the evening more comfortably when she imagined she would be able to tell Laurent about...the thing she needed to discuss with him.

She felt a shudder of foreboding.

Why is it our secrets always come to cause our ruin? Have I learned nothing in my seventy-five years on this earth?

One thing she did know, no matter how much she tried to tell herself otherwise, and that was that her secret would without a doubt affect all of the people she loved so much.

11

Maggie ordered *poulet à la moutarde* with a green salad and *pommes frites* for dinner at Le Trésor. She was feeling very relaxed from the bottle of wine she and Grace were sharing and decided that once more, Laurent had been right about her needing this weekend trip. She could literally feel the knots unkinking in her neck and the worries that she kept as constant companions beginning to fall away.

She'd overindulged a bit on the *pommes frites* and was slightly uncomfortable as a result, but she wouldn't have done it any differently. She even photographed her plate for Laurent and although he professed to thinking that photographing one's plate was ridiculous, she knew he would be interested in the dish and would likely try to deconstruct it to see how it was made.

She turned in her seat to face the street where the parade was about to begin. She and Grace ordered coffees and two chocolate *pots de crème* to justify the fact that they intended to stay longer at their table.

"So how did you meet the owner of La Nuit Est Belle?" Maggie asked with a lilt to her voice.

"I told you. I met him shopping while you were out walking."

"And he just came up and introduced himself?"

"Well, no. He commented on the little plastic airplane I was buying for Philippe. I believe he has a grandson, too. I didn't know he was the owner of La Nuit Est Belle until I saw him in today's tour."

"And you didn't think to mention any of this?"

"Why in the world would I? Do you imagine I intend to date him? I'm practically a married woman."

That was the opening Maggie was looking for.

"Have you heard from Windsor?"

"Of course. He and Philippe are having a lovely visit with Peoria."

Grace smiled pleasantly and then turned her attention to the street. Maggie had never been so blatantly lied to—at least not by Grace. She had to assume her friend had her reasons.

"That's nice," she said.

"Yes, isn't it?" Grace pulled a brochure out of her purse. "We need to book our tours early for tomorrow," she said.

Maggie knew a change of subject tactic when she heard it but decided not to press. Grace would talk when she was ready.

Thank goodness the weather was holding, Maggie thought as she watched the first few floats pass by the restaurant terrace. Most of the floats were ablaze with neon-colored lights, outlining massive butterflies, trees and enlarged icons of the star-shaped jasmine flower itself. The effect was breathtaking with float after float seeming to outdo the one before.

Maggie tried to deduce a pattern to the floats beyond what she'd read, which was that they represented the "battle of the *flotter*." Some floats were no more than a single woman decked out in battery-operated costumes of dramatic size and flashing color, from sparkling headdresses to trains of pulsating, colored lights to depict the flower in all its glory.

The series of decorated floats drove through the town and past their terrace with young women in skimpy costumes on board, throwing flowers, confetti and spraying scented water into the crowd. The fire department—with its colorfully dressed *sapeurs-pompiers*—had filled their fire truck with jasmine-infused water and drove down the street spraying the delighted crowds that lined the boulevards into town. Live music poured out from every street corner and as soon as the evening sky had dimmed enough, fireworks exploded overheard like fiery flowers erupting in the night air.

At one point, Maggie spotted Capuccine Dix in the crowd. She was wearing sunglasses—*á la* Vogue's Anna Wintour—although Maggie would've thought it much too dark to need them. She watched her as she slipped away into the crowd, ignoring the noise and fanfare exploding around her.

That's odd. Since this parade is about the fragrance business, I would've expected her to be riding one of the floats, not skulking around in the audience eager to get away.

She turned to see that Grace was watching the parade but something about the expression on her face made her believe she wasn't really seeing it.

"Are you okay?" Maggie asked.

Grace instantly frowned. "Stop it, darling. I'm fine."

Definitely not fine.

"Is it Windsor?" Maggie asked.

"It's nothing. Can we please watch the—" Suddenly Grace's face contorted into a pained visage of horror and surprise. To

Maggie's astonishment, she stood up from her chair, knocking it backward behind her, and bolted from the table.

"Grace?" Maggie felt a fluttering in her stomach and then suddenly, her mouth fell open as she watched in astonishment as Grace ran to the float that was slowly inching by them. Grace raised her arms as if trying to flag down the driver of the float, an elderly gentlemen dressed as a large rose bush.

"*Arret! Arret!*" Grace shouted.

What in the world?

Maggie jumped up from the table and hurried to her friend's side. She had no idea why Grace was acting like this, but she was pretty sure there must be a good reason for it.

As soon as she reached the float, she saw what that reason was and her blood ran cold.

A pale naked arm hung limply off the side of the floor of the float.

The float had finally stopped, the driver's drunken and irate cursing filling the air. Maggie put a hand out to touch the arm —as if needing to prove to herself it was real. It was then she began to hear screams ring out all around her.

The body was covered in a thin layer of bright pink flower petals. The thick matting of tangled red hair was easily visible through the flowers, even if Vivienne's face was not.

12

As soon as Maggie recognized who it was, she pulled Vivienne's long red hair from her face. With chills racing up and down her arms, she'd gently touched the girl's neck to check her pulse. But by the flat, glazed look in Vivienne's eyes, it was clear she was dead.

It took the police nearly fifteen minutes to arrive and by then the crowd had swarmed the float, their screams and cries punctuating the night air. The other floats—not realizing what was going on—had maneuvered around the stopped float. As many of the float drivers were inebriated, those fifteen minutes were ones of chaos and confusion.

Maggie and Grace returned to their café table to wait until the police could take control of the crowd and the scene.

"I can't believe it," Maggie said, feeling a heaviness in her chest and arms. "I just saw her this afternoon."

"How did it happen?" Grace asked, reaching for her second glass of Merlot since they'd returned to the table.

That was a good question. Vivienne was a young, seemingly healthy woman.

"She was covered in flower petals," Maggie said.

Grace turned to her. "That's macabre."

Maggie shrugged helplessly.

"You think someone *did* this to her?" Grace asked.

"I mean, what was she even doing on the float? She wasn't dressed in costume. Did she fall? And her face—"

Maggie swallowed hard as she recalled what she'd seen. "She had a white powdery substance around her lips."

"Are you saying you think she was murdered?" Grace repeated, aghast.

Maggie thought of Vivienne's boyfriend. She scanned the crowd, but she hadn't seen him all night. *Could he have done this?*

"I don't know what I'm saying," she admitted.

As soon as the police came, they watched them cordon off the float and a section of the street as well as erect a canopy over Vivienne's body where it lay on the float. The sounds of the police scene blended in Maggie's head in a blurry amalgamation of walkie-talkies burping, people shouting and the loud frenetic murmuring of the gathered crowd outside the blue and white tape that cordoned off the float where she had found Vivienne's body. She easily identified the man who had to be the detective on the case.

He was, Maggie thought, the man they created the term *ruggedly handsome* for. Tall, dark hair, strong jaw, eyes that missed nothing. Full lips. And the affect of someone who'd just sucked a lemon.

Maybe two.

Maggie reached for her phone and searched the Internet for the name of the lead detective in major crimes for Grasse. She found a photo of the very man she was looking at, now directing his men and what was left of the street crowd.

August Landry, Detective Commandant of the Grasse Police.

A man dressed in street clothes but clearly a part of the police activity walked onto the café terrace and a woman standing by a tall planter pointed to Maggie and Grace's table. He turned and walked over to them.

"Lieutenant Joseph Baldar," he said, identifying himself but not bothering to show his badge. "Are you the ones who stopped the float?"

Maggie was used to the police in the smaller provinces acting like a good Samaritan had ulterior motives—especially if that Samaritan was American. But being used to it didn't make it any less aggravating.

"We saw an arm protruding from the lower platform of the float as it passed us," Grace said imperiously.

Maggie nearly smiled at her tone. Grace knew her effect on people—especially men—and sure enough, as she spoke, the detective sergeant turned to her as if seeing her for the first time. There was something in the way he regarded her now that made Maggie think he imagined he was about to speak to Catherine Deneuve.

"I see, Madame...?"

"Van Sant," Grace said. "And this is my friend, Maggie Dernier. We are both naturalized French citizens."

"Very good, Madame," he said, smiling at Grace warmly. "Thank you. France is very glad to have you."

Suddenly Detective Commandant Landry appeared seemingly from out of nowhere.

"Canvas the crowd," he barked at his man. "Since you are incapable of taking a simple statement."

Maggie and Grace glanced at each other. Their unspoken assessment was immediate and unassailable: They had met men like Landry before.

"Names please?" Landry said, as he whipped out his notebook.

"We already gave them to the other detective," Maggie said sweetly and then felt Grace kick her under the table.

Landry narrowed his eyes at Maggie.

"Perhaps it would be more comfortable for you to tell me your details downtown," Landry said.

Grace gave both their names again.

"You say you spotted the body on the float?" Landry asked. "Explain."

Grace calmly described how she'd seen a limp arm draped over the side of the float and had run into the street to stop the driver while Maggie went to see if the owner of the arm was injured or worse.

Landry turned to Maggie and scowled. "You touched the body?"

"In order to see if she was beyond help," Maggie said. "Yes."

"Do they not know in America not to interfere with crime scenes?" He clenched his jaw in annoyance.

"So, you believe this to be a crime?" Maggie asked.

Landry looked furious that Maggie had made him admit that to her.

"Why are you in town?" he asked.

That was an incredibly stupid question since almost everyone within sight was here to take the factory tours and buy perfume, but Maggie realized Landry was flustered and attempting to buy time in order to get control of himself.

"We are here to take the factory tours," Grace said.

Was he seriously considering them suspects? Maggie wondered. Did he intend to ask everyone on the street where they were today?

"And it can be confirmed," Maggie said. "We went to the morning and afternoon factory tours at La Nuit Est Belle."

Behind Landry, Maggie could see someone who appeared to be a medical examiner. He was tall and balding with tired eyes—preparing Vivienne's body for removal from the float and transport. She saw the body being zipped up in the body bag and she felt her eyes burn as she fought to keep tears from falling.

"And after the tour?" Landry asked abruptly.

"I was at a create-a-fragrance workshop at Fragonard," Grace said.

"And I went for a walk in the village," Maggie said.

She wasn't sure why she decided not to mention the fact that she'd spent a good half an hour with the victim this afternoon.

Probably because there was something about this detective that told her he couldn't be trusted.

13

As soon as the unpleasant detective dismissed them, both Maggie and Grace paid their restaurant bill and gathered their things. It had been a long and unpleasant night and Maggie was longing to call Laurent. She needed to touch base with his good sense and security right about now.

The street was thickly carpeted with confetti and jasmine petals along with spent balloons and the inevitable detritus of a pedestrian audience, drink cups, cigarette butts, and candy wrappers.

Seeing the flower petals, reminded Maggie of how she'd seen Vivienne on the float with the petals everywhere as if they'd been dumped on her body.

Who could have done that? Why arrange her body and then put flower petals on them? And why was she on the float? Surely, it's the sort of thing she'd have mentioned during the tour? Or if not then, then when she and Maggie had sat in the garden and talked.

Maggie felt a wave of sadness descend upon her and her energy seemed to seep out of her.

The day had gone from delight to absolute horror and Maggie felt herself shivering despite the warm spring evening temperatures. The apartment they had rented was down a less-travelled avenue off the main artery and for some reason Maggie felt uneasy walking it tonight. It was fully dark now, and she could hear the sounds of police walkie-talkies crackling in the distance behind her.

Suddenly a figure emerged from the darkness, blocking their path. Maggie screamed before she could stop herself. Grace grabbed her arm in a panic.

"We're Americans," Grace said loudly. "And we're armed."

The figure staggered a few steps toward them until Maggie realized she recognized him. It was Mathys Tremblay.

"Monsieur Tremblay?" Grace said. "Are you alright?"

Tremblay looked at them as if he'd never seen them before which was technically true, Maggie thought, since they only knew him because he'd been introduced to them in front of a crowd.

"Who are you?" he asked, his words slurring.

Before Grace could speak, Maggie stepped forward.

"We're friends of Vivienne's," she said.

Immediately, his face contorted into a grimace but with only the light from the moon, Maggie couldn't tell if it was anguish or fury.

But what she could tell was that he had a scattering of rose petals down the front of his shirt.

Tremblay pushed past them to stagger down the alley toward the main artery of the village.

"Rude," Grace muttered, brushing nonexistent dirt from the sleeve of her floral crepe de chine sundress where he'd touched her.

"But did you notice?" Maggie asked eagerly. "He had rose petals down his front. Did you see?"

"Not really darling. Is that pertinent? I imagine as a perfume maker he plays with rose petals quite a bit."

"Vivienne had rose petals all down her front!"

Grace frowned and the two began walking again to the apartment.

"She did? Are you sure?"

Maggie cursed the fact that she hadn't taken some of the petals at the time but it had not occurred to her.

"Well, she had flower petals and they looked like what I just saw on Mathys Tremblay."

"But they might not have been rose petals?"

"Does it matter if they're roses if they're the same on both?" Maggie said in agitation.

They walked in silence the rest of the way home. Maggie looked around as they walked, determined she wasn't going to be surprised again by not paying complete attention to her environment. They stood in front of the door to their apartment as Grace rummaged in her purse for the key.

"What a night," she said. "Poor Vivienne. I can't believe that lively, lovely girl that we spent most of the day with is gone."

She pulled out her key.

"I know," Maggie said.

"I wonder how much trouble the police will go to in order to confirm my alibi," Grace said.

Maggie frowned. "What?"

"My *alibi*, darling. You heard me tell them I was at the Fragonard class."

"That should be fairly straightforward. How many were in your class? You are fairly memorable."

"I don't know how many were there since I didn't go."

"You didn't go?" Maggie said in astonishment.

"Can we talk about this inside?" Grace inserted the key in the door. "I'm not completely sure I trust Monsieur Handsome

Detective not to follow us home with a recording device in his pocket."

Maggie followed Grace inside and switched on the lights.

"Why didn't you go to the class?" she asked in exasperation. "And why did you tell the police you did?"

Grace kicked off her Jimmy Choo leather slides and padded into the kitchen.

"Honestly, I'd gotten a bit of a headache from all the fragrances I'd inhaled up until then. Wine, darling?"

Maggie pulled off her own shoes. Suddenly she felt as if the weight of the world had landed on her shoulders. Grace used the corkscrew opener on the bottle she took from the kitchen shelf.

"I just came back to the apartment to lie down," Grace said. "But of course, nobody can confirm that. I was astonished when you just told him outright that you were wandering around town. Clearly you have more confidence in the local police than I do. Or maybe my memory is just better than yours."

Grace pulled the cork out of the bottle and poured two glasses. She walked over to Maggie and handed her one.

"You shouldn't have lied to him," Maggie said. "If he wants to confirm your alibi it will be easy enough to do."

"Did he strike you as the diligent type?" Grace said with mild sarcasm.

"I don't know how he struck me," Maggie said tiredly. "I'm hoping he'll do his best to find the truth of what happened to poor Vivienne."

"They wrapped things up pretty quickly, didn't you think?"

Maggie frowned. Now that Grace mentioned it, they *had* processed the scene in record time. Almost as if they hadn't bothered dusting the float for prints or collecting any DNA evidence.

"You think it was a sham?"

"I don't know, darling. I just know that as soon as the blue tape went up, I saw an awful lot of policemen standing around drinking coffee and not doing very much."

"Landry came over and talked to us."

"He took a statement so he could wrap the case up and put it to bed. Hardly the same thing as trying to solve it."

Maggie put her wine down and went and got her laptop.

"What are you thinking, darling?" Grace said as she sat back in her chair and closed her eyes. "Are we leaving tomorrow? Because I'd still like to take that create-a-fragrance workshop."

Maggie looked up from her laptop screen.

"I have a hunch," she said. "Didn't you think Tremblay acted weird tonight?"

"Yes, but if he was grief-stricken, appropriate surely?"

"Did that look like *grief* to you? I mean, was he really even her friend?" Maggie looked at the laptop screen in front of her. "It says here on the La Nuit Est Belle website that Tremblay is the nose and chemist and also the vice president of the company."

"So?"

"So that means there were only three people working for La Nuit Est Belle aside from the growers and the warehouse packers. Two, now that Vivienne's gone."

"Your point, darling?"

"Your friend Florent Monet—"

"Stop that. He's not my friend."

"I wanted to see what Tremblay's role was in the company and there's an announcement on the website that Monet appears to have just posted referencing the passing of Vivienne Curie and how much she meant to the company."

"Again, appropriate, no?"

"You don't think it's a little fast? She's been dead, what, an hour?"

Grace frowned. "Now that you mention it."

"There's more," Maggie said as she looked at her computer screen. "Florent assures his customers that all tours will go on as scheduled tomorrow."

"Seriously?"

"He says he's going to do the tours himself."

Grace sat down with her glass of wine.

"He would've had to have gone straight home after hearing of Vivienne's death and jumped on the Internet to post that announcement," she said. "I mean, I know it's a small operation, but what about decorum?"

"I counted nearly a dozen people in our tours," Maggie said. "Both the morning one and the afternoon. I know everyone was buying stuff in the gift shop hand over fist. Is it the tours keeping La Nuit Est Belle propped up?"

"Remember Vivienne said it's less about quality these days than branding and celebrity endorsements?"

Grace wrinkled her nose. "Did she?"

Maggie shook her head. "Never mind. I guess she just said it to me. I bumped into her this afternoon, and we chatted."

"Oh?" Grace raised an eyebrow. "I don't remember you telling Herr Detective about that."

But Maggie wasn't listening anymore. She was thinking of how strange it was for Florent to be replacing Vivienne so quickly—almost as if he'd known he might have to—and how strange Tremblay had acted tonight.

And why was he covered in flower petals?

Maggie sipped her wine and was quiet for a moment. On top of all that, if what Grace said was true—and now that she thought back on it—there *had* been a certain cursory manner about the police processing of the scene—then Vivienne's death would remain a mystery.

And *that*, Maggie could not allow.

14

The evening wind had picked up and was blowing in sharp angry gusts that flapped the *Dormir* sign hanging on a chain outside the main house. The rain itself came slashing down sideways.

Laurent stepped outside with the dogs, wishing, as he hadn't wished in a long time, for a cigarette. He'd gotten back to *Dormir* by lunchtime. The day had been unsatisfying and even frustrating. He turned toward the house and could still hear Amelie's screams.

The child had done surprisingly well being cooped up all day on a rainy day, but she'd finally given in to her nature and the provocation. This tantrum—a long time coming—had been one for the ages.

Laurent ran a hand over his face.

Maggie was better at dealing with this sort of thing. His first instinct was to leave—not an option. His second wasn't much better but at least he knew that. Removing his belt to threaten corporal punishment was never going to get anyone to calm down and he'd learned that well enough over the years. Besides, who would have the heart to do such a thing to a child who'd likely been beaten before and likely for the most trivial of offenses? No, threatening to spank her wasn't an option either.

But neither was the option of accommodating her since she was presently too upset to be appeased, even if he had the power to stop the rain or conjure up playmates. He cursed the fact that Windsor had taken Philippe with him.

More than anything, Laurent believed that the child was missing Maggie whom she very much considered her mother and whom she had not been separated from since she'd arrived.

He'd be lying if he said he hadn't been tempted to call Maggie and ask her to cut her weekend short. But Maggie lived on the front lines with the child day in and day out, and as much as she adored her, she needed this weekend where she only had to worry about which cocktail to order or how late to sleep in the morning.

No, today's storm would just have to be weathered. It would've helped if the boys had come over again. Especially since Laurent hadn't been able to stay for their visit last night. Unfortunately, it appeared that the American girl had promised Amelie that they would come back today.

Unless you have children, it's probably difficult to understand how important keeping your promise is. Laurent hoped that he'd raised his sons to know that keeping one's word was important.

He felt a hardening in his stomach as he pulled out his phone and called Jem, but the call went to voicemail. The dogs ran back to the shelter of the house and Laurent knew he couldn't stall for much longer. As he turned to join them, Jemmy texted him.

<What's up?>

The text message sent a shiver of annoyance through Laurent.

"What's up" is that you promised Amelie you'd come back today,

Laurent wanted to say. *"What's up" is that I haven't seen you for longer than five minutes since you've been back.*

Instead, he shoved his phone back in his pocket and turned his collar up against the wind that was picking up stronger still, the sounds of his granddaughter shrieking behind him for Danielle to deal with.

Even Danielle's patience had begun to fray with Amelie. He would insist that she take a book and some earplugs and go up to her room.

He sighed as he opened the door to the suddenly increased volume of Amelie's howls and the three wet dogs who went charging past him into the interior. As he stepped inside, he found himself wishing yet again that Maggie would decide to come home early.

15

The next morning, Maggie noted that it must have rained again during the night. At the moment the clouds overhead were bunched, dark and ominous. She and Grace decided to breakfast at the nearby Café Constant again on rue des Palmiers. They took folding umbrellas with them and picked their way through the streets that were strewn with leaves and fronds from last night's weather as well as remnants from the parade itself.

Even though it wasn't raining, Maggie felt there was something bereft about the streets—unusually vacant for this time of morning—that gave a gray pallor to the scene in front of the café.

After much discussion the night before, she and Grace had decided that they would stay at least another day, rather than leave in the middle of their weekend, so that Grace could go to her build a fragrance class and not end the trip on such a dark note.

They ordered coffees and croissants with fruit and sat on the terrace facing the quiet street before them.

Maggie sipped her coffee and scoured the Internet on her

phone for any news of Vivienne's death or of how the police were handling it but there was only a single line referencing it.

"You don't think that's odd?" she asked as Grace added a dollop of jam to her croissant.

"What's odd?"

"That a woman is killed in the biggest village event of the year and there's no mention of it in the news?"

"I suppose," Grace said as she signaled the waiter for another cup of coffee.

"I've got a bad feeling," Maggie said.

"How so?"

"I'm wondering if the police are treating this as a suspicious death."

"Why would they?"

"*Because*, Grace," Maggie said with exasperation. "The body was covered in rose petals! I told you that! She had white foamy stuff on her mouth."

"A suicide perhaps?"

"Do you seriously think Vivienne arranged flowers on herself before she drank poison?"

"What makes you think she drank poison?"

"I told you, because of the white powder on her face. She either drank it or...well, I don't know how it got there. But how else do *you* account for the white powder?"

"I'm sure we'll find out, darling. The police will do their little forensic magic and voila, all will be revealed."

"Unless they don't. And it isn't," Maggie said with a frown, still scrolling to find any mention of the incident. "I need more information."

"Well, before you get any ideas, darling, I can tell you right now that that hunky detective is not about to share a bottle of Evian with you, let alone any details of this incident. I may not be a world class detective but on that much I am certain."

"He *was* a pill, wasn't he?"

"Little Man complex."

"He was easily six foot two."

"I was being metaphorical, darling. Speaking of handsome giants, have you talked to Laurent today?"

Maggie was scrolling through her phone again for any mention of Vivienne's death.

"Not really," she said absently.

"Well, you either have or you haven't."

Maggie looked up. "I haven't. I texted him last night."

Grace sipped her coffee and looked off into the distance. There wasn't much to see from this vantage point except still-closed shop fronts.

"I thought we'd go back to La Nuit Est Belle," Maggie said. "What time is your build-a-bear workshop?"

"Very funny, darling," Grace said as she signaled the waiter for the bill. "It's this afternoon."

Maggie booked two spots on her phone for the factory tour at Dix Fleurs for later that morning. They had plenty of time to run by La Nuit Est Belle first but when she checked the factory website, she saw it was closed for the foreseeable future.

"Rats," Maggie said, frowning at her phone. "I guess Florent changed his mind about carrying on as usual."

"Someone must have had a word with him," Grace observed, as she paid the bill and gathered up her purse. "Ready, darling?"

Maggie tucked her phone away and left the café with Grace. She told herself she was going to do everything possible to try to enjoy the rest of her trip. She wasn't a detective. It wasn't her job to find out what had happened to Vivienne.

On the other hand, if in the process of enjoying her weekend, she happened to talk to a few people who could tell her why a healthy young woman died suddenly in an explosion of rose petals, all the better.

16

Maggie couldn't help but notice that the interior of the Dix Fleurs factory was considerably more stylish and streamlined than La Nuit Est Belle. Everywhere she looked was chrome and gleaming white shelving set against clean monochromatic backgrounds. The showroom itself looked as if it had been designed and built this year, it was so contemporary and ultramodern.

Maggie smiled at the Canadian couple, Sheila and Bernie Williams, standing with Karen and her husband both of whom nodded their greeting as they entered the factory atrium.

Capuccine Dix, the owner of Dix Fleurs, stood at the front of the room. She was likely in her late fifties, but as Maggie had noticed before her skin was as creamy and smooth as a woman much younger. Her golden blonde hair was short and styled expertly to frame her face. Maggie always admired how French women tended to look so put-together with much fewer outside aids than any other nationality that she knew of.

"We have lost one of our own," Capuccine was saying, her face impassive except for a bare hint of sorrow. "Vivienne Curie was a beloved mainstay in the world of fragrance, and she will be missed both professionally and personally."

Capuccine allowed a moment for the audience to nod appreciatively before she continued.

"If you have been to even one other tour during your visit to Grasse," she said turning to gesture to a poster behind her showing a field of lavender, "you will have discovered that the main activity of our beautiful village is the production of natural raw materials—flowers, to you." She smiled. "The essential oils and concentrates distilled from these raw materials are the main products that, when diluted in alcohol, becomes perfume."

Capuccine turned back to smile at her audience, almost fondly before picking up a fragrance strip and holding it delicately to her nose. She closed her eyes as she smelled it, a small, satisfied smile forming on her lips.

She tossed the strip in a nearby container.

"It might interest you to know," she said with that same smug smile, "that the same fragrances we love so much can also make you sick."

Grace nudged Maggie at Capuccine's words.

"It is a fact," Capuccine continued, "that one in three people report health problems when exposed to fragranced products. Some of these problems include headache, dizziness, breathing problems, rashes, and seizures."

"What about death?"

Maggie recognized Karen's abrasive voice and was interested to see how the ever cool and composed Capuccine would deal with the interruption. Capuccine turned her gaze on the American woman who this morning was wearing a large, brightly colored t-shirt touting a midwestern football team.

"I don't think I know of any perfume that has ever resulted in death," Capuccine said coolly.

A young woman standing next to Karen seemed engrossed

in the exchange. Her face was serious, creased in a frown. She looked vaguely familiar to Maggie. For a moment she wondered if she was a waitress who might have served them at one of the many cafés she and Grace had visited during their stay.

"Not even if you drink it?" Karen goaded, looking around the room as if expecting laughter.

"Many things are not good for you if you put them in your mouth," Capuccine said sweetly before turning away.

The crowd tittered in amusement and Maggie saw, to Karen's credit, that she took the one-upmanship with good grace. Capuccine had gotten the laugh that *she'd* gone after, but it had been a decent *bon mot* and Karen clearly appreciated that.

"She really is the living end," Grace whispered to Maggie.

"I will now bring you into the heart of Dix Fleurs," Capuccine said, "where you will see how we create the magic."

"Isn't it true that the Grasse perfume industry can't compete against the large chemical multinationals?"

Maggie turned to see the question had come from the frowning young woman who looked so familiar to her.

Capuccine ignored the question, but Karen wasn't about to.

"Hey, that's a good question," Karen said loudly. "What about that?"

Capuccine turned to look first at Karen and then the young woman.

"It is true," she said, "that the larger laboratories toil to create what we make here from natural raw materials. When money is involved, the need to find shortcuts even if it results in an inferior product is only natural."

"So how can you compete against that?" Karen asked.

"Somebody needs to muzzle that woman," Grace said under her breath.

"Essential oils such as jasmine, rose, vetiver, ilang-ilang, iris, vanilla, sandalwood and lavender cannot be synthesized in the laboratory," Capuccine said. She turned to wave a hand at the perfume organ against the wall.

"Every bottle you see here is made from raw materials whose quality and cost are sensitive to changes in agriculture, politics, natural disasters, climate and disease. It is what makes the perfume unique."

"You mean it's what makes it expensive!" Karen brayed.

"How can you possibly protect those raw materials?" the angry young woman said. "Isn't it true that the very resources Grasse depends on are dwindling by the day?"

Capuccine laughed and looked at the audience who grinned back at her.

"The young ones are always so passionate, are they not? But perhaps the situation is not quite so dire as they believe," she said. "Shall we move on?"

The rest of the tour was fairly uneventful and while Maggie had intended to keep her eye on the mysterious young woman, she seemed to have left the tour before the inevitable visit to the Dix Fleur gift shop.

Maggie followed Grace to the gift shop where shelf after shelf of soaps, candles, creams, home fragrances and atomizers, and bottles of scent in every imaginable size and shape were displayed.

"I thought you'd already bought out the gift shop at La Nuit Est Belle," Maggie said to Grace as she watched her friend put a slender glass flagon of an orange blossom eau de toilette into her shopping basket.

"I'm just doing my share to help the perfume economy in Grasse," Grace said.

"Single-handedly, it looks like," Maggie said as she picked up a bottle of rose scented shower gel.

"Wasn't Karen the living end today?" Grace said. "Honestly. I wish she could hear herself."

"Madame Dix handled it well, I thought," Maggie said, putting the shower gel back on the shelf.

She glanced around the gift shop and saw that Karen was practically clearing the shelves of one particular perfume, loading every form of it into her shopping basket. Beyond her, DJ and the Canadian Bernie Williams were leaning against the counter talking.

Maggie had to admit it took a certain kind of man to follow behind his wife for hours on end—especially if she was the kind of woman who tended to leave wreckage in her wake as Karen did.

Since she'd already picked up more fragrance products at La Belle Est Nuit the day before than she'd ever use in a lifetime, Maggie put her hand on Grace's arm and pointed to the exit.

"See you outside," she said.

Maggie stepped out of the gift shop into a small adjoining garden and courtyard where three more bored-looking husbands were standing by a defunct fountain. One of them was smoking, and Maggie realized that even in France it was becoming more and more unusual to see people smoke. Laurent had given up the habit nearly eight years ago and although Maggie was sure he missed it from time to time, he never mentioned it.

She walked down a path filled with pea gravel and spotted a bench that would make a good place to wait for Grace. As she headed toward it, mindful of not catching her new Stuart Weitzman jelly sandals on the rough cobblestone pathway, she realized that there was someone standing near the bench.

For reasons she couldn't explain, Maggie instinctively stepped off the path into the interior of the garden. Perhaps hiding in order to eavesdrop was a reflex she wasn't even aware she had. Her heart began to speed up when she realized she was hearing Capuccine Dix's voice. She moved quietly from her spot in the garden to a closer vantage point beside a tall cluster of hyacinths.

She could see Capuccine standing and facing the direction where Maggie hid. She was talking to a man with his back to Maggie. His voice was strong and even distinctive, but Maggie didn't recognize it.

Suddenly the man drew Capuccine into his arms and held her, pulling back briefly to kiss her. The lines in the older woman's face relaxed and then stiffened when she spotted Maggie watching them.

Capuccine pulled away from the man's embrace and spoke a few abrupt words to him. When he turned around, he spotted Maggie and glared at her.

She started in surprise.

It was Vivienne's boyfriend.

17

The last time Maggie had seen the young man he had been publicly wrangling with Vivienne.

Looks like he's recovered from her death.

She emerged from her hiding place, casually dusting off leaves and bits of dirt clinging to her sundress and walked over to the pair.

"What are you doing here?" the man said in a snarl, taking several steps toward her.

"Jean-Luis, *non*," Capuccine said, grabbing his arm and pulling him back to her. "It's all right."

"It's *not* all right!" he said, his face a twisted grimace of indignation and fury. "I asked you a question!"

"What I'm doing here," Maggie said pointedly, "is wondering what Vivienne Curie's boyfriend is doing snuggling up to another woman twelve hours after her death."

"How dare you, Madame!" Capuccine said, her voice shaking with indignation.

But Jean-Luis's reaction surprised Maggie. His face went from anger to surprise. And then he laughed.

"What I do is none of your business," he said, walking

toward Maggie and forcing her to step off the path for him to pass.

Maggie watched him go and then turned back to Capuccine.

"I suppose you're each other's alibis for the night in question?"

"How dare you say such things to me?" Capuccine said, jutting her chin out.

"I dare because a woman was murdered yesterday, and I saw your boyfriend have a knock-down drag out fight with her just hours earlier."

"Jean-Luis is my son, you....you...."

Okay. That makes more sense.

Maggie swallowed hard but forced herself to recover. She'd learned long ago that, wrong assumption or not, she couldn't let a few mistakes derail her. After all, she'd made much bigger blunders than this.

"Are you going to tell me he was with you yesterday?"

"*Of course,* he wasn't with me! As if it is any of your business. He was where half the population of Grasse was—watching the annual Jasmine parade."

"How about you? I remember seeing you during *apèros* that day. You had words with Florent Monet."

Capuccine's eyes widened in astonishment. "You...have you been following me?"

"Nope. Just hanging in all the same public spaces. But I didn't see you again after drinks. So were you watching the parade too? By yourself? And before you answer, if you say you were, that's just weird."

Capuccine sputtered.

"How dare you! Three hundred people watched the parade yesterday."

"Can any one of those three hundred people confirm where you were during the time that Vivienne was killed?"

Capuccine whitened visibly. And her fury seemed to ramp up.

"You people," she snarled. "All of you with your bad manners and rudeness. I am sick to death of all of you. I wish they would just let us make perfume and send you tourists back to the Côte d'Azur! Or Hell!"

"My, my," Maggie said calmly. "The public relations train just came off the rails. But let's stay on topic. What I want to know is how Vivienne Curie died and if she had help doing it."

Capuccine snorted derisively but Maggie saw her hands were trembling.

"The police have not indicated it was murder," the older woman said.

"Well, Vivienne didn't die of natural causes," Maggie said. "So *you* connect the dots."

While it was true Maggie didn't have access to any of the forensics on Vivienne's death, she'd seen what she'd seen. And to her eyes, that said murder.

"I don't need to," Capuccine said stiffly. "I have every confidence in our police to handle this terrible tragedy. Now if you will excuse me, Madame, I've frankly had quite enough of pushy Americans for one day."

On that word, Capuccine shoved past Maggie to walk down the path toward the door of the factory gift shop. Maggie watched her go—and watched her briefly stumble in her two-inch ankle-strap heels on the uneven pathway, before catching herself and striding away.

Capuccine had behaved defensively, Maggie thought as she watched her disappear into the gift shop.

Guilty or not, whatever was going on, it was clear she was definitely hiding something.

~

The café Maggie and Grace chose for lunch was on a less populated street. It was more terrace than interior but the weather was presently fine and Maggie always preferred dining outdoors if she had the choice.

"So do you think Capuccine knows something about Vivienne's death?" Grace asked as she cut into her Croque Madame.

Maggie knew Grace would only eat a few bites of her meal while Maggie fully intended to wipe her plate with the left-over toast. She squinted into the sunlight and wished she'd brought a light cardigan with her. Sunny or not, it was chilly in the shade of the café awning.

"I don't know. But she acted guilty," she said.

"Well, what does it mean that Jean-Luis is her son? I mean, the boyfriend of the victim—who worked for her competition—is her son? That seems significant."

"I agree. The question is: in what way is it significant?"

Maggie was hungry and a Croque Madame was one of her favorite lunches with its savory ham and fried egg and smooth, gooey cheese all atop crunchy toast. She'd often thought few meals on earth could compare with its perfection.

Looking at her plate suddenly made Maggie think of Laurent who loved to cook and who firmly believed that good food was the answer to any problem or dilemma that might come up. She had missed two calls from him but when she tried to call him back her call went to voicemail. She was sure things were fine at home. But even if they weren't, there was no one on the planet more capable than Laurent to handle it. And what could be the problem anyway? Both boys were home and Laurent was getting any other help he might possibly need with Amelie from Danielle.

"She tried to tell me that the police were handling the case just fine," Maggie said.

"Seriously? There's been only a one-liner in the news about the death and no hint that there might be a killer on the loose."

"I know. It makes me think that since the fragrance industry owns Grasse, maybe it also owns the police."

"Dix Fleurs has only about twenty employees," Grace said with a frown. "Granted it's larger than La Nuit Est Belle, but buying off the police? That seems a stretch."

"You're probably right. And I might be reading something into Capuccine's affect that wasn't there. I was just so shocked to see Jean-Luis with her."

In any case, Maggie made a mental note to get on her laptop when she got back to the apartment to see what kind of information she could find on Dix Fleurs.

"Have you heard from Laurent?" Grace asked.

"I missed a call from him," Maggie said. "But I'm sure he's fine. He always is. What about Windsor?"

Grace put down the piece of baguette she was buttering.

"I haven't talked to him since he left," she said. "He texted me. That's it."

"What is going on?"

"I don't know."

"You don't seriously think he's going back to Susie," Maggie said firmly.

Grace looked up at her.

"I know he talks a lot about how he hated the fact that he missed out on so much of Zouzou's childhood."

"So you think he'll go back to Atlanta in order not to miss Peoria's?"

"I wouldn't blame him."

"He has a commitment to you, too," Maggie said gently.

"Does he? He hasn't proposed or anything."

"He has a responsibility to Philippe."

"Yes, but the obligation one owes to a grandchild is not the same as what you owe your own child. In fact, I think having

Philippe around is making it worse for Windsor in some ways. He sees Philippe getting all this attention and love from me and Danielle and him, too, and he wonders how Peoria is doing in Atlanta without him."

"It's not an ideal situation. Divorce when kids are involved never is."

"Who are you telling, darling?"

"Sorry."

Suddenly, Maggie's eye was caught by the sight of a figure moving purposefully toward their table. She realized it was the serious young woman who'd badgered Capuccine Dix that morning on the Dix Fleurs tour. Before she could imagine what she might want, the woman pulled out a chair at their table and sat down.

Grace stared at her in mild surprise and then at Maggie.

"May we help you, Mademoiselle?" she asked.

The girl was breathless, and Maggie noticed that her hands were trembling in her lap.

"I am, Annabelle Curie," she said. "Vivienne Curie's sister."

18

Laurent held the large slip-joint pliers in one hand as he eyed the leaky faucet in *Mirabelle* cottage. Along with the main house, *Dormir* was comprised of three separate cottages, all named for fruit to help Grace communicate with her elderly handyman Gabriel. Laurent had given Gabriel the weekend off since he himself would be onsite this weekend.

While *Dormir* had no paying guests at the moment, Grace was expecting a full contingency next week. She worked hard to provide a premium resort-style experience—from the high-end bed linens to the very best food from the region to the flowers in the garden. Americans especially were particularly picky about things working properly—especially plumbing.

Laurent turned off the water supply and removed the faucet housing, checking for the nut which he saw was loose. He didn't mind doing basic maintenance; in fact he found it soothing in its mindlessness—like doing the dishes which he never minded either. It was easier than the afternoon he'd signed up for at *l'Abbaye de Sainte-Trinité*. Frère Jean had asked him to speak to some of the incoming refugees to let them know what would be expected of them working in the vineyard. It was nearly four months before harvest time and Laurent really didn't want to take the time, but he'd told the monk he would come.

Amelie and Danielle were gardening, or at least Danielle was. The last time Laurent had left Amelie, she had been digging for worms alongside Danielle as Laurent had promised to take her fishing later at the small pond on the property. As he tightened the nut at the base of the handle, Laurent heard his cellphone ring and looked around to see where he might have left it.

It was on the bathroom counter. He picked it up, sorry to see that it wasn't Luc, Jemmy or Maggie.

"*Allo?*"

"*Allo*, Laurent," Frère Jean said. "I am glad I caught you."

Laurent felt a chisel of impatience drill into him. "*Oui?*"

"Monsieur Jacquard just called to say he saw a boar this morning near *Dormir*."

Laurent frowned. That was unusual and definitely something to be on the alert for. Boars were unpredictable animals and could be deadly.

"*Bon*," he said. "Thank you. We will watch for it. *Merci.*"

A few minutes later, he left *Mirabelle* cottage to shower and change clothes. He stepped out into the garden and Amelie ran to him, all smiles.

"We are planting *haricot verts!*" she said. "In the *ground!*"

"Very good, *ma petite*," Laurent said before turning to Danielle. "I want to stop by Domaine St-Buvard to check on something. I shouldn't be long. If you need anything, call. I have my phone with me."

Danielle smiled and nodded.

"Can I come too, *Opa?*"

Laurent hesitated but decided he didn't want to wait for her to get cleaned up.

"Not this time, *chérie*," he said. "But I will be back after your nap to inspect the caliber of your bait. *Oui*?"

Amelie grinned and ran back to the small can she was filling with worms.

"I'll be ready!" she said.

The drive to Domaine St-Buvard was only fifteen kilometers from *Dormir* and Laurent had driven it many times over the years. He parked on the rim of the vineyard which was cut into four quadrants by two narrow dirt roads. The larger section the two—often used by tractors—sliced down the center of the field past an ancient shed with an abandoned well at its threshold.

A stand of gnarled olive trees was set at the perimeter of the vineyard and the house garden, providing nothing useful but a nod to their historical role. Laurent thought they'd probably been fruitful during his uncle's time, but now they weren't even good for shade.

On the far side of the vineyard was an apple orchard but it too was not harvested. He'd often threatened to bulldoze it to enlarge his vineyard but Maggie had argued against it.

As had Jemmy.

Laurent felt a flinch of annoyance at the thought of his first-born son. Even after eight years, after Jem had left to get his education in the US and become an engineer, even after all the times that Jem had insisted he wanted nothing to do with the winemaking business, Laurent had harbored a hope that the boy might reconsider and one day take his place next to him at Domaine St-Buvard.

He'd assumed that Luc would join him here but now after the years of him living in California, Laurent began to think that that was a fool's dream too.

That just left Mila. And while she continued to say she would return home to work at Domaine St-Buvard after her studies in America, Laurent was no longer holding his breath. He gazed out over his fields and felt an unusual sense of sadness at the thought.

He always enjoyed the time he spent in his fields and even though he was only at *Dormir* for the weekend, he missed the solitude and serenity of walking his vineyard at any time of day or night.

He left the car and set out walking down a few rows of tidily tended vines, checking that the wires he'd used to tie up the quickly growing shoots were holding well. After a few minutes, he decided to stop in at the *mas* to see how the boys were doing.

It was a quick walk to the *mas* from the fields. Whether he approached it from the front or the garden side as he was doing now, he never ceased to appreciate the gem he'd inherited—and of course what he'd managed to do with it.

Domaine St-Buvard itself was an old farmhouse that he'd had inherited from an unmarried uncle. It was built with materials from the landscape, so stones of varying sizes were cemented into its sloping knee walls that corralled the thick hedges of lavender. The *mas* itself featured cherry-colored roof tiles that spanned the entire roof and its iconic Provençal blue shutters had been crafted in the village, latched with ironware forged in the seventeen hundreds.

Except for his children, this home was what Laurent was proudest of all he had accomplished, and that included a successful winemaking business.

He passed through the house garden, his *potager* to his left, and crossed the slate flooring of the terrace to the French doors that led into the house. He was surprised to find the doors unlocked. He found that mildly annoying but in truth, someone would have to break in from the back—and traipse through one hundred and fifty hectares of open vineyard first—to do it. He recognized that he was just looking for an excuse to be peeved since he and Maggie often left the house unlocked, especially if they were only as far as the village. He walked through the large dining room.

"*Allo?*" he called.

There was only silence in the house as answer.

He was tempted to text the boys to ask where they were. But he knew he was irked, which he didn't want to convey unless it could serve a purpose. Except for venting, which he personally found no merit in.

The kitchen was off the dining room. He'd designed the open cabinetry to give easy access to plates and mugs, preferring the organic feel of the stonework and exposed wooden beams overhead. The walls were painted a pale ochre yellow and the window over the sink faced the front driveway. It brought in the Mediterranean sun that infused the kitchen—whenever the dreaded Mistral wasn't tormenting the front topiary.

He'd arranged the room to suit his height and his cooking style with counter and appliance placement. Unless it was sandwiches, he cooked almost every meal for the family. Along with the vineyard it was his indisputable domain.

He stepped into the kitchen and frowned. Dishes were piled in the sink, dishtowels hung on backs of chairs and counter tops showed congealed food.

Laurent went to the sink and began to fill it with hot sudsy water. He looked out the kitchen window to the driveway to confirm that Jem's car was not there.

He felt a stiffness develop in his neck and jaw. He found himself hoping that the act of plunging his hands into the hot water and inhaling the soapy fragrance might help calm him. In truth, that and habit were half the reason he'd decided to clean up. He was the one who normally did the dishes as it gave him pleasure to tidy up his space after he'd wrecked it.

At the moment, he wasn't getting anywhere near his usual emotional redress. In fact, the more dishes he washed, rinsed and set in the strainer, the madder he became.

19

Annabelle looked as much like Vivienne as to be her twin. She had dark russet hair down to her waist and green probing eyes. Those eyes were reddened at the moment and her long hair hung in her face in the picture of despair.

"I've been to the police, but they were horrible, so I didn't know who else to go to," she said. "And when I saw you confront Jean-Luis, I thought maybe—"

"Wait," Maggie said. "You were following me?"

"I was not," she said indignantly. "I was on the other side of the Dix Fleur courtyard. I went there to talk to Jean-Luis when I saw him go up there. But when his mother arrived, I hung back. And then you showed up."

"Sorry," Maggie said, feeling more than a little embarrassed since it was entirely possible that Annabelle had seen her attempt to hide from Capuccine and Jean-Luis.

"And then when you spoke to Jean-Luis, I realized that you and your American accent—well, you were exactly what I needed to help me find out what happened to my sister."

Maggie glanced at Grace who seemed to be listening attentively.

"How does our being American help you?" Grace asked.

"Seriously?" Annabelle said, shaking her head as if in bewilderment. "It's because you won't take no for an answer and because you won't be intimidated by our police. Everyone else around here —unless they have them in their pocket—is afraid of them."

"Why is that?"

"Because the police have all the power, of course! And they use it, too. Detective Landry could throw any one of us in jail and toss away the key but not if you have an American embassy behind you."

Maggie had to admit she felt a certain layer of security knowing precisely that.

Annabelle turned to Maggie, leaning forward in her earnestness.

"I read about you on the Internet," she said. "I googled your name and found out how you helped that boy who the police in St-Tropez were going to indict for a crime he didn't commit."

Maggie wondered if Annabelle had read enough to know that "that boy"— thirty years old if he was a day—still ended up going to prison, just not for murder. In any case, she felt a flush of pride that Annabelle had heard of her.

"I need your help," Annabelle said. "Vivienne was killed—I know she was—and the police are going to pretend it didn't happen."

"Why would they do that?" Grace asked.

"Who knows? Because it's easier? Because someone is in bed with someone else? Because someone is getting paid to look the other way?"

"You don't have a very high opinion of Detective Landry," Maggie said.

Annabelle snorted.

"I know him, is why," she said. "Vivienne said he made a pass at her and when she rejected him, she got *two* speeding tickets in a week!"

"Is there any possibility she was actually speeding?" Grace asked.

Annabelle gave her a withering look.

"He's crooked," she said. "If he says Vivienne's death is accidental—even if she had a knife sticking out of her chest—there's nobody in Grasse with the *vaillance* to argue." Her eyes teared up. "I'm all Vivienne has. I'm the only Curie left."

"I can only imagine how you must feel," Maggie said. "But we don't know anything about this crime. We don't even know for sure that the cops *won't* treat it as a suspicious death."

Annabelle crossed her arms against her chest. Her mouth trembled slightly.

"I thought you'd be different," she said.

"All I'm saying is I think we need to give them a chance," Maggie said.

Annabelle looked from Maggie to Grace and then reached into her purse and pulled out her cellphone. She scrolled through it for a few seconds and began to read.

"*The Grasse tourist bureau has announced the building of a new six-million-euro welcome center off the main green past the Place aux Aires.*"

She looked at them.

"What does a village population of fifty thousand need with a six-million-euro welcome center?" She turned back to her phone and read out loud.

"*Albert Montague, a known vagrant and thief, was found at the bottom of the LaBaix quarry last spring. Police do not suspect foul play.*"

She looked up again.

"Albert was twenty-five. He didn't do drugs and he didn't

hang with the wrong people. How did he die? He had no family to push the issue, so we'll never know."

Maggie had to admit it was starting to sound as if Grasse had a police corruption problem. But she also knew that those sorts of things didn't usually start in the police ranks. More likely, someone up the food chain had made Landry an offer he couldn't refuse.

"I understand how you feel," Maggie said. "And I agree on the face of it that this doesn't sound good—"

"Come on, Maggie," Grace said with exasperation. "You said yourself you thought it was odd that Vivienne was covered in rose petals."

A shudder of dismay emitted from Annabelle, and she clapped a hand over her mouth.

"She...she was covered in rose petals?" she said in an agonized whisper. "How...how do you know this?"

"I'm afraid because we were the ones who found her," Grace said gently.

Annabelle looked from Maggie to Grace, her eyes filled with tears again.

"You have to help me," she said hoarsely.

"You need to give the police time to do the right thing," Maggie said.

Why was she hesitating? Didn't she believe all that Annabelle was telling her about the Grasse police force being corrupt? So why was she hesitating?

"Is twelve hours long enough?" Annabelle said as she scrolled through her phone again before turning it around to show Maggie. "This email to me as next of kin states that their public affairs department has deemed the case involving the death of Vivienne Curie closed. As of noon today."

Maggie felt a wave of dizziness at Annabelle's words.

"How is that possible?" she said. "They've barely had time to do an autopsy."

"Nonetheless," Annabelle said, reading from her cell phone. "Detective August Landry said that the tragic death of Vivienne Curie on the night of April tenth during the village Jasmine festival has been resolved as an accident."

She looked at Maggie.

"How does someone *cover herself in rose petals* before she accidentally dies?"

That is a very good question, Maggie thought, as her mind began to race.

Could it truly be a police cover-up? For what possible reason? Were the cops just lazy? Were they afraid of bad optics for their town as a fragrance capital? Without doubt, murder had a certain stench to it that wouldn't play well with the village's brand.

"Will you help me?" Annabelle begged. "Please? I know you didn't know my sister, but she was a wonderful person. She didn't deserve what happened to her. I don't deserve to lose her. And the police aren't going to find out the truth."

"Of course, we'll help you, *chérie*," Grace said, reaching across the table to take Annabelle's hand. "Won't we, Maggie?"

"Yes, of course," Maggie said but her smile was tremulous. She was anything but sure that this was the right thing to do.

As she accepted Annabelle's tearful gratitude, Maggie couldn't help but think that one thing she'd learned from years of working with the police was that if they didn't want to investigate a murder for whatever reason, they certainly won't want anyone else doing it either.

20

That afternoon it was decided that Grace would go to her build-a-fragrance workshop if for no other reason than she would be able to honestly talk about it if questioned by the police. Maggie and Annabelle would go back to the Airbnb to create a game plan for what they would do next to find some answers.

Maggie had no contacts within the Grasse police department and no pull aside from being a concerned American tourist who had witnessed the aftermath of a disturbing crime.

She certainly had no expectation after her brief interaction with Detective Landry that he would be willing to answer her questions—or even take a phone call from her.

Landry had struck her as callous and uncompromising. If he was crooked, too, he would be seriously inclined to protect himself. The question was, if he *was* bent, how bent was he?

Maggie had known plenty of police willing to work outside the lines or bend a rule a time or two, but she had yet to work with a corrupt policeman who might stop at nothing to protect himself.

Was that what she was dealing with here? Was Landry so corrupt he would break the law?

Perhaps even commit murder?

As she opened the apartment door Maggie did her best to shake that particular thought out of her head. Landry had no motive that she knew of to want Vivienne dead, and just because she had taken an immediate dislike to him, was no reason to make him a suspect in the murder.

Had he known Vivienne?

"Make yourself at home," she said to Annabelle. "I'll make tea."

Annabelle sat on the couch and Maggie watched the young woman's shoulders sag as she did. There was a familial resemblance between her and Vivienne and it was obviously that which had caught Maggie's eye when she noticed her at the tour this morning.

She brought a small tray of cups and saucers into the living room and set it on the coffee table in front of Annabelle.

"So, you mentioned that Vivienne knew Detective Landry," Maggie asked as she laid out spoons. "But nothing ever happened between them?"

Annabelle frowned. "Beyond the pass he made and the two tickets? She never mentioned it if it did."

Maggie went back to the kitchen to pour the boiling water into the teapot and added the tea bags. Suspect or not, bent cop or not, that would have to be the first thing she attempted to discover—how well had Landry known Vivienne?

She collected a small ewer of milk from the fridge and a bowl of sugar cubes and returned to the living room.

"Will you talk to Detective Landry?" Annabelle asked as Maggie poured tea into her cup and handed it to her.

"I will," Maggie said. "It'll probably be useless, but I'll at least try."

It occurred to her that Grace was actually the better choice for approaching Landry. She hadn't missed his not-so-subtle double-take when he first laid eyes on Grace. Maggie was used to Grace's effect on men and was well aware of those cases where that effect came in handy.

On the other hand, with Windsor's nonsense going on—and Grace's insecurity about it—it might not be a great time to put Grace on the front lines. Maggie had rarely seen her so vulnerable. She made a mental note to ask Laurent to reach out to Windsor to see if he could find out what was going on in Windsor's head—or if it was all inside Grace's. Maggie decided that Jean-Luis was a better person for Grace to approach. He was less overtly venal than Landry and Grace always had a way with the younger men.

"What do you want *me* to do?" Annabelle asked.

"Well, since you're the grieving relative, I think we'll keep you in the background. At least at first. I'll go talk to the people who owned the float to see what they saw."

"There's no way Vivienne would have voluntarily been on that float," Annabelle said.

"Really? Why not?"

"It's the sort of thing we did in *le lycée*. Vivienne was proud of her status now. She'd consider riding a parade float a backward step."

"Even if someone asked her to do it?"

"Who would do that? There are plenty of fifteen-year-olds who would die to ride the floats. There's no way Vivienne would've agreed to be on that float."

"So you think she was killed somewhere else and moved to the float?" Maggie chose her words carefully.

"How else? There were too many people on the float for her to have been killed there in broad daylight."

Annabelle shook her head, her voice catching.

"I can't believe that this is my sister we're talking about."

"I am so sorry for your loss, Annabelle. Were the two of you close?"

"We used to be. Not so much in later years. She was here and I live on the farm still."

"Oh? I didn't realize you were still growing flowers for the fragrance industry."

"Oh, not like that. I mean, yes, I'm growing flowers but in seriously small quantities for a ridiculous sum that does nothing to keep food on the table. And it's not for the perfume industry. There are a bunch of smaller operations around Grasse selling ingredients for unguents for pharmaceutical companies." She shrugged. "They don't need Chanel 5. They just need a benign salve that smells good."

"But you're still in the family business," Maggie said.

"I'm not, Madame Dernier, no," Annabelle said firmly. "Make no mistake about that."

After chatting a bit longer, Annabelle left to do some shopping in town before returning to the farm which was an hour's drive away.

Before separating she advised Annabelle to keep a low profile while Maggie and Grace did the leg work. Maggie got the sense that Annabelle was the kind of person who was led by her emotions. She might lash out at someone who otherwise might prove to be helpful to their investigation. It was best that she stayed out of the spotlight.

After Annabelle left, Maggie glanced at her watch and realized that Grace would still be in her workshop for another hour. That gave Maggie time to start talking to the float people. As she put away the tea things and rinsed out the teacups, Maggie felt a twinge of discouragement.

It's bad enough when the cops think you'll be in the way, she thought grimly.

It's a lot worse if they have something to hide and might do something desperate to keep it that way.

21

The garage on rue Amiral de Grasse was a long, squat building made of concrete blocks painted white. From where Maggie stood, she could see three large garage bays, and a loading area. The roll up door to one of the garage bays was open. Maggie stepped inside, noting the oil stains and cracks on the concrete floor.

Long, thick hoses and greasy looking wheels, levers and cables snaked across the concrete floor. Loose tires were stacked in rows straight ahead of her and an older station wagon was parked against the far wall.

"Hello? Is anyone here?" she called.

"What can I help you with, Madame?" a deep female voice said before the owner of it stepped up from a shallow maintenance bay.

"My name is Maggie Dernier. I'm making inquiries on behalf of the Grasse police."

Maggie had debated saying she was writing an article for the American Embassy on tourist traps but opted for this approach instead—even though, if she were to be reported for the lie she could be detained, fined or thrown out of town.

At the very least.

"Is this about Vivienne?" The heavyset woman with a ruddy face snorted. "It's about time."

Maggie frowned.

"Am I to understand that the police have not taken full statements from you yet?" she asked.

"Full statements? They haven't even talked to us!"

This confirmed what Maggie had been afraid of. It also went a long way to confirming in her mind that Landry might indeed be corrupt.

"Well, I'm here now," she said. "May I ask your name and how well you knew Vivienne Curie?"

"Known her all her life. Knew her folks too."

"And your name?"

"Marie-France Delmas. I'm a mechanic. Well, I do a bit of everything."

"Can you tell me what Vivienne's role was on the float?"

"Her role?"

"I know she wasn't the driver but was she supposed to be waving to the crowd? Throwing candy or flowers?"

"Her role was not to be here at all!"

This was as Annabelle had suggested.

"Can you show me the staging area for the float where Vivienne's body was found?"

"I can do better than that. I can show you the float."

Maggie was stunned to hear that the float was not off limits as a possible crime scene. She followed the woman across the garage to where a *flotter* was parked. Most of the floral decorations from the night of the parade were gone.

Maggie went to the spot on the float where she had first seen Vivienne sprawled. Amazingly, much of the petals that had covered the body were still there. Chilled, Maggie dug in her purse for a plastic baggy and began scooping the petals into it while Madame Delmas watched with interest.

"Where were you situated on the float?" Maggie asked as she stepped back to examine the float from a distance of several feet.

"Me? Do you think I had something to do with her death?" the woman said indignantly.

"I'm just trying to figure out what time Vivienne's body got put on the float," Maggie said. "What was your role in the parade?"

"I'm the Lilac fairy," Madame Delmas said huffily. "They're not all skinny, you know."

"So it was supposed to be just you and the driver on the float? What's his name?"

"You really are barking up the wrong Jacaranda bush if you think Louis had anything to do with this. He was drunk. He's always drunk."

"Does Louis have a last name?"

Madame Delmas sighed. "Frere," she said. "And trust me, he had no idea anything was going on."

"Could you tell me when you left the garage and when you joined the other floats in the street?"

Clearly torn between wanting Maggie to know what an imposition her questions were and feeling a little pleased to be the center of attention, Madame Delmas crossed her arms and affected to be thinking.

"Last year we went earlier but that was before Louis got into it with one of the parade organizers so this year, we were next to last. The first *char allégorique de parade* was on the move around eighteen hundred hours, and we were scheduled to pull out behind the blue garden one."

"What time was that?"

"I didn't look at my watch, but I think it was around nineteen hundred hours."

If that was anywhere near accurate it meant that Vivienne would have been dead no later than seven o'clock. Since

Maggie had no access to her autopsy or the forensics reports, she didn't know how much before that Vivienne might have been alive.

"Okay, so you were sitting on top, right?" she asked.

"Yes. There's a ladder on the far side of the float and then a chair on top."

"And you never came around to this side?"

Madame Delmas frowned again as if thinking.

"I walked all around the float before we started, but I didn't see anything."

Which meant that Vivienne's body was hidden just enough when, combined with the fact that Madame Delmas wasn't specifically looking for her, would account for why she hadn't spotted her. Or it might mean Vivienne hadn't been placed there until after the older woman had walked around the float.

Maggie wanted to rip her hair out in frustration.

There were so many questions with no facts or DNA to help fill the holes!

"Here comes Louis himself, if you want to hear what he saw that night," Madame Delmas said as an elderly man shuffled into the garage.

Even from six feet away Maggie could tell the man, easily in his seventies if not older, was inebriated.

"Monsieur Frere," she said, walking over to shake hands with him. "I'm Maggie Dernier."

"She's working with the police about what happened to Vivienne," Madame Delmas said.

Instantly the old man's face contorted into one of deep grief and Maggie was shocked to see tears pour down his face.

"Poor little one!" he said, reaching out to support himself on the float next to him. The waves of alcohol came off him in a steady haze. "It is catastrophic. Just catastrophic."

"Louis knew Jean Curie," Madame Delmas said. "Vivienne's father."

"In the old days," Louis said, mopping his wet cheeks with his threadbare flannel shirt sleeve. "We picked together, we drank together. I was there when he got the news of Vivienne's birth." He shook his head. "He would have been heartbroken today."

"Do you have any idea of how or why Vivienne would be on the float, Monsieur Frere?" Maggie asked.

He cracked his knuckles and snarled at her.

"Anyone with half a brain would know the answer to that question! She was murdered!"

"You don't know that, Louis," Madame Delmas said.

"Why else would she be there?" he asked her, his eyes bulging in incredulity.

"The police haven't said anything about murder," Madame Delmas said. "I've been reading the news trying to find information, but there's nothing."

"Was there any time *before* you got on the float when the float was not being watched?" Maggie asked them.

"Not watched?" Louis asked, confused.

"She wants to know if there was a time when someone might have had time to stuff Vivienne's body onto the float without our knowing it," Madame Delmas said.

Louis's face whitened as he was clearly imagining the scenario.

"We saw nothing," he said softly. "We failed her."

Maggie wanted to comfort him by saying that by then Vivienne would have been beyond saving. On the other hand, she knew that would be pretty cold comfort.

Instead, deciding she'd upset both of them enough, she gave her condolences, and left.

22

Grace took the only seat available on the terrace of the café. She ordered a quiche Lorraine with a salad and a glass of Sauvignon Blanc and turned her attention to the street. But she couldn't concentrate on what she was seeing.

The fragrance workshop had been worth the money, but Grace had felt so distracted throughout the session with thoughts of Windsor and poor Vivienne and now poor Annabelle that she'd not enjoyed a moment of it. Even so, she *had* been able to cobble together a fragrance for *Dormir*—one full of heavy floral notes which she thought appropriate since *Dormir* was situated practically in the middle of a lavender field. But the pleasure of the experience had been lost.

She picked up her phone and looked again at the text message from Maggie. She'd worded it as if to make her request no big deal, but Grace read right through it. Anyone with half a brain knew that one of them should be talking to the detective to see what information could be gleaned. Only Maggie hadn't asked Grace to do that. She'd asked her to talk to the bratty boyfriend instead.

Has she lost confidence in me?

She looked at her phone again and scrolled to the single text message she'd received from Windsor. <*cant talk now will call later*>

She'd tried calling him but received an automated message back saying he was currently unavailable. It was the sort of impersonal response one would send to a client or perhaps an annoying customer. Grace computed the time in Atlanta. It was one o'clock in France so it would be seven in the morning in the States. Surely, he would be awake by seven?

She tossed down a few euros for her coffee and uneaten meal and gathered up her bag.

Talking to Jean-Luis wasn't a taxing assignment, but at least it was something she could do to help. And right now, she needed to feel like that was something she could do.

She stepped out on rue Amiral de Grasse and looked both ways down the street.

The question now was where did one find a rich bad boy in a town dripping with them? As she walked down the street gazing in the shops as she passed, she found herself amending her assessment. Cannes and St-Tropez were more choc-a-bloc with playboys. In fact, Grasse was so overflowing with tourists, it made the Louvre Museum look positively undiscovered.

She stopped and looked down a narrow winding street.

So how would a rich young man, bored with life spend his days? Grace stepped into the street. Overhead loomed ochre yellow apartments. She mounted the seemingly endless series of stone steps where an impressive stone obelisk stood in front of Grasse Cathedral which dated back to the thirteenth century. She stopped for a moment to study the obelisk which, like most French villages, was a monument erected to honor those who'd served in one of the world wars.

Garlands of jasmine still draped over the rifle barrel on the soldier in the war memorial at the center of town from the festival two nights ago. She glanced past the monument to marvel that she could see for miles down onto the village and past it to the Mediterranean where she caught a glimpse of a glimmering sliver of a cruise ship.

Turning back, Grace read the plaque on the monument which listed every single man in the village of Grasse who'd fought in World War II, whether they'd returned or not.

She sighed and moved on. Surely a bored rich kid would not be spending a single minute sightseeing or reading war memorial plaques. Her stomach started to hurt as she realized how much time she was wasting.

She was letting her anxiety over Windsor affect her dedication to what she was supposed to be doing to help Annabelle! Whatever was happening with him, she'd know soon enough. And if it turned out he wanted to stay in the States—or even return to Susie—well, she had no control over that. She resolved to put the matter firmly tucked away in the back of her mind until the truth could be revealed. The truth. She would deal with that when the time was right. Not all this what-if nonsense that only weakened and distracted her.

Taking a long breath to match her conviction, she turned and wound her way back down the steep stone steps into the historic part of Grasse where the Dix Fleurs factory was sited. She glanced at her watch. It was well past lunch time. She didn't know if that meant Jean-Luis was more or less likely to be at the factory.

She debated going inside and decided that a revisit to the gift shop couldn't hurt. She stepped inside, instantly engulfed by the heavenly scent of the many competing fragrances, all of them heady and mostly floral. She walked around the shop's aisles, lightly touching a few items as she did. The walls in the gift shop were covered with brightly colored murals depicting the history of the fragrance industry in Grasse.

The artist had placed Grasse at the center of the Mediterranean, and piled the stone village high like Mont St-Michel. Grasse was neither of those things, but Grace didn't fault the artist for attempting to create a magical representation of the village. Another mural showed a vast field of intensely colored flowers, another of people from all over the world spraying scent on themselves.

The gift shop was busy. One of the tours must have just finished. As Grace turned down the final aisle toward the cash registers, she was surprised to see behind the counter none other than Jean-Luis Dix, himself.

She felt a throb of satisfaction that she'd found her prey. She imagined that her brief walk around the village in the sunlight and brisk wind had given her cheeks a glow, but she nonetheless ducked behind a conveniently located postcard carousel to inspect her makeup to make sure it *was* glow and not shine. She refreshed her lipstick and headed toward the counter where she watched an extremely bored Jean-Luis finish waiting on a stout female tourist, her arms loaded down with shopping bags from other stores.

When the woman finally turned away, Grace stepped up to the counter. Jean-Luis was focused on his phone, his brows knit into a web of concentration.

Grace smiled at him as if bemused by him.

"Yes?" he said sourly. He wasn't looking at her.

"That is a very interesting scent you're wearing," she said, ready with her best eyebrow arch to follow up on his soon-to-be unequivocal interest in her comment.

He didn't look up from his phone.

"If you're not going to buy anything," he said, "the next tour starts in an hour."

"I have taken the tour," Grace said, feeling the beginning threads of unease begin to pulse in her shoulders.

"Great."

"I must say, I found it lacked a personal touch," she said,

suddenly feeling too warm. "I was wondering if you might help with that."

Never in her life had she ever had to take such a brazen tack, but the woman behind her in line was pressing in and Grace didn't have time to finesse her approach.

She suddenly saw an image in her head of Windsor leaning in to kiss his ex-wife.

"Do you mind, Madame?" Jean-Luis said to her, still not looking at her. "I have customers."

Grace allowed herself to be nudged out of line by the woman behind her, her arms laden with bottles and boxes of Dix Fleurs scent.

She turned and walked to the exit, her face burning with humiliation.

23

Danielle kept an eye on the simmering lentils while she whisked a Dijon mustard vinaigrette. Amelie was watching cartoons in the living room. The child was being compliant today, which tended to worry Danielle. She knew the girl had her heart set on doing something—picking apples in the forbidden orchard or combing honey through little Nougat's fur—but was content to behave at the moment.

Danielle put a pan of cold water on the stove and added a half dozen fresh eggs for the boiled eggs she'd serve with lunch. Then she went to pull out a handful of rocket lettuce from the refrigerator for the salad.

Laurent had come back from his morning visit to Domaine St-Buvard out of sorts and ill-humored. She'd tried to ask him about it but one thing she knew about the man—if he didn't want to tell you, he wouldn't. She knew she needed to talk to him and sooner rather than later. She wasn't sure she could go through one more day without telling him—

Amelie was suddenly at Danielle's side in the kitchen. "Is *Opa* going to take me fishing today?" she asked.

Danielle carefully moved between the stove with the boiling pan of water and the girl.

"If he said he would, then he will," she said. "Have you washed your hands for lunch?"

Amelie frowned at the activity on the stove and Danielle could see her brain processing her interest—and temptation. She knew that a scalded hand would cure the girl, but she hated knowing that was the way Amelie needed to learn.

"Besides, you still have to dig up the worms, *n'est-ce pas, chérie?*"

Amelie's eyes widened as she realized that Danielle was correct. But before she could turn and run out of the kitchen, Danielle grabbed her arm.

"After lunch," Danielle said firmly.

Amelie hesitated and then nodded, moving toward the small bathroom off the salon to wash her hands.

Danielle was proud of the fact that even though Amelie wasn't immediately getting her way, she wasn't throwing a tantrum.

Petit à petit l'oiseau construit son nid.

Little by little the bird builds its nest.

As she turned back to the stove, she saw Laurent coming across the garden path from Prune Cottage.

"You may watch TV until I call you for lunch," Danielle said to Amelie.

Laurent came into the kitchen and glanced first at Amelie in the salon and then at what Danielle had on the stove. He had a fresh baguette in his hands.

"*Ah, bon,*" Danielle said, holding her hand out for the baguette.

Laurent grunted in response but before he could turn away, she spoke up again.

"Did you see the boys at Domaine St-Buvard?"

Laurent grunted again.

"I've been meaning to ask you how you feel about them being there...on their own?" she said.

"It's different times, Danielle," Laurent said, but she could see in his face that he wasn't happy about it either.

"I thought Jem and Luc would spend more time with us," she said.

Laurent leaned against the counter and crossed his arms. "I know what you're doing, Danielle."

"*Moi?*" she said innocently. "Well, I suppose they are young. And there's a girl."

"Do you think that's a problem?"

Danielle frowned for a moment.

"Maybe," she said. "I'm just not sure how serious it is."

"Which one does she belong to?"

"Possibly neither. Maybe *that* is the problem."

"Or she belongs to one but hasn't made that clear to all parties," Laurent said.

"Ah. Yes. That would do it."

It occurred to Danielle as she scooped up the boiled eggs in a slotted spoon and settled them in the bowl of waiting ice water, that she and Laurent rarely interacted, just the two of them. For twenty years, the busy family dynamic had always ensured that someone else was around. Usually, several someone else's.

When Jean-Luc was alive, he and Laurent practically had their own private language. She felt a shiver of foreboding that she quickly shook off. She had been glad for Laurent to have had a father figure and for Jean-Luc, who was childless, to have had the son he'd always dreamed of.

"Something is on your mind?" Laurent asked.

Danielle laughed. There was never any hope of keeping something from Laurent. She wondered how Maggie managed all these years or if she just accepted that he would always uncover her secrets.

"I am seeing someone," she said bluntly and found herself digging her fingernails into the palms of her hands, awaiting his response.

"Yes," Laurent said. "Bernard."

Danielle gave him an incredulous stare.

"You...you knew?"

He frowned. "Was it supposed to be a secret?"

Danielle hid her smile with a hand that she realized was shaking.

Of *course,* Laurent would know that she'd had the odd coffee with Bernard. He would have heard about Bernard's few impromptu visits to *Dormir,* the picnic that time when it rained, and he'd deposited her back home sopping wet. Laurent would know Bernard as the retired postmaster in the village. As usual, what one thought Laurent was seeing was always just the tip of what he was actually seeing.

"I think it's serious," she said softly, more afraid than she could ever remembered being.

If Laurent turned away from her or shared his concerns with Maggie, Danielle didn't know if she could ever face either of them again. Jean-Luc had been a beloved member of the family. The closest thing to a patriarch, the one they all looked to.

Laurent reached out and took her hand.

"I'm glad, *chérie.* Bernard is a decent man."

Danielle smiled tremously. "He is. But...what about Jean-Luc?"

"Are you asking me or yourself?" Laurent asked, arching an eyebrow but then relenting. He squeezed her hand.

"Jean-Luc would be happy for you, *non*? Could I be anything less?"

"I'm not sure Jean-Luc would be happy for me at all," she said, wiping away a tear.

"Well, since we'll never know, let us assume the best, eh? Jean-Luc wouldn't want you lonely."

"I haven't been lonely."

"Yes, but there is more to life than child minding and playing cards with your girlfriends. If you have the offer of more, you should take it."

"You don't mind?"

Laurent snorted in amusement and then seeing how upset she was, he patted her hand.

"Jean-Luc was my first real step into becoming a family," Laurent said. "I will honor him all the days of my life. Nothing can push the memory of that away."

Danielle nodded. "I miss him."

"I know you do."

"I can't help but think that you or the children might think I'm forgetting him if I...if I allow Bernard to join us."

"They know how much you loved Jean-Luc," Laurent said. "And they will learn to love Bernard, too in time."

"Oh, Laurent, do you think so?"

Danielle's eyes sparked tears. It was all too much to hope for. To imagine Bernard sitting at this kitchen table, perhaps Amelie on one knee, and everyone knowing him and his little jokes and his small ways.

Laurent leaned over and kissed her. "I do, *chérie*. Invite the man to dinner. Here at *Dormir* or, if you'd rather, Domaine St-Buvard."

Danielle dabbed at her eyes.

"I'd rather he came here," she said. "But I would appreciate your help with the cooking. Bernard is a bit of a *gourmande*."

Laurent grinned. "I like him already."

∽

After leaving Danielle in the kitchen with her happy thoughts to finish making lunch, Laurent went back out to check on his morning plumbing project. And to think.

The path to Mirabelle Cottage was gravel and narrow. It needed weeding. He'd have to have a word with Gabriel again. It occurred to him that it was the sort of work that any of the children could manage easily enough, even Amelie. He frowned.

Regardless of what he'd just told Danielle, not all his feelings about the situation were happy ones. But of course, like so much in his life, those thoughts were not ones he could share.

24

After leaving the garage, Maggie wasn't completely sure what she'd learned, short of the fact that the police hadn't bothered to get statements from their main witnesses.

She glanced at her watch. She still had thirty minutes before Grace would be back at the apartment. She'd texted her about the possibility of her interviewing Jean-Luis and was hopeful that she'd have something to report when they met up again. As for herself, aside from confirming what they already knew—that the police weren't working the case—she had nothing new to report.

Maggie set her jaw and strode down the street to the rue Jean Ossola where La Nuit Est Belle was located. From fifteen yards away she could see a sign on the door announcing the factory was closed to visitors. But that didn't deter her. She felt sure that Florent and *le nez* would be working.

As she approached, she slowed her steps when the side door to the factory opened and Mathys Tremblay stepped out, lighting a cigarette as he went. Maggie frowned. She was positive that Vivienne had said that smoking was the biggest no-no of all for the proper working of a "nose" in the fragrance business. She watched as Tremblay turned to make his way toward a side alley, clearly intending to smoke in private.

Too bad, she thought as she walked to the alley.

She touched both sides of the rough stone walls to steady herself so she wouldn't trip on the lumpy cobblestones which hadn't been replaced in centuries.

Tremblay stood leaning against one of the walls taking in big gulps of smoke and spewing it out until it circled his head in a cloud of noxious vapors.

Maggie's shoe made a scraping sound as she approached and he snapped his head around, his fingers poised to throw away his cigarette. When he saw her, he hesitated and then brought the cigarette back to his mouth.

Clearly, Tremblay was preparing to hide his habit from his boss, but a lowly tourist was not worth losing a whole cigarette over.

"I thought smoking was bad for *le nez*," Maggie said as she approached.

"Bugger off," he snarled in French.

"Goodness. Is that anyway to talk to a paying customer? Are you so far removed from the retail side of your business not to know proper etiquette?"

He glared at her and for a moment, Maggie could imagine him throwing his lit cigarette in her face.

Now that she knew how little the police were interested in solving Vivienne's murder—although she didn't yet know why—she had to assume they never bothered talking to either Tremblay or Florent. Now was her chance to amend that little oversight.

"I was wondering where you were during the parade," she said. "You and Vivienne seemed close. Did you watch it together?"

She watched his face as initial astonishment gave way to a

growing fury. Now he did throw down his cigarette. He turned to face her, drawing himself up to his full height of at least six feet.

"What are you implying?" he growled. "That I killed Vivienne?"

"Did you?" Maggie pointed to the cigarette butt on the ground. "I'm sure she didn't love the fact that you were polluting your abilities as a nose. Vivienne believed in the company. A company you are clearly intent on taking advantage of."

He approached her angrily and it took everything Maggie had in her not to take a step backward. It was a risk but, in her experience, provoking unstable people often resulted in them telling her things they otherwise wouldn't.

Of course, it often resulted in other things, too. Things much less desirable.

"You don't know what you're talking about! Vivienne was no more loyal to…" But he caught himself and lifted a lip in a sneer as if realizing what Maggie was trying to get him to admit.

"Are you saying she *wasn't* loyal to La Nuit Est Belle?" Maggie asked. "Because I spoke with her the day she died, and I know differently."

This was a bluff of course. Maggie hadn't known Vivienne well enough to really know her. But she'd certainly given an amazing impersonation of someone loyal to her company and the perfume business.

"You don't know anything," Tremblay spat out, raking Maggie from head to toe with his eyes. "Vivienne—she was so pretty, and such a good actress with the tourists. But she was going to be the death of our business."

"I thought she was the face of your business," she said, goading him.

"The lying face! She wanted to destroy what we were building, and nobody knew! Nobody could imagine that sweet little

Vivienne—" his voice cracked and he expelled an audible breath.

"How was she lying exactly? She promoted the fragrance business to every visitor to Grasse, every single day. Your own boss Florent said she was irreplaceable."

He laughed roughly.

"Did he now? That is not what he told *me* when he told me to—"

He caught himself in time and his eyes became guarded.

"Who are you, Madame? Why are you here in this alley with me?"

Maggie was mildly surprised that he would dare to make such an overt threat to her.

"I'm working with police," she said.

"That is a lie."

Tremblay's face showed no doubt at all. He knew the police, she realized. And he knew they would not be investigating Vivienne's death.

Did he also know why?

"Well, then, I'm a concerned citizen of the world. I met Vivienne. I liked her. She was murdered and nobody seems to care. Not even you and I thought you were her friend."

His laugh was a harsh bark.

"Friend? Yes, we were friends. Friends enough that I wasn't looking in her direction when she stuck the knife in my back."

"Sounds like you had a motive for wanting her dead, Monsieur Tremblay."

He snorted.

"Me and everyone who knew her," he said before pushing past her and walking away.

25

As Maggie made her way back to the Airbnb, she put a call in to the Grasse police station, asking to speak with Detective Landry. She wasn't surprised when she was told he was unavailable to take her call. The act—as fruitless as she was sure it would be—nonetheless helped her feel better about what she would need to do going forward.

Annabelle had done her shopping and was waiting for Maggie at the door of the apartment. Maggie was surprised since she thought the young woman had intended to go back to the farm.

"Hello, Annabelle," Maggie said. "Is Grace not back yet?"

"I don't know," Annabelle said. "I knocked but nobody answered."

Frowning, Maggie unlocked the door and stepped inside. Immediately she could feel the moisture in the air that told her Grace was in the shower. She led Annabelle into the living room.

"Where are your groceries?" she asked. "I thought you were going to the produce markets."

"I put them in my car," Annabelle said. "I got an idea as I

was shopping that you might agree to come with me to Vivienne's apartment."

"Yes, of course," Maggie said. Why hadn't she thought of that?

"I don't know if it will tell us anything," Annabelle admitted. "But I am not really up to looking at her things by myself. I hope you don't mind."

"Not at all," Maggie assured her, as Grace stepped into the living room in a casual tie-dye slip dress, her hair styled in careful curls around her shoulders.

"Hey, how was the fragrance workshop?" Maggie asked. There was something *off* about Grace and Maggie noticed it immediately. Something brittle and artificial. Maggie had seen Grace through many bad stages in her life—divorce, bankruptcy, substance abuse, estrangement from her children to name just a few. She knew when Grace was putting on a brave front to hide what she was feeling.

Had something happened?

"It was lovely," Grace said breezily. "I now have a unique, signature scent for *Dormir* that will allow my guests to imagine themselves bedding down in a lavender field as cookie sheets of macarons are being baked in the next room. Shall I make coffee?" Grace smiled a greeting at Annabelle.

"Annabelle has suggested we check out Vivienne's apartment," Maggie said. "I guess we can probably assume the police haven't been there so we might actually find a clue or two. Meanwhile, were you able to track down Jean-Luis?"

"Oh, sorry," Grace said woodenly. "I caught him in the middle of something and he was too distracted to be helpful, so I cut the interview short. How about you? Any luck?"

Maggie had already decided to keep her interview with Mathys Tremblay to herself. It would only serve to upset Annabelle to see how reviled her sister had been by the chemist.

"Not really," Maggie said. "The people on the float said the cops didn't even question them. I didn't see anyone after that."

"Is this going to work?" Annabelle said fretfully. "Neither of you were able to talk to anyone? Is this a wild-goose chase?"

"Not at all, Annabelle," Maggie assured her. "It's always a bit hit or miss in the beginning of any investigation. This is totally normal. Right, Grace?"

Grace smiled too broadly. "Absolutely. Totally normal."

Now Maggie was *sure* something had happened.

26

Vivienne's apartment was in a medieval building down a narrow lane. The building's yellowing walls were cracked, with grooves and black spots where they'd aged irregularly. Its sooty windowsills were clogged with dust and grime.

Maggie shivered in spite of herself as the three of them walked down the street to Vivienne's front door.

The barely leafed-out branches of a towering elm tree rustled overhead as the breeze gathered itself.

Maggie was not at all surprised to see that there was no police tape barring the door of Vivienne's apartment. But when Annabelle used her key to unlock the door, Maggie was shocked to see that the place gave evidence of having been systematically and roughly searched—drawers were pulled out and emptied on the carpet, side tables turned over, couch cushions ripped, their stuffing strewn about the living room.

Annabelle emitted a cry of anguish.

"I can't believe this!" she said. "That the police could do this! The bastards!"

Maggie and Grace shared a glance. It was obvious that

neither the police nor their results-happy forensic techs had done this. This mayhem was created by someone who was looking for something. Desperately looking.

"How could they?" Annabelle said as she went to a small writing desk in the corner, laying on its side. A pen cup, potted plant, and framed photos that must have sat atop it, were now scattered and broken on the floor.

Maggie picked up one of the picture frames. In it was a black and white photo of two girls, clearly Vivienne and Annabelle. They looked to be in their early teens, their arms around each other, smiling broadly.

"The police didn't do this," Maggie said as she handed the photo to Annabelle.

The young woman's head snapped around to stare at her. Her face was bleached of all color.

"Are you sure?" she asked and then looked again at the room as if assessing it from this new perspective. "Then...who? And how did they get in?"

Maggie went to the window and saw that it was open an inch. Since the front door hadn't been jimmied or bashed in, this was clearly the way the vandal had gotten into the apartment. She thought it odd that whoever had done this had bothered to close the window behind him—or her—on the way out.

"Looks like they came in through the window," Maggie said. "Would Vivienne have left it open?" It didn't look as if it had been forced.

"The nights have been cooler lately," Annabelle said. "Vivienne might have opened it for the air."

She sat down heavily on the single bed. It too had been sliced apart by the same knife that had gone to work on the couch. She put her head in her hands.

Maggie was tempted to comfort her but decided there was nothing she could say to temper what Annabelle was seeing. She turned and went into the kitchen instead.

In many ways, the scene here was even worse than the living room. Drawers were pulled out, pantry items tossed on the floor, dishes broken.

In Maggie's mind, the concern that was only slightly less worrisome than the fact that Vivienne's apartment had been so ruthlessly searched was the fact that the police hadn't bothered processing it at all.

"I don't suppose you have any idea what they were looking for?" Grace asked Annabelle.

Annabelle's face clouded over and she shook her head.

"I can't even imagine," she said. "Do you think it was the same person who killed her?"

"Probably," Grace said gently.

Maggie went over to the desk and knelt beside it.

"Did Vivienne own a laptop?" she asked.

"Not that I know of," Annabelle said. "But as I said, we'd been drifting apart the last few years."

Maggie noted that Annabelle had *not* exactly said that before now.

"What about a cellphone?" she asked.

"Everyone has a cellphone," Annabelle said with a frown.

It seemed likely to Maggie that whoever killed Vivienne—and whoever tossed her room—was now very probably in possession of her cellphone. She blew out a breath of frustration.

"Is there any hiding place that you can think of?" she asked, looking around the room.

"Do you have hiding places in *your* home?" Annabelle asked. "What normal person has a hiding place? I certainly don't."

As the young woman spoke, getting more and more agitated, Maggie went to the built-in bookcase by the upturned desk. Vivienne must not have been a great reader since there were no books on the shelves, only small sculptures, perfume bottles and framed postcards. Maggie reached into each of the shelves, probing to the very back. On the bottom shelf, her fingers touched something hard and small.

Suddenly Annabelle jumped up from the bed.

"None of this is helping," she said, wringing her hands. "The cops haven't searched her place. Only the creature who killed her has been here. And whatever he was looking for, he probably found. What's the point of any of this?"

"Annabelle, I know this is hard," Maggie said as she got to her feet and dusted off the clinging debris of errant pillow stuffing and lint from her knees.

"How do you know?" Annabelle said glaring at Maggie. "Has somebody killed *your* sister?"

Maggie swallowed hard but before she could answer, Grace went to Annabelle and took her hand.

"Actually," she said. "Maggie may be the only person here who does know how you're feeling."

Annabelle took a moment to process what Grace was saying and then turned back to Maggie, her eyes filling with tears.

"Oh, Maggie," she said. "Forgive me."

Maggie smiled sadly at her. Elise's murder had been a long time ago and, in the end, Maggie had succeeded in getting justice for her. Even so, it wasn't until this moment that she realized that the driving force for her to want to help Annabelle was unquestionably connected to the murder of her own sister.

"It's fine, Annabelle," she said. "I'm not upset. And what you're going through—angry one minute and sad the next—it's perfectly normal."

Annabelle sat down on the destroyed bed once more.

"Had you fought with your sister before she died?" she asked. "Had you said unforgivable things to her and then never got the chance to take them back?"

Maggie came and sat down next to her.

"My sister and I were not close," she said. "She left home

when I was a teenager, breaking our parents' hearts in the process, and with only a handful of letters in the ensuing years before I was called to identify her body in the Cannes police morgue."

Annabelle swallowed hard.

"What were the harsh words about?" Maggie asked gently.

A part of her thought it might help Annabelle to unburden herself. Another part of her needed to know if the fight between the sisters could be related to Vivienne's death. She wasn't consciously thinking of Annabelle as a suspect. Not really.

Annabelle ran a trembling hand over her face. Her shoulders seemed to curl in over her chest in shame.

"I need help on the farm," she said. "I tried to talk her into coming back with me. When she refused, I told her I needed her to at least help financially."

"Was this financial aid request in order to keep the farm afloat or for you?" Maggie asked carefully.

Annabelle narrowed her eyes.

"To keep the farm," she said. "My family has owned that farmland for nearly two hundred years. My parents are gone. It's just me now. It's a legacy. One that mattered to me. It once mattered to Vivienne, too."

"So, she refused to give you money?" Grace asked.

"Oh, she offered me a place to stay." Annabelle waved a hand around the room. "*Temporarily*, she said. Until I found a job. She just wasn't listening. She didn't care enough to listen."

Maggie could well imagine the sort of bitter exchange that kind of fundamental schism might prompt.

"I try not to think of the things we said to each other," Annabelle said in a soft voice, her shoulders sagging under her guilt and despair.

The three of them sat quietly for a moment. Maggie wanted

to give Annabelle time to digest what had happened to her and her sister. Then she got up and pulled a pillow free of its case.

"Why don't you take a few things now?" she said. "And we can come back later for the rest."

Annabelle nodded miserably and took the pillowcase from Maggie. She stood up and listlessly began picking up strewn items from around the apartment. Grace shook her head sadly as Maggie went to the refrigerator to see if any food might possibly be salvaged.

27

Laurent leaned over the bathroom sink to inspect his morning's work and was satisfied that it was holding. He turned the faucet on and off. It was no longer leaking.

The truth was, he was glad that Danielle felt like she could talk to him about Bernard. And he was glad to know that she hadn't given up on love. It pleased him to know the woman to whom he owed so much would get a third chapter at love. He grimaced in memory of Danielle's first chapter—a man who had brought her to this very property as a young bride—and kept her emotionally and physically captive before finally freeing her by committing a crime that nearly decimated Domaine St-Buvard, itself.

Laurent often wondered how Danielle felt about living in her old home—now operated as a bed and breakfast. Eduard Marceau had allowed Danielle to divorce him while he was in prison and when she married Jean-Luc she'd gone to live in his house. When Eduard died a few years into his sentence, he left this property to her. She'd sold it with its surrounding vineyards and all its bad memories to Laurent.

After Danielle moved in to help run *Dormir*, Laurent often wondered at the sad reminders Danielle couldn't help but have of nearly every room in the place. Or was it now so changed by the ring of children's laughter and moments around the salon stove—with good food and loving friends—that those memories never generated?

Yes, Jean-Luc was a good man, salt of the earth and solid. But Laurent's relationship with him had begun with a betrayal —and the near destruction of Domaine St-Buvard. It was true that Jean-Luc had become a loving and trusted father figure for many years afterwards, but it had been Laurent's ability to forgive him that had allowed it to happen.

Laurent's own father—a war hero, renowned and *fêted* throughout Paris—had been a cold man and disconnected to both his sons. Giving Jean-Luc a second chance after his treachery was one of the hardest things Laurent had ever done. And one of the most rewarding.

He smiled to himself. That had been largely Maggie's doing. She'd pressed him to forgive Jean-Luc, for his own sake if not Jean-Luc's.

As Laurent looked around the cottage, he glanced out the window and it hit him that, flawed though he was, Jean-Luc had been the kind of father Laurent had always tried to be. And he realized that the generous, indulgent grandfather that Jean-Luc had been with Jemmy, Mila and Zouzou was a personal template for Laurent for being the kind of *Opa* to his own grandchild.

He went to check on the faucets in the cottage's small kitchen before recognizing he was feeling a strong urge to talk with Maggie. He stepped outside onto the small deck and put a call in to her. The sky held a threat of more rain, but that would be beneficial for the grapes and for the red poppies that grew wild at *Dormir*.

The call rang and rang before finally going to voicemail.

Laurent didn't leave a message. He tried to remember the last time he'd spoken to her.

They've probably had to turn their phones off for the tours.

He put his phone away and went back to the bathroom to pick up his tools. He had a lot on his mind, not least of which was figuring out what was going on with Luc and Jemmy and whether it was something he could fix. He had no doubt that whatever it was would require fixing. Then, he thought with a heaviness creeping into his bones, there was that talk Frère Jean was expecting him to give later this afternoon at *l'Abbaye de Sainte-Trinité*.

But as he hefted his bag of tools onto one shoulder and locked the cottage door behind him, he forced himself to shove aside his dour thoughts. He stepped off the porch and headed back to the main house.

Because before all that, I have a date with a little girl and a can of worms.

28

After leaving Annabelle at her car with a small bag of groceries from Vivienne's apartment and a few mementos and framed pictures, Maggie and Grace walked back to their apartment.

Neither of them spoke until they were at their front door. For a moment Maggie imagined how *she'd* feel if she'd returned to a loved ones' apartment to find the shocking and heinous scene that Vivienne's apartment had revealed to Annabelle.

Who had broken into her apartment? Was it truly the killer looking for something? Had he tried torturing Vivienne first? Her glimpse of the body had been too brief to determine something like that. She felt a wave of frustration at having so little information from the police.

It's not even like they don't want to help.

They don't want anyone else to help either.

Inside the apartment, the air had the light jasmine scent from one of the candles that Grace had been burning earlier that she'd bought from the La Nuit Est Belle gift shop.

"Annabelle just about broke my heart today," Grace said wearily as she unwound the brightly colored Hermès scarf from her neck and dropped it on the quilted chair in the living room.

"I know."

"I'm sorry if I was insensitive, darling. You know. About Elise."

Maggie waved away her words.

"That was a long time ago. And I was nowhere as close to Elise as Vivienne and Annabelle were."

"Are you sure about that?" Grace asked. "Didn't it sound as if they'd had a falling out?"

"Sisters," Maggie said with a shrug.

"If you say so. Tea?"

"Sounds good," Maggie said as she pulled her laptop out of its sleeve. "Meanwhile, now that Annabelle's gone, can you tell me what happened with Jean-Luis?"

Only silence came from the kitchen.

"Grace?"

Grace came into the living room. "I did speak with him," she said. "Sort of."

"Yeah, okay. Good. So?"

"So, nothing, dearest," Grace said but Maggie saw her eyes glistening.

"Grace?"

"Oh, stop it, Maggie! Nothing happened, okay?" Grace said, a pained expression on her face. "I approached him with my best come-on, and he basically asked me if I had something in my eye."

"No, he didn't."

"No, he didn't. Because that would have taken too much effort on his part."

"What are you talking about?" Maggie asked impatiently.

"He treated me as if I were a pest," Grace bit out.

Maggie nearly laughed but stopped herself.

"Welcome to my world," she said, raising an eyebrow at her friend. "Half the people I know treat me like that."

"You don't understand," Grace said crossly. "Jean-Luis didn't even look at me! Except maybe to...to sneer."

"Don't be ridiculous."

Grace turned to her, her cheeks burning with emotion.

"I'm not!" she said hotly. "He looked at me the way we look at Karen Dixon! Like he could see right through me and what he saw was a forty-six-year-old woman trying too hard."

"That is absurd, Grace!"

"Did you or did you not send me to interview Jean-Luis because he was vain and liked women and you thought I might disarm him?"

"Well, yes, but..."

"And didn't you decide *not* to have me approach Landry for the same reason?"

"Now wait a minute, Grace," Maggie said, standing up. "I didn't want you batting your eyes at Landry to get information out of him because at the moment you seem to be a little vulnerable with whatever is going on with Windsor. I didn't want to make things worse for you."

"I don't know if that's better than what I thought or not," Grace said. "In any case, I'm a liability."

"Just stop it," Maggie said firmly. "I'm happy to indulge you up to a point, but you thinking you're a liability is ridiculous."

"That's me, ridiculous."

"Okay, so this conversation is over. If you didn't get anything out of Jean-Luis, fine. I was sure he was going to be a pill anyway. Shake it off, please."

"Whatever you say."

Maggie threw up her hands in helpless frustration. She understood what Grace was saying, but honestly, the fact was that she herself, although pretty enough, had never experienced every man in a restaurant turning their heads when she walked into a room. And that had always been life as normal for Grace.

What happens when a beautiful woman ages?

Grace was still beautiful. But it was also true that she didn't command the unbridled admiration that she had in her thirties. Who does? Even in France, where French men happily ogle women well into their seventies, there comes a time when the power of attraction wanes.

For a woman of Grace's dynamic and neverending attraction, the loss of that could be devastating.

After Grace retired to the kitchen to finish preparing the tea, Maggie turned her attention back to her laptop and felt in her pocket for the jump drive she'd found at the back of the shelf in Vivienne's apartment.

She inserted it into the USB port on her laptop and woke up her machine. She wasn't sure why she hadn't announced her discovery to Grace or Annabelle at the time, but something had told her not to mention it. She felt a flush of guilt as she saw the folder from the jump drive appear on her desktop. The folder was named *Top Secret*, interestingly, the same in French as English.

Grace came into the room and set down a steaming mug of tea on Maggie's desk.

"I was wondering," Grace said, now fully composed—every golden hair in place in her perfectly coifed hairstyle, not a smudge of mascara to indicate anything but total control and self-possession.

"If we can't get any help from Detective Landry," she said, "you could always ring up Roger Bedard. He's always happy to help."

Maggie gave herself a moment by taking a tentative sip of her hot tea. The fact was, she'd been debating whether to call Roger for the past day. The rub lay in the fact that she had a complicated relationship with him which was made increasingly more complicated every time she reached out to him.

Currently a *Capitaine* in the Central Directorate of the Judicial Police in Nice, Roger had been the head homicide detective in Aix-en-Provence for years until he'd been unceremoniously demoted and shifted to the coast as a result of a favor he'd done for Maggie eight years ago.

A dear friend but with dangerous strings attached, Roger had repeatedly proved himself immeasurably helpful to Maggie. The trouble was, reaching out to him always involved much more than a simple favor.

Laurent had been extremely patient with her unusual friendship with Roger. As a result, she was always aware of those moments when she might be tempted to take advantage of that patience when she didn't absolutely have to. Usually, she waited until her need for Roger's help was literally life and death. She told herself it was the least she could do since she knew he continued to love her in a mutually acknowledged one-way street of devotion.

But still, it *would* be very helpful if she could at least find out if Jean-Luis Dix had a record of any kind. And Roger could get her that information easily. A few keystrokes on his computer, that was all. And Grace was right that they certainly weren't going to be getting that kind of information from Detective Landry.

"He's my avenue of last resort," Maggie said. "Unless Detective Landry decides *you* killed Vivienne—or me—I'm keeping the Roger card firmly in my back pocket."

"Mm-mm, I'm sure that's exactly where Detective Bedard is only too happy to be," Grace said.

"Very amusing," Maggie said turning back to her laptop and the ominous folder.

"What are you doing?" Grace looked over Maggie's shoulder. "Researching La Nuit Est Belle?"

"Something like that," Maggie said as she clicked on the folder, her excitement building.

She felt her mouth go dry when she opened the single document inside the folder and saw with mounting astonishment what she would never have expected to see.

She skimmed the document, and then read it line by line two more times before emitting a gasp that made Grace look over at her.

"What is it?" Grace asked.

Maggie felt the goosebumps race up and down both arms as she closed the document, entitled *Sport du Sang*—Blood Sport—and then opened it back up again. Somewhere in the back of her brain she was aware of Grace getting up to stand behind her again.

"Darling? Did you find something?"

"Grace," Maggie said breathily, as she read the brief contents of the document for the third time. "You are not going to believe this!"

29

Maggie stared in disbelief at the open document before her on her laptop screen. At first, it didn't seem possible what she was seeing. But the more she read and reread the document, the more undeniable it became.

Vivienne had stolen the formula for *Mon Sang,* Dix Fleur's international breakout seller.

Here it was—along with at least a dozen other fragrance formulas—including the exact engineering information, method and production processes for Dix Fleur's biggest selling fragrance.

"What does it mean?" Grace said in a horrified voice.

"It means Capuccine has a motive for murder," Maggie said grimly. "It means that a lot of what we thought we knew is wrong. Like Vivienne being who she pretended to be."

"Where did you find the file?"

"It was on a jump drive I found at Vivienne's apartment."

"You stole a jump drive from her apartment?"

Maggie twisted around in her seat to look at her.

"I think you're focusing on the wrong thing," she said.

"Don't you understand what we're looking at? *Vivienne stole trade secrets.*"

"How are you going to tell Annabelle what you found without telling her you stole the jump drive?"

Maggie pinched her lips together.

"Look," she said, "I didn't tell Annabelle because I couldn't take the chance she would insist the jump drive belonged to her. Was I supposed to let her walk off with it without seeing what was on it?"

"You don't trust Annabelle?"

"I don't know who I trust. Can we table that particular question for a bit? Because what we know now is that Vivienne was doing something illegal. Something that could get her killed."

Grace looked unconvinced. "It's perfume, for heaven's sake."

"You heard what Vivienne said! Fragrance is big money in Grasse."

Maggie gestured to the documents on her screen.

"*Mon Sang* is Dix Fleurs' biggest seller," she said as opened another browser window. Her fingers flew over the keyboard until she found what she was looking for.

"The company made well over a billion euros last year. Do I need to look up the exact amount they made the year before *Mon Sang* when they were only selling soap fragrances to the shampoo companies?"

Grace sat down beside Maggie and put a hand to her head as if it had begun to ache.

"So you think Vivienne stole the formula for *Mon Sang* in order to sell it to one of the other fragrance operations?" she asked.

"Maybe. My first thought is that the other factories are all too big to involve themselves in something like this. It's too big a risk."

"Okay, so then, she was stealing it to give to La Nuit Est

Belle. Do you think Florent asked her to do it? And how did she get the formula? Through Jean-Luis?"

"I don't know. All good questions."

Maggie's brain raced back to her conversation with Mathys Tremblay. Was this the reason he was so angry with Vivienne? Did he know what she was doing? Why would he be angry about receiving a money-making formula like this? La Nuit Est Belle could tweak it just enough to make it different, slap their own label on it and step back to rake in the profits.

Or did Tremblay think that Vivienne had dishonored the company in some way? He was angry at her. Did he believe that her theft jeopardized the integrity of the company he was vice president of?

Another thought slithered into her brain as cold and quick as a cobra.

Or was he in on the theft and afraid that if it ever got out that La Nuit Est Belle was stealing competitor's secrets, it would ruin him and the company?

Either way, it was motive for wanting Vivienne Curie dead.

August Landry eased back into the basketweave chair on the terrace of the Café Constant. It was his favorite place, and the waiters all knew him. They knew what he liked before he knew himself. He grinned at the thought that French waiters have a reputation for being surly and rude. And yet the ones he knew made it clear they'd shine his shoes for him if he wanted.

The rain had slacked off so that what was left was a clean scent with a floral underlay. Or perhaps he was imagining that. He'd just received his packet from the Grasse tourist board and it had been fatter than usual. He'd hinted to them at the last meeting that a bonus would be appropriate considering how

Grasse's reputation for cleanliness and lack of crime was down to him.

Making a dead body disappear in the middle of the Jasmine parade—especially with Vivienne not an insubstantial member of the community—*that* had truly been worth a little extra in the bonus department.

He ordered a plate of oysters and a bottle of champagne knowing there would be no bill, and also knowing that a clear head was not required for the rest of his afternoon. An impromptu visit to his lover to recharge his batteries and then perhaps a nap before dinner were definitely in order.

His phone rang and he glanced at the screen and smiled.

Speak of the devil, he thought. He picked up the phone and said smugly, "Landry, Commandant de police."

"Perhaps you will not be for much longer," the voice said on the line.

The smile dropped from Landry's face. "Monsieur Shibel? Is there a problem?"

"You tell me, *Commandant*," the voice said snidely. "It was our understanding that the news of a certain popular tour guide being found dead in the middle of Grasse's biggest annual festival would not become public knowledge."

Landry switched hands holding the cellphone and shifted in his seat.

What in heavens was the man talking about? Landry had made the entire incident disappear!

"I don't understand," Landry said, pushing his dish away, no longer hungry. "That case was put to bed and closed with no press to indicate it ever happened."

"Oh, really?" Shibel said in a raised, agitated voice. "Well, perhaps you should tell that to the two American women running all over Grasse asking questions of anyone who might know something about it! *They* don't seem to think the case is closed!"

Landry ground his teeth in frustration.

"They have been sent packing," he said. "I assure you, they are no longer in Grasse, nor are they asking any questions."

Or at least they soon won't be.

"Make sure that is the case. We are not in the habit of handing out bonuses for nothing."

After his caller had hung up, Landry switched his order from champagne to whiskey. But even that didn't seem to help put out the fire that had suddenly begun to smolder deep in his gut.

30

That evening before dinner, Maggie put a phone call in to Laurent to update him on what was going on and to let him know that she and Grace would be staying a day longer, but he never picked up. This wasn't unusual for Laurent who often left his phone on the kitchen counter before leaving for the day.

She tried calling Danielle too and felt a throb of unease when *she* didn't answer either before sending off texts to both of them.

<Anything going on? Call when you get a moment.>

She was tempted to text Luc and Jemmy too but decided she didn't want them to think she was freaking out. She was not freaking out. She was just wondering where everyone was.

After a quick shower and a change of clothes she and Grace decided to split up their efforts to interview more possible suspects. Especially without any help from the Grasse police they both knew that time was of the essence. If they couldn't move the needle on the investigation—or encourage the police to reopen the case—they would have to leave Grasse with no answers. Maggie knew she couldn't stay indefinitely. She had people at home who depended on her. Amelie.

The thought of her granddaughter made her smile. This was the first time since the child had come to live with them at Domaine St-Buvard that they'd been separated for longer than a few hours. And while she was sure Amelie was perfectly happy with her two older brothers—technically an uncle and a nephew—and of course with Danielle and Laurent, Maggie also knew how important stability was to a child. And to a child who'd been ripped away from the only parent she'd ever known, it was particularly important that she feel safe.

As she locked the apartment behind her and gazed down rue Amiral de Grasse, Maggie tried to think what it meant that Vivienne had stolen the formula for *Mon Sang*, and what those implications were beyond the obvious. Had she really stolen the formula on her own? To what end? To impress Florent? It didn't make sense. Vivienne had seemed so proud of her role in the history of Grasse's fragrance industry.

Stealing someone else's winning formula didn't conform with that picture. At all.

Thinking of Florent, she and Grace had decided that Grace would track down the La Nuit Est Belle owner in order to gauge whether he was aware of the theft. That would tell them a lot right there.

As for Maggie, she would approach Capuccine again to see if she had the same knowledge.

As she walked down the narrow stone alley that led to the main artery in the village, Maggie couldn't help but feel uneasy about this case. There was something indefinable going on that she just couldn't put her finger on. She wasn't sure if it was the fact that Vivienne—whom Maggie had spoken with on a fairly intimate level and with whom she'd felt some kind of personal connection—had shown herself to be someone other than she'd appeared to be, or because just about everyone Maggie had spoken to seemed to have something to hide.

Even Annabelle. Although, granted, Maggie didn't know her well enough to know if her suspicious affect meant anything, she was aware that she didn't trust Annabelle completely. A flutter of nausea settled into her gut. Because now, with the theft of the thumb drive, Maggie herself had something to hide.

Even Annabelle.

After she and Grace split up, Maggie headed to the center of the town's historic district. Along the way, she indulged an uncomfortable moment of worry that all of the processes and means to every end that she was in the habit of allowing might be chipping away at her integrity.

Or as Danielle was only too happy to remind her: *You can't play in the mud and not expect to get dirty.*

Grace lifted her face to the sun and allowed the frustration of her wasted morning seep out of her. She'd found this café down a quaint alleyway lined in cobblestones. There were only three tables on the tiny terrace, but it was quiet. A cup of lavender tea sat before her, a pleasant relief after all the endless cups of high-voltage coffee she'd drunk this weekend.

Her efforts had come to nothing—unless you counted a broken heel on all these cobblestones—and she was once more left with the prospect of meeting up with Maggie empty-handed. She drew in a long breath and let it out in an attempt to ease her frustration.

She picked up her phone and stared at the screen. She'd texted Windsor a cheery *what's-up?* text and still he hadn't replied. Whatever was going on with him, she decided, unless he was hooked up to life support at Grady Hospital, nothing was going to excuse him for ghosting her for the last twenty-four hours.

She felt her throat constrict in discouragement.

"Madame?"

She looked up to see a balding man with glasses in his mid-forties. He had a thin, unremarkable face and was holding his hand on the empty chair at her table. It took her only a few seconds to place him. He was the Medical Examiner she'd seen at the crime scene at the float after she and Maggie had discovered Vivienne's body.

"This seat is available?" he asked, ready to whisk it away to his own chair-less table.

Grace put her hand on the chair as if to stop him from taking it.

"It is," she said with a slow smile. "But only if you sit in it at my table."

31

The talk at the monastery had been tedious. Laurent had discerned no interest at all in the faces of the audience listening to him. He didn't blame them. These people had escaped lives of hell and poverty. They were in France and safe, but they were also homeless, friendless and broke.

He never took it personally if he didn't see interest or passion in the work he described that would be their employment in the coming summer.

But still.

On his way back to *Dormir*, Danielle texted him to stop at the bakery in Éguilles—the nearest village—to pick up a baguette. He'd been in a hurry to get back to relieve Danielle of her child-minding duties but as she'd also texted that Amelie was content watching afternoon television he relaxed a bit and rerouted.

It occurred to him that Éguilles was barely five kilometers away from Domaine St-Buvard. He'd run by there again to see if he could catch Jem and Luc at home and invite them to dinner tonight.

The fact that Jem was home for an extended stay—although wonderful for his mother—worried Laurent. *How is it he can leave his job for an indefinite period of time? Something must have happened.*

As for Luc, he'd been living in Napa after college for the past four years, but Laurent hadn't heard anything specific from him about his plans for the future in a long time. Did he intend to stay in the States? And apply for his green card? Just the thought was discouraging. Laurent had counted on Luc to come back to Domaine St-Buvard to help him with the family vineyard.

As he maneuvered up the long gravel drive from the main road to the *mas*, Laurent saw Jem's car parked in the driveway. He felt a prick of annoyance that neither Jem nor Luc had texted or called since their one dinner at *Dormir* the night before.

He parked next to Jem's car. Both dogs were at *Dormir* which was just as well since the boys seemed to have trouble washing their own dishes, let alone feeding and walking two dogs.

Laurent hurried up the front steps and stopped. Sounds of muffled shouting came to him from around the house. There wasn't a fence around that portion of the property, so his mind went first to the possibility of a break-in. The sounds were louder and among them was laughter. Girlish laughter.

He jumped off the porch and hurried around the house to the side yard and then stopped abruptly.

At first he couldn't make sense of what he was seeing. Both Jem and Luc were on the ground, wrestling. Laurent could see fists flying and hear grunts and cursing.

Were they subduing an intruder? But no. It was just the two of them. Out of the corner of his eye he caught a glimpse of movement and turned to see the girl Natalie, leaning against a blooming dogwood tree, and laughing behind her hand.

"What's going on here?" Laurent bellowed.

32

The oldest section of Grasse was full of shops and fountains, Maggie noted—not unlike Aix or even Arles. But it was the fragrance shops—one right after another—that made this town so different. She walked down Route de Cannes marveling at them all when it suddenly occurred to her that because of its hilly setting and all the steps, Grasse vaguely reminded her of Mont St Michel.

The narrow streets smelled wonderful with their surrounding *parfumeries*. And of course there were the souvenir shops on literally every corner showcasing the copious lavender products—soap, pillows, sachets, sprigs, and perfume—found all over Provence.

She stopped when she came to the end of the street. She had decided to try her luck at Café Constant, the same café where she'd first spotted Capuccine, the night of the parade, hoping that perhaps the place was her usual watering hole.

After her previous run-in with the woman, she didn't think Madame Dix would willingly talk to her, so she was hoping to make the meeting look like an accident. She was glad that she and Grace had decided to take the full afternoon for their separate missions. They wouldn't feel rushed this way.

Regardless of Grace's current insecurities, she was still a striking woman and memorable. It wouldn't have helped Maggie get information out of Capuccine if she was threatened by Grace's impeccable style—American or not—or if she felt she was being ganged up on. She and Grace would meet back up before dinner and compare notes.

Maggie stood on the perimeter of the café's terrace and scanned the tables for Capuccine. When she spotted her, sitting in the sunniest portion of the terrace, Capuccine was already glaring at her.

Maggie rarely let a frosty reception keep her from doing what she set out to do. She strode over to Capuccine's table and smiled—knowing that most French find someone smiling for not obvious reason disconcerting at best.

"Madame Dix," she said, pulling out a chair.

"Do not dare," Capuccine said, her eyes snapping. "I will call the waiter."

"Good," Maggie said, seating herself. "He can get me a Kir Royale."

Capuccine pulled out her cellphone and punched in a number before holding it to her ear.

"You're right. Perhaps the police would be a better call."

"Got the chief of police on speed dial, do you?" Maggie said lightly. She'd only meant it to goad the woman, but the expression on Capuccine's face told her it had done much more than that.

"Oh, snap," Maggie said, sitting up straight. "You and the police chief?"

"Don't be crude," Capuccine said placing her phone on the table without completing her call.

"Or maybe the detective? He's pretty cute."

"What do you want? Say what you have to say and leave."

"Okay," Maggie said, waving away the waiter who had glanced questioningly her way. "I was wondering how close you were to your son's girlfriend, Vivienne."

"You are not seriously suggesting *I* killed Mademoiselle Curie because I didn't like her as a prospective daughter-in-law?"

"People have killed for stupider reasons."

"My son was not serious about her. The liaison would not have led to marriage."

"Especially if one party were dead," Maggie said wryly.

"But to answer your question," Capuccine said, ignoring her comment, "I was friendly with Mademoiselle Curie and wished her no ill."

"Even if it became known that she had stolen something valuable from you?"

Capuccine narrowed her eyes and Maggie saw her pale under her tan.

"I have no idea what you are talking about."

Maggie couldn't tell if that was true. Capuccine was a master at hiding her emotions. Did she know that the formula had been stolen?

Another thought occurred to Maggie. What if Vivienne stole the formula and then attempted to extort money from Capuccine to keep it secret?

Capuccine was standing with her elbows pressed into her sides as if attempting to make her body as small as possible.

"I heard La Nuit Est Belle was working on creating a competing fragrance for *Mon Sang* that was so similar as to be nearly identical," Maggie said.

Capuccine seemed to relax a bit.

"Are you talking about creating a reverse formula? Let them try! It'll never be as good."

So, she doesn't know about the theft.

"I'm not talking about a reverse formula," Maggie said. "I've heard that the actual formula to *Mon Sang* is floating around Grasse, available for the right price."

"That is a lie," Capuccine said, her face contorted into an ugly mask of panic.

She looked like someone who'd just been kicked in the stomach. Or someone who'd just heard they'd been betrayed by someone they trusted.

"I guess we'll find out," Maggie said. "Where were you during the parade?"

Capuccine folded her arms protectively across her chest, her eyes snapping.

"Get out! Leave me! And if I hear you spreading pernicious gossip, I will have you arrested!"

Maggie stood up.

"I'm not too worried about being arrested, Madame Dix," she said. "The police don't appear interested in pursuing any leads pertaining to murder, so I can't imagine someone being annoyed by a tourist will get their attention."

"I am not just someone," Capuccine said, her smugness mixing with her anger, distorted her expression into a haughty grimace.

"That's right," Maggie said as she gathered her bag and prepared to leave. "You have a special relationship with the detective of police, don't you?"

Capuccine snatched up her phone again, her eyes boring into Maggie, but she made no real attempt to use it. Maggie turned and left the terrace, looking back just once, to see Capuccine staring at the table in front of her.

Maggie thought she could still see her hands trembling.

33

Grace stretched out her legs and crossed her ankles under the table, completely aware that Docteur Anouilh was watching her movements closely. He had indeed opted to join her at her table and had wasted no time in attempting to charm her.

"I saw you on the job," Grace said. "Very impressive."

"Most people don't notice the medical techs," he said.

"I imagine the detectives rake in all the attention," Grace said, frowning as if indignant on his behalf. "Yet where would they be without the information you uncover?"

"Exactly!"

"How long have you worked for the Grasse police department?"

"Four years. And it's only work if you attempt to do your job properly."

Grace raised an eyebrow and Anouilh took the gesture for the hint to continue that Grace intended it to be.

"Unlike Toulon, where I worked before," Anouilh said, "Grasse is, shall we say, uninterested? It doesn't care to follow the dots to form the picture."

"How so?"

She smiled encouragingly at him, her heart thudding with excitement as she realized what a miraculous boon it was to have run into him. It had never occurred to Maggie that they might get inside information on this case. And yet here Grace was, talking to one of the main people beside Detective Landry himself who knew the details of how Vivienne died and what had been uncovered about her murder.

"It is a network of old family relations," Anouilh said with a sigh. "Even now. For every case that does not get log jammed by red tape, there is always a newer, inappropriate obstacle to have to navigate."

"Inappropriate?"

Anouilh blew out a huff of exasperation and drained his drink, making Grace fear he was about to leave. He quickly gestured to the waiter to bring them two more of the same.

"I can't say for sure," he said. "And he's my boss after all."

He's talking about Landry.

"A real taskmaster?" Grace prompted, knowing that was not the problem at all.

He snorted. "Hardly." He looked around the café as if looking for anyone who might be able to overhear him. Grace leaned in conspiratorially and he dropped his voice.

"He's protecting certain…people," he said enigmatically.

"Criminal people?"

Anouilh grimaced and waggled his hand as if to hedge his answer.

"But people who have done something wrong?" Grace asked.

"Possibly."

Grace eased back into her chair. So, Landry was being paid off in some manner not to do his job. It was as much as she and Maggie had already supposed but hearing it confirmed was still discouraging.

"I saw the body," Grace said. "I was the one who stopped the float."

He smiled at her, his eyes twinkling. "Trust me, Madame. I remember you."

Grace smiled sweetly. "Oh? I'm flattered."

"You wore a silk off the shoulder sundress. I thought the evening air perhaps a bit too harsh for your skin which is as pale and supple as the silk itself."

Grace made a show of stretching out her arms as if to see for herself and then turned to him, suddenly serious.

"I couldn't understand about all the rose petals," she said. "You know. The ones that poor Vivienne was covered in?"

"Ah yes," Anouilh said, his eyes watching Grace's face closely, hungrily. "The rose petals. I wanted to bring them in for analysis but was told to leave them," he said with disgust. "I could have found out so much if forensics had simply bagged them and let me do my job."

"That's a shame," Grace said. "But you did do a proper autopsy, didn't you?"

"One wasn't ordered," he said. "Can you imagine? I'm as surprised as you are." He leaned over and dropped his voice further.

"I performed one anyway," he said and then sat back, smugly. "I did my job. If they question me about it, I'll say I only intended to examine the body for bruises, abrasions and so forth. Otherwise, why am I here?"

"Why indeed?" Grace said. "Goodness, that was brave."

Anouilh puffed out his chest. "I was only doing my job."

"What did you discover?"

He leaned forward again in his chair, his eyes glowing.

"I found out that she'd been poisoned," he said excitedly. "I found traces of a toxic cocktail of synthetic musk in her throat and nasal passages."

"Oh, my goodness. What did the detective say to that?"

An unsettled look flitted past the ME's face.

"I didn't report my findings. How could I? I was not told to do the autopsy in the first place."

"But when you found she'd been poisoned," Grace said reasonably, "surely your colleague—Detective Landry—would have been grateful that you went ahead anyway?"

He shook his head. "Disobey a direct order? It would have gone on my permanent record. Not that I uncovered proof that a murder had been committed, but that I'd overstepped the bounds of my rank."

"Unbelievable," Grace said and this time she wasn't acting.

"I am sorry for the victim," he said sadly. "She will get no justice. Her family will get no comfort from the law."

"It is indeed sad. Do you know why the case was closed so quickly?" Grace asked. "It's almost as if Detective Landry was trying to protect someone."

The waiter came and deposited two more drinks on the table and then left. As Docteur Anouilh lifted his drink, he smiled sadly at Grace.

"It does, doesn't it?" he said.

34

As Maggie rounded the narrow stone road of rue Jean Ossola—now actively trying to dodge the rain drops—she spotted Grace on the restaurant terrace. Even from a distance, she could tell that Grace had had a good afternoon. Her face was flushed and a smile tugged her lips as she scanned the crowd looking for Maggie.

Maggie hurried over to her table.

"You look like you had some luck," she said as she sat down.

"I'll say," Grace said. "You're not going to believe who I ran into."

"Florent?"

"No, sorry about that. I never found him. Instead, I spoke to the ME on Vivienne's case."

"Oh my gosh, Grace. That's amazing!" Maggie leaned over and hugged her. "You're like having an inside contact in the police department!"

Grace smiled happily.

"And wait until you hear what I found out," she said before quickly outlining her hour spent with Docteur Anouilh.

"We ended with him promising to call me with a confirmation of the substance he found in Vivienne's nostrils," Grace said. "I think I inspired him to go a little further than he might normally. But at least we'll know for sure that Vivienne was in fact poisoned."

"Unfortunately," Maggie said, "that means the police know too. And then they'll definitely be no help to us because they'd have to admit that they knew it was murder but did nothing."

"Surely you weren't expecting help from them anyway?"

Maggie shook her head. "Not really," she admitted.

"What did you find out?" Grace said, gesturing to the waiter to bring menus.

"Not as much as you did," Maggie said. "I was able to interview Capuccine, but she was super cagey."

"Was she able to give you an idea of what Landry's relationship with Vivienne might have been?"

"No, but I got a pretty good idea of what Capuccine's relationship with him is."

"The village copper is having an affair with Capuccine Dix?" Grace asked, clearly impressed with Maggie's morning's work too.

The waiter brought their menus and took Maggie's drink order and disappeared.

"So what does this mean?" Grace asked.

"Well," Maggie said, trying to put the few pieces she knew together, "we know Vivienne was stealing secrets from Dix Fleurs. And now we think the person she would have harmed by that—Capuccine Dix—is sleeping with the police detective."

"That doesn't seem to connect with anything, does it?"

"It might, if Capuccine wanted Vivienne dead and needed her boyfriend detective to sweep the murder under the rug."

Now Grace frowned.

"Do you seriously think Capuccine would kill Vivienne for stealing secrets? Why not just have her boyfriend cop arrest her?"

"One possible reason is because she knew she'd never get satisfaction." Maggie picked up her phone. "I found this article when I was researching Dix Fleur. It's about a case five years ago between two different fragrance companies. A guy who worked for one company took a job at another and brought more than the company stapler with him when he left. He actually admitted he took secret formulas! It went to court, and he was found not guilty."

"Seriously?" Grace's eyes widened in surprise.

"In the article it said that there has never been a meaningful claim of trade secret misappropriation upheld in the entire history of the fragrance business."

"So, people can just steal trade secrets and suffer no consequence?"

Maggie shrugged.

"Not from the courts anyway. So not only would Capuccine be facing huge lawyer bills to try to prove that Vivienne stole her formula, but in the end—win or lose—her secret formula would then be published for the whole world to see."

"Yikes," Grace said shaking her head. "It would be a lot easier to just kill the guilty party."

"*Et voila.*"

"So do you think Capuccine had her killed?"

"Well, poison *is* a woman's weapon, after all, and we both saw Capuccine near the parade route before the festival began. That gives her means, motive and opportunity."

"And Vivienne would have trusted her so Capuccine could have gotten close to her."

The waiter came and took their orders. Grace—ever mindful of her figure—ordered a Niçoise salad, and Maggie, the chicken *cordon bleu*.

Grace took a sip of her Sancerre.

"What do you think of Annabelle?" she asked.

Maggie frowned. "Do you mean do I believe her?"

Grace shrugged. "I'm just wondering."

"It's interesting that you would wonder about her," Maggie said. "I was going to mention something to you but wasn't sure I should."

"Let's hear it."

"So, I found myself wondering why Annabelle thought Vivienne was murdered in the first place. I mean, I'm not sure it's the first thing a normal grieving family member would jump to, you know? That they were murdered?"

"So, you think Annabelle is a suspect? Why would she come to us for help then?"

"I don't know. Unless it was to make it look as if she had nothing to hide? Or to see what kind of evidence the police had?"

"Surely, she couldn't have imagined the police would share anything with us."

They were silent for a moment.

"You know," Maggie said, her mind reaching out to a place she really preferred not to go, "when I talked with Vivienne the day she died, she said the fragrance industry in Grasse was essentially a family business—or at least it used to be. Her family were growers for three generations."

"If Vivienne was stealing secrets," Grace said in a low voice, "she would be tarnishing the family name."

"Yes, but if Annabelle killed her sister, why would she lead us to the evidence of her crime?"

"You mean Vivienne's apartment? Annabelle didn't know she had, remember? When you took that jump drive, you slipped incriminating evidence out from under her nose."

"But if Annabelle doesn't know about the theft of the *Mon Sang* formula, then there's no motive," Maggie said.

"Maybe she knows about the theft and was hoping to uncover the evidence so she could destroy it. Maybe *she* was the one who trashed the place. How do we know she wasn't?

Maybe she wanted us to help her, all the while hoping we'd do the work and then just hand over what we found."

"Grace, you're talking about someone killing her own sister. That's a whole new level of depravity."

"Granted."

The waiter returned with their starters, smoked salmon canapés.

When he left, Maggie frowned.

"I'm wondering if we're looking at this from a skewed perspective," she said.

"Explain."

"Well, putting Annabelle to the side for now, we're thinking Capuccine could have killed Vivienne because she had opportunity and motive and from what Docteur Anouilh told you, this toxic substance you found out about could be found in any of the chemist's laboratories at any of the factories, which she had access to."

"True."

"But that means anyone near any perfume lab could've killed Vivienne, and don't forget Tremblay, who's a chemist, hated her."

"And then there's Jean-Luis," Grace said with a grimace. "Thanks to me, we don't know his motive *or* his availability during the window of the crime."

"Grace," Maggie admonished. "Stop beating yourself up about that. We'll get to him before we're done. But along those same lines, there's also Florent Monet. He had access to the same lab that Tremblay did."

"What in the world would his motive be? Vivienne was stealing secrets to benefit his company."

"That's what we assume," Maggie said. "But when I talked to Trembley, he implied that Vivienne was not loved—particularly not by Florent."

"That makes no sense," Grace said, picking up one of the

salmon canapés. "Wouldn't he favor her if she was doing his dirty work?"

"Maybe he had a problem with her *because* she was doing his dirty work. It would make Florent very vulnerable, don't you think?—knowing that Vivienne had this kind of information on him?"

"You think she was blackmailing him?"

Maggie shrugged.

"I don't know. But I think we need to talk to him again before we try to hang this on Capuccine or Tremblay. Or Annabelle."

Their dishes came and Maggie immediately cut into hers. The cheesy interior of the *cordon bleu* oozed out onto her plate.

"Oh, that looks amazing," Grace said.

"It does, doesn't it?"

It smelled as incredible as it looked and Maggie found herself thinking again of Laurent—for whom food was always so important. It never mattered what they were discussing—when food was served, it always got his full attention.

"Before we talk to Florent," Maggie said as she tore a piece of bread from the half baguette on the table, "I think we need a little more in the way of evidence."

"Evidence of what? That he knew of the theft or that he put Vivienne up to it?"

"Either. Both. Because if we found out that, it would give him the biggest motive of all for wanting Vivienne out of the picture."

"Agreed. But how are we going to find out?"

Maggie smiled and dropped her voice.

"You enjoyed the tour of his factory yesterday, didn't you? How about we go again? Only this time, when there's nobody there."

35

A hush had descended over the yard, the kind of quiet that often foreshadowed a storm. Both boys were bloodied and surly standing in front of Laurent. The giggling girl had fled the scene as soon as Laurent had spoken.

"I asked you a question," Laurent said, baring his teeth.

"We...we..." Jem started, his right eye was already beginning to blacken and swell. He stopped speaking when it became clear he had no sane explanation for what they'd been caught doing.

"Stop," Laurent said, interrupting him. "You're beating each other's brains out for a reason and I'll know what it is."

Both boys looked down at their feet except for an occasional glare at each other.

"Fine," Laurent said. "I'll make my own guess, how's that?"

"Dad—" Luc started.

Laurent held up a hand and turned to Jem. "Who is this young woman you have brought home?"

"Her name is Natalie," Jem said.

"I *know* her name," Laurent said, his tone dangerous. "Does she belong to you?"

"Natalie is her own person," Luc said. "She belongs to no one."

Laurent turned to Jem. "Who do *you* think she belongs to?"

Jem shrugged uncomfortably, clearly not wanting to say the girl wasn't her own person. But neither wanting to be seen agreeing with Luc.

"I met her at a club in Atlanta," he said.

Laurent turned to Luc. "And you met her for the first time here?"

"So?" Luc said, his voice high with indignation.

"*So*," Laurent said deliberately, trying to hold his anger in check, "she came with Jem. Has she chosen to be with you instead?"

"It's not like that, Dad," Jem said. "Couples today don't match up like they did in your day."

Laurent held up a hand to stop him speaking. That this scamp was going to tell *him* how romance worked was laughable in a moment he definitely didn't want to be seen laughing.

"Luc, you will come back to *Dormir* with me," Laurent said over Luc's groans. "Jem, you will drive your friend to Aix and find her a hotel room."

"Dad, no! She wants to know about a working vineyard!"

"That makes one of you," Laurent said bitterly and was instantly sorry for the retort.

"Take her to Aix," Laurent said. "Domaine St-Buvard is locked until your mother gets home."

"But why?" Luc asked in frustration. "There's eight bedrooms and nobody here! Half the time you have homeless people living in the guest rooms."

Laurent turned to look at him and silently counted to five. It was the best he could do. He'd never have made it to ten.

Six years ago, Luc himself had been one of those homeless people before he'd become a part of the family. Although it was against Laurent's personal credo to give an explanation for any order he delivered, he took a breath and looked at both boys.

"I'm sorry that your friend is causing a rift between you," he said. "But I won't have Amelie or Danielle or your mother see it and I will not have you hiding here so you may behave in any way you like. The girl goes and both of you are coming to stay at *Dormir*. Now which one of you wants to go tell the American girl what's happening?"

Both boys turned on their heels and left the side yard. As Laurent watched them go, he wondered if they'd start slugging each other as soon as they were out of his sight.

A part of him thought that might actually be just fine.

36

The window from Landry's office revealed the bull pen next door that was used as a workstation for interdepartmental meetings, impromptu birthday celebrations, a training class or two, and, upon occasion, a place to strategize investigations.

Upon rare occasion.

Landry turned away from the view and rubbed his hands across his face in agitation. Instead of going over to Capuccine's and then on to his nap, the call from the dispatcher had forced him to come back to the office. He couldn't afford to lose the deal he'd established with the Grasse tourist board's public relations division.

Over the years, he'd been paid steadily growing bonuses under the table to make sure Grasse had the lowest crime rate in the area. He did that by closing cases without solving them. And by dumping bodies of transients without registering their deaths.

The result? A village with virtually no crime.

It was astonishing to him that his own supervisor, based in

Nice, forty kilometers away, didn't think it odd or miraculous for Grasse to have such a pristine record.

He probably thinks nothing happens here because it is provincial. He dismisses Grasse in the same way he dismisses me. And for the same reasons.

As he waited for his men to gather in the adjoining room, Landry remembered the day he joined the police. His grandfather had been so proud of him. Landry felt a sliver of guilt knife into his heart. His grandfather had been a renowned grower in Grasse. Even today, the Landry name was remembered by some of the old ones. Landry easily recollected all the Sunday lunches of the surrounding farms when they would come to his grandparents' farm to pay homage to his *Papi*.

His gut churned as he wondered what *Papi* would think of what he was doing. He bit his lip at the thought but quickly replaced the feeling of guilt with an indignant eruption of anger.

I am presenting Grasse to the world as flawlessly as it can be, he thought angrily. *It doesn't matter that they pay me to do it. I am giving the gloss to the golden reputation that is Grasse.*

He felt fury stab into him that the memory of his grandfather would make him feel inferior or even dirty.

Times have changed. You didn't need someone like me in the old days. But Grasse is a multi-billion-dollar enterprise now. With over two million tourists coming through every year. Without me, it would all fail.

"Commandant?" Thierry, his second in command stuck his head in the door. "We are all waiting in the briefing room."

Landry signaled to him that he was coming. But he didn't stand up and he didn't follow his subordinate. His eye had fallen on his computer screen and the email from Anouilh, the department ME. The subject line was: *Curie autopsy.*

Landry stared at the email without opening it and felt a visceral charge of shame erupt deep in his stomach. His family had known the Curies. For generations both families had grown the flowers together, gone to war together, rejoiced when the weather was good, rallied together when it was bad.

Vivienne Curie was the great granddaughter of *Papi's* best friend.

He pulled at his collar as if the room had suddenly become too warm. Abruptly, he got to his feet, turning away from the computer screen and Anouilh's email.

Screw that. The old man would have no idea what today's fragrance industry is like. I won't cow before his antiquated version of moral superiority.

And with that conviction firmly in place, he picked up his cap to meet with his men in the briefing room.

They had a problem to solve and, by God, they would solve it.

One way or the other.

37

Maggie and Grace stood in the shadows of the dank alley, opposite an inauspiciously plain door that led into the office section of the factory. Maggie fully expected the factory itself to be protected by state-of-the-art alarms and electronic motion sensors and cameras. But she couldn't imagine a small operation like La Nuit Est Belle would shell out for that level of security for its office—likely only a couple of desks, computers and perhaps a filing cabinet.

If she was wrong, they'd have to try this again in the light of day and *that* would be much trickier.

"Are you sure we won't get caught doing this?" Grace whispered loudly.

Maggie shushed her, her own nerves starting to hum annoyingly. She pulled out a slim case of lock picks she had gotten in the habit of carrying with her—in case she got locked out of her car or hotel room, she told herself. She'd tucked this packet into the glove compartment of their rental car as a matter of habit.

Glancing both ways down the alley, she stepped across the narrow cobblestone street to the door. Grace hurried behind her and then shone her cellphone light onto the lock beneath the handle. Maggie was relieved to see it was a simple lock. She slipped the slimline pick into the lock and probed the interior gently until she felt it ping in her hand. She opened the door, holding her breath against the possibility of an alarm sounding. She could feel Grace tense and rigid behind her.

"Are we in?" Grace whispered excitedly.

"We are," Maggie said and stepped inside.

It was just as she thought—although both she and Grace had been ready to run if she'd been wrong. Florent wasn't going to bother protecting the office if it didn't contain cash or inventory or anything else of value.

The space was small with two facing desks, a wall of bookcases full of binders and several potted plants, most of them dead or dying.

Maggie and Grace pulled on latex gloves and moved silently into the interior of the office. There was a desktop computer on one desk that had to be twenty years old. Maggie went to the desk and shined her small penlight on the papers there. A stapler, scissors, pens, notepads, highlighters, a headset and a tangle of electrical cords, along with a coffee mug—much as one would expect to find in any office. No personal touches or photos, she noted.

She touched the computer keyboard to wake it up and when the prompt came up for the password, she typed in *LNEB*. When that didn't work, she gave up.

She knew that people usually tended to use special birthdays or anniversaries of loved ones for their passwords, but she hadn't done enough research on Florent to be able to guess at those. She didn't have time to try without any Intel or history. She could kick herself for taking such a risk tonight without first gathering every tool imaginable to help her find the answers she needed.

"Did you find anything?" Maggie whispered loudly to Grace who was opening cabinet doors in the adjoining room.

"I don't know what I'm looking for," Grace answered.

"Just anything that hints that Florent knew what Vivienne had done," Maggie said. "Anything that looks like it doesn't belong."

"Do you mean like a bottle of *Mon Sang*?" Grace said, turning around and holding a bottle of the competitor's best-selling fragrance in her hand.

"Why would they have a bottle of that here?" Maggie asked in surprise. But then Capuccine's words came back to her. "Maybe they really *were* trying to reverse-engineer the formula?"

"If that's so, then why get Vivienne to steal it from Dix Fleurs?"

"Good question. Put it back. It doesn't tell us anything. Check the trash baskets," she said. "Then we should get out of here."

Maggie pulled the trash basket nearest the desk where she was standing and dumped its contents onto the desk before shining her light on the pile. If she could just find something to implicate Florent or that would suggest he knew what Vivienne had done!

She quickly sorted through old receipts, sandwich receipts, and a crumpled cigarette packet that she recognized as Mathys' brand. It reminded her that even though he spent most of his time in the lab, he was still the VP of operations. The desk with the computer she couldn't access must be his.

She found a piece of partially burned paper and shined her light on it. She could see it was an email printout.

"I think I found something," she said as her heart began to beat quicker.

"Did you hear that?" Grace said. "I thought I heard a car door slam."

But Maggie was too excited about what she held in her hand.

"Look at this, Grace! It's an email from Florent to Mathys. It says here that *something needs to be done about Vivienne.*"

Grace came over to her and squinted at the paper. "Why is it burned?"

"Why do you think? He was trying to get rid of the evidence. It's practically an admission of guilt! Florent is asking Mathys to kill Vivienne!"

"Are you sure? It could be read a couple of different ways. And you only have part of the entire message."

"What different ways?" Maggie was starting to feel a headache forming at the base of her skull. "When I spoke with Mathys yesterday he practically admitted that Florent had asked him to get rid of Vivienne."

"Seriously? You never mentioned that to me before."

"I didn't have proof before."

Suddenly the room was an explosion of noise and light as the front door burst open before it slammed against the abutting wall. Maggie jumped nearly out of her skin at the sound.

"Police! Stand with your hands up!"

Five policemen wearing flak jackets and face shields stormed into the room, their guns pointing at Maggie and Grace who carefully raised their hands in shocked surrender.

38

The office had been armed with a silent alarm. Maggie knew she should have expected that. Maybe on some level, she *did* know it and thought she would just take her chances with talking her way out of the consequences. Sometimes she got so frustrated with no results and with people stonewalling her that stepping out of line felt like it was worth the risk.

Sometimes, however, in all the excitement and determination, she forgot what it was she was risking.

She sat now in a large cell in the Grasse detention center with Grace, iron bars on the solid metal sliding door, a hard metal bench that wrapped around the room shared by no fewer than twenty other people—mostly male. Someone thankfully at the far end of the bench was vomiting onto the cement floor.

Next to her, Grace was clearly making an effort to hold herself as far away from anything that might touch her as possible. She sat with her shoes touching the floor only by the toes, and she hugged herself as if afraid she would be infected by the accidental touch of the wall or another person.

They'd been cuffed at the scene and transported to the jail

but as far as Maggie could tell they hadn't been processed in any way or even arrested.

Outside the sliding metal door, Maggie heard guards speaking, door buzzers going off from somewhere and other mechanical iron doors sliding open and shut. She looked around the cell dejectedly and suddenly recognized the man who'd thrown up. It was DJ Dixon, Karen's husband. He looked up at her with startled eyes.

"Oh, God," he groaned.

"DJ?" Grace said, leaning forward to squint in his direction. "Is that you?"

"I'm begging you," he said, his eyes bloodshot and forlorn. "Please don't tell Karen."

Maggie frowned.

"Isn't she going to wonder where you were all night?"

He shook his head and then winced, the motion clearly more painful than he'd expected.

"She thinks I sacked out with some guys I met at some bar last night," he said. "Things were getting late, and I was so polluted—she hates it when I drink too much."

"Imagine that," Grace said with a raised eyebrow.

"I know, I know," he said, rubbing his face. "Look, I know what people see when they see Karen. I do. But she's not like that. She's got a heart as big as God's and she'd do anything for you."

Maggie saw he was getting emotional, and she could only imagine what it felt like to love someone the rest of the world was appalled by.

"I feel like an idiot," he said. "It's one thing if Karen thinks I had too much to drink and crashed with my new friends. But it's a whole different ball game if she finds out I was arrested for public drunkenness." He groaned. "Just my luck. I didn't think the French cared how much you drank!"

Maggie wanted to say that he seemed to have a slightly

skewed vision of the French, but he looked so miserable that she couldn't help but feel sorry for him. He'd clearly been having a boring time in Grasse—and that's when Karen *wasn't* publicly embarrassing him—but on top of that to have his few free hours of hanging out with likeminded souls turn out this badly had to be the epitome of bad luck.

"We won't tell her," Grace assured him. "Will we, Maggie?"

"No," Maggie said, "but I'd make sure you make it to your hotel shower before you see her."

"No worries about that," he said ruefully. "She's got a whole day of tours today."

"You really love her," Grace said.

He grinned. "Does it show? She was my first love. I know how she comes off to everyone else, but for me, well, I've never met anyone to compare."

Which just goes to show there's someone for everyone, Maggie thought.

"So what are you two doing in here?" he said. "You don't look drunk."

"Why, you old flatterer," Grace said. "Thank you so much."

"Aw, you know what I mean," DJ said, grinning ruefully.

"We were brought in for trespassing," Maggie said.

He blinked. "Seriously?"

"It's just a misunderstanding," Maggie said.

"Boy, I'll say," he said. "I can't see how this is much of a tourist town if they can lock us up for having a few drinks or walking on the grass."

"Well, it was a tad more than that," Grace admitted. "What happened to the guys you were hanging with?"

"They were smart," he said ruefully. "They all went home to their wives while I decided to find one more drink somewhere."

Maggie smiled sympathetically before standing up. First love or not, there was nobody who ever met Karen who could blame the poor guy for that.

As she and Grace turned to stand at the front of the cell where they'd spent the last four hours, Grace pulled out her purse and pulled out a small mirror to check her makeup. While the police had taken their phones, they'd allowed them to keep their purses which was another odd thing, Maggie thought, about their detention.

"So what are we going to say when they get us under the hot lights?" Grace asked as she slipped the compact back in her purse. "We can't plead innocent. They have your safe-breaking tools. And we were both wearing latex gloves."

Yes, that was annoying, Maggie thought. It would be nearly impossible to claim they didn't know what they were doing. Although she would probably try anyway.

"Maggie?"

"I'm thinking," Maggie said.

"Better think fast, darling," Grace said. "I hear footsteps."

Maggie stared through the bars as Detective August Landry walked up, his shirt freshly pressed, a definite spring in his step. She thought she could even smell the espresso he must have just had.

He looked beyond Maggie to Grace and then back at Maggie before signaling to the guard who was standing behind him.

"Bonjour, Madame Dernier," he said pleasantly. "Madame Van Sant."

"We are outraged by this heinous and outrageous action on your part," Maggie said as she crossed her arms and stiffened her posture. "You cannot hold American citizens without charging them."

"That can always be amended," he said as the guard opened the cell door.

"My embassy will hear of this," Maggie continued, willing herself to appear as indignant as she knew an innocent person would be. "It is a violation of our civil rights."

"Your civil rights are not relevant here," Landry said as he motioned for her to step out of the cell.

Behind her, Maggie felt Grace begin to move too but Landry immediately put up a hand stopping her.

"Depending on my conversation with Madame Dernier," he said to her, "I will return for you."

He turned to Maggie.

"But that will depend on how satisfied I am with our conversation. As you say, Madame, I cannot hold you without charging you." He smiled evilly. "After you."

39

The interview room was freezing.

It was furnished only with a plain table and two chairs, handcuff rings hanging from the underside of the table, and a stack of paper pads. Maggie shivered uncomfortably, knowing that its austerity was the point. Landry signaled for her to sit down and took a seat opposite her.

"I fear you have had an unpleasant night, Madame Dernier," he said.

"Thanks to you."

"Is it typical for Americans not to take responsibility for their actions? You were found after hours on the premises of a private business."

"We got lost."

He opened his jacket and pulled out the packet of lock picking tools and tossed them onto the table.

"Those aren't mine," Maggie said.

"We have two sets of CCTV cameras that state otherwise."

"Did your cameras see me take these tools out of my bag or pocket or use them to gain entrance?" Maggie asked boldly.

She knew they couldn't possibly have. She and Grace were

in the darkened alley when she took them out of her bag. She had scoured the alleyway and seen no cameras.

"So you deny these are yours?"

"I absolutely deny it."

He cocked his head as if trying to figure her out. Clearly the interview was not going precisely as he'd imagined.

"And the gloves?" he asked.

"We are very careful of germs," she said. "You never know where the next pandemic will pop up."

"Of course. Very sensible. What were you doing in La Nuit Est Belle after hours?"

"I told you. We got lost."

Maggie wanted so much to tell him what she'd found, the evidence that made it clear that both Florent Monet and Mathys Tremblay had had something to do with Vivienne's death. But if she had ever counted on her instincts to direct her before, she knew they were telling her now not to trust this man.

"You want me to believe that you got *lost* in a village with one main street, and somehow found your way inside a locked building?"

"Clearly it wasn't locked," she said.

"What were you doing in there?"

"We were looking for a map to help us find our way back to our Airbnb."

"Is that why the cameras caught you rifling the desk drawers and attempting to access the computers?"

Maggie flushed at his words. She hadn't even looked around for cameras inside the factory office.

"If that's what they recorded," she said with a shrug.

Landry said nothing for a few moments.

"Perhaps instead of charging you," he said, "I should just give you a different identity and send you to *Baumettes*."

Baumettes was the maximum-security prison in Marseille. Even Maggie had heard the horror stories of it over the years.

She felt her adrenaline spike and a line of sweat appeared on her top lip. She couldn't wipe it off in case he hadn't noticed. The last thing she wanted was for him to see he'd unnerved her.

"That is an egregious threat," Maggie stuttered.

The sickening part of it was that she knew he could do it. He could make her disappear. And she didn't know him well enough to know whether or not he might actually be considering doing it.

"All I am asking is one simple little thing," he said in mock reasonableness. "Merely that you tell me what you were really doing in the offices of La Nuit Est Belle so that you are then able to enjoy the rest of your vacation—the rest of your life—in comfort and freedom. Is that so much to ask?"

"Unless the arresting officers planted evidence on us," Maggie said, "which I am not putting past them, I assume nothing was found on our persons to suggest we stole anything."

Landry made a noncommittal gesture.

"So if we didn't steal anything—"

"It only means you didn't find what you were looking for."

"How did you know we were there in the first place?" she asked suspiciously.

"We have our ways," he said.

"Ways based on Gestapo methods? Wait, were you having us followed?"

Landry didn't answer but he smiled as if pleased with himself making a chill pebble over Maggie's bare arms.

How had he known we were in the factory?

Suddenly, Landry picked up the lock picking tools again and slammed them on the table, making her jump.

"What were you looking for?" he shouted.

"Nothing!" Maggie said, her heartbeat racing. "We didn't know what we were looking for!"

Landry frowned. Maggie's response echoed in her ears. It sounded like it was given in spite of herself. In other words, it sounded like the truth.

Clearly, Landry thought so too. He sighed heavily.

"You will leave Grasse today. You will not return, and you will not contact anyone here."

"By *anyone*, you mean Annabelle Curie," Maggie said and was immediately sorry she had. Landry had been seconds from allowing her and Grace to leave. Now he looked, for one moment, alarmingly like Laurent sometimes did when he was negatively considering one of her wilder ideas. And neither reaction promised a pleasant outcome.

"I mean *anyone*," he said. "But yes, Mademoiselle Curie absolutely. You are not helping her to grieve or to process what happened to her sister."

"Neither are you," Maggie retorted. "And it's your job."

"Go home, Madame Dernier. Buy your perfume at *Gallerie Lafayette* like a normal tourist or perhaps from the Internet? I'm told the fragrance websites have become very sophisticated."

"Someone killed Vivienne Curie," Maggie said, not sure why some small part of her stubbornly still thought this bullheaded man might be convinced to help.

"Mademoiselle Curie's death was an unfortunate, tragic accident."

"Exactly how is being sprayed in the face with a toxic cocktail of synthetic musk in any way accidental?"

Landry narrowed his eyes at her, looking suddenly predatory, the smile gone from his face.

"You have been talking to people who know nothing about what happened," he said coldly.

"I think I'm talking to one of those people right now."

His lip twitched almost as if he was attempting to keep from smiling but instead, he shook his head.

"Mademoiselle Curie broke her neck when she fell from the top tier of the float."

Maggie looked at him in astonishment.

"That's not true," she said. "Your own ME confirmed she was poisoned. And Annabelle Curie is going to be demanding a copy of the autopsy—which is her right."

He stared at her. Her mind raced trying to decipher his expression. Hadn't Grace said that the ME had done an autopsy? Maggie's long night in the cell had given her a mental fuzziness. If there *hadn't* been an autopsy performed—and from Landry's expression—that was starting to look very likely, what possible reason could he have had, besides incompetence or negligence, for not doing one?

"Don't tell me you didn't do an autopsy?" Maggie said, looking around in an exaggerated parody of bewilderment. "What kind of backwater Mayberry outfit *is* this?"

Instead of reacting to her taunts, Landry appeared relaxed and even satisfied. He abruptly signaled to the guard who had been standing motionless in the room and then stood up himself.

"Go home, Madame Dernier," he said. "Or risk spending much longer with us than I'm sure you or your family would be comfortable with."

"This isn't Rwanda," Maggie said tartly. "My family will find me even if you bury me in a drum barrel in the remote marshes of Mont St-Michel."

He laughed.

"My, you Americans are all so dramatic. Is it all the television you watch, I wonder? I will not need to do anything like that, I assure you. And I welcome your family—a husband, perhaps?—although I must say that would surprise me—to hire all the lawyers they want, to come to Grasse and examine my investigation of Vivienne Curie's death—and your subsequent detention—if it comes to that—in detail. I have every confidence it will stand up to whatever questions they may have."

"I'm not ready to leave Grasse just yet," Maggie said obstinately, standing up, too.

There was no way she would let this small town Barnie Fife chase her out of town before she had the answers she'd promised Annabelle.

"As you wish," Landry said with a philosophical shrug before turning back to her as if he'd just remembered something. "Remind me again of the reason why your friend Madame Van Sant lied to me when she said she was somewhere during the murder she was not?"

Maggie stared at him and closed her mouth when she realized it had fallen open. She hadn't forgotten that Grace had lied about where she'd been during the afternoon of the murder, but in truth she *had* relied on Landry's slipshod tendencies to ensure it wouldn't be a problem.

The expression on her face must have told him as much—clinching his victory.

"I will expect to see your taillights leaving the village before dark," he said with a cold smile.

40

Maggie and Grace spoke very little on the walk back to the Airbnb. Maggie briefly told her of Landry's insistence that they leave Grasse immediately and about the final straw that had bought Maggie's acquiescence. A mushroom cloud of guilt hung thick between them.

Grace knew it was her fault they were being forced to leave without helping Annabelle. But there was nothing for it. As for Maggie, she'd had a good hour in the police station lobby while she waited for Grace's release, enough time to come to terms with Landry's ultimatum.

She wouldn't risk Grace's freedom for answers to questions that would ultimately change nothing anyway. It galled her to be forced to let the pompous and no doubt bent policeman win but she couldn't balance her desire to help Annabelle and find out the truth against her need to keep Grace safe.

One was satisfying to have, the other essential.

Now as they silently packed their bags and had their own thoughts there was a sudden pounding on the front door. Grace looked toward the door, alarmed.

"I thought you said Landry was giving us until nightfall," she said.

Maggie went to the door and opened it to find Annabelle on the other side, her face pained and distraught.

"I got my neighbor to agree to watch the livestock for today," she said, anxiously. "Tell me what you want me to do."

Maggie was glad that Annabelle had come in person because pulling the rug out from under her over the phone would have been even worse.

"Come in, Annabelle," Maggie said. "Grace? Tea?"

"On it."

Maggie led Annabelle into the living room.

"What's going on?" Annabelle said, glancing over Maggie's shoulder to the open bedroom door with the luggage visible on the bed. "You're leaving?"

"Some things have happened since we saw you last, Annabelle," Maggie said.

"You said you were going to talk to Capuccine Dix."

"Yes, and I did that, but something else happened. For reasons I won't go into now, Grace and I broke into La Nuit Est Belle after hours."

"You did what?" Annabelle said, her mouth falling open.

"We broke in and we found incriminating evidence against Florent Monet. Evidence that suggested he might have had something to do with Vivienne's death."

Annabelle gasped. "What kind of evidence?"

"It was a half-burnt printed email," Maggie said.

"Where is it?"

Grace came in with a tray and three mugs of tea along with a small dish of macarons. She set the tray down on the coffee table between them.

"We no longer have it."

Annabelle fisted her hands and sputtered. "Why not?"

"Because we tripped a silent alarm," Grace said. "And the

police came and arrested us."

"Correction," Maggie said. "They didn't formally charge us, but they did make credible threats against us until we agreed to leave town."

Annabelle looked around the room in bewilderment as if hoping to find a different answer than what she was hearing.

"But the evidence!" she said.

"I know," Grace said. "But we can't get our hands on it now."

"Landry has probably destroyed it," Maggie said to her.

"But you can testify as to what you saw!" Annabelle said.

Maggie took a sip of her tea to keep from speaking immediately. She couldn't tell Annabelle the reason they were being forced out of Grasse. It wouldn't help or change anything, and it wouldn't be fair to Grace.

Suddenly, Grace's phone chimed, and she went to the kitchen to fish it out of her purse.

"Maggie," Annabelle said. "I am begging you. You can't leave. You can prove that Vivienne was murdered."

"But how? Who will believe me?" Maggie said in frustration. "The court of public opinion? The police certainly don't want to know. In fact, I'm not sure it wouldn't be very dangerous for the police to know what we know."

"So we're going to just let Vivienne's killer get off? Just tell no one and go on as if nothing happened?" Annabelle stood up and placed her hands on her hips. Her eyes flashed dangerously.

"That was the Grasse ME," Grace said coming back to the room.

"Who?" Annabelle asked.

"Grace got some information from the Medical Examiner on Vivienne's case," Maggie told her.

"He'd done an unauthorized autopsy on Vivienne," Grace said. "I asked him to send me the report, but he wasn't quite that drunk." She turned to Maggie. "Sorry."

"You did great, Grace," Maggie said. "Just knowing that an autopsy report exists is big."

"Anyway, he said he'd call me to confirm that the substance he told me about—the synthetic musk—was what killed Vivienne, and he just did that. He confirmed that the substance itself was not necessarily lethal. It depends on the dose. And it can be found in any basic laboratory."

Grace flushed with pride and satisfaction and then grimaced.

"I think I also may have a date later tonight but that's a problem I'll deal with another time."

Annabelle sat back in the couch as if stunned. "It's proof Vivienne was poisoned," she said in awe.

"It does seem to be," Maggie said. "Good work, Grace."

"For all the good it does us," Annabelle said. "You can't leave now! We can go to the press! Or get that ME to testify! Show the cops the text message he just sent you!"

"None of that will be admissible," Maggie said. "And it won't be enough to open a case that the police have closed. We'd need to be prepared to bring a suit against the entire Grasse police station."

"Then do it! I'll do it!"

Maggie felt ashamed that she'd doubted Annabelle before now. The young woman was clearly distraught. There was no way she could be behind Vivienne's murder.

"Look, Annabelle," Maggie said tiredly. "There's more."

A part of Maggie was hoping she wouldn't have to tell Annabelle what they'd discovered on the jump drive. Learning it would undoubtedly finish the young woman off in short order. She was clinging to her love for her sister—and to their shared family legacy of the fragrance industry. All that would be gone as soon as Maggie told her that Vivienne had committed economic espionage.

"Maggie, don't," Grace said. "What's the point? It's over."

"No, tell me," Annabelle said looking from one to the other. "I need to know, whatever it is."

"There is some evidence," Maggie said slowly, "that Vivienne was...that she took trade secrets."

Annabelle looked perplexed.

"What do you mean? What kind of trade secrets?"

"Maggie found a jump drive in Vivienne's apartment," Grace said. "It showed that Vivienne had possession of the formula for *Mon Sang*."

Annabelle looked at Grace in confusion for a moment and then at Maggie.

"You found a jump drive in the apartment? You didn't tell me."

"I'm sorry," Maggie said. "I'm telling you now."

"Now is a little late, *non*?" Annabelle said, standing up again. "You have the nerve to accuse my sister of trade secret theft? Show me these documents! How do you know she stole them? How do you know *how* she came into possession of them?"

"You're right," Maggie said, placatingly. "I don't. I'm sorry."

"You accuse Vivienne of doing this despicable thing and then you just leave town?" Annabelle shouted, her face purple with fury.

A distant roar erupted and rattled the plates on the counter, knocking framed pictures from the wall. All three women leapt to their feet as the rumbling shuddered through the building.

Maggie was the first one to rush to the front door, flinging it open, half expecting to see an advancing tank or an exploded bomb crater in the street. Instead, she saw a plume of black smoke billowing into the sky from the historic section of the village.

It was coming from the exact spot where Grace and Maggie had been last night—from La Nuit Est Belle.

41

That evening, Luc sat sullenly at the outdoor dinner table while Amelie did her best to cheer him up and get his attention.

Dinner was grilled pork chops with a side of sliced cucumbers from the *Dormir* garden served with mint and yoghurt dressing, and green beans from the Aix farmer's market. Danielle had been delighted to hear the boys would be there for dinner and would in fact be moving into *Dormir* for the remainder of the weekend.

Unfortunately, Jem had not come home in time for dinner although Laurent had called him twice to find out what was keeping him.

Danielle suspected that Luc *knew* what was keeping Jem. His affect during dinner was dark and contrary in spite of Amelie's best efforts to distract him.

"Would you like more pork chops, *chérie*?" Danielle asked him as he glanced up from his phone, looking at her as if not understanding her words.

"*Uh, non,*" he said. "*Merci.*"

"The phone goes into the grill if I see you look at it one more time," Laurent growled.

"Oh, yes, *Opa*!" Amelie cheered. "Throw it in the fire! I want to see it burn!"

"Calm down at the table, *mon cher*," Danielle said to her. "Are you finished? Would you like to be excused?"

"Can I watch TV?" Amelie asked, her eyes bright with hope.

Danielle glanced at Laurent who gave a nearly imperceptible signal of assent. She then nodded at the child. Amelie jumped up from the table and ran into the house.

"Just the television room!" Danielle called after her. She turned back to Luc who was pouring himself another glass of wine.

"Will someone tell me why Jem and his girlfriend are not joining us?" she asked.

"Natalie's not joining us," Luc said hotly, "because Dad threw her out. And Jem's not joining us because he's too busy scr—"

He stopped himself in time and glanced at Laurent who glowered threateningly at him.

"Why did you throw the young lady out?" Danielle asked Laurent.

"She was proving to be a bad influence," Laurent said, pouring himself a glass of wine.

Strong scents of rosemary mingled with the woodsmoke of the grill and seemed to fill the dark, empty spots over the garden. If the mood at the table hadn't been so tense, Laurent would have found the sensation quite pleasant.

"I thought she seemed sweet," Danielle said. "Very...cheerful."

"May I be excused?" Luc said, gulping down his wine.

"Clear the table first," Laurent said. "Without breaking anything."

Luc emitted a snort of irritation as he stacked the dishes and carried as many glasses as he could manage.

"And check on Amelie, please, *chérie*," Danielle called to his back before turning to Laurent.

"Was it necessary?" she asked.

"Removing the girl? I thought so," Laurent said, honestly not sure now that he hadn't overreacted.

They watched Luc move into the house and Danielle turned back to Laurent.

"He'll get over it," she said.

"It seems that has been my mantra for the past ten years."

Danielle laughed. "Yes, the teenage years are *très difficile*."

Laurent began stacking dishes. He needed to move, to take action, to *do* something.

"The girl has come between them?" Danielle probed.

"I caught them fighting over her like street brawlers," he said, glad to share the incident with her. If Maggie had been here, she would've insisted on "processing" it with him. And incredibly, it often helped. He smiled inwardly. Perhaps he was more accustomed to her American ways than he realized.

"But Luc and Jemmy never quarrel!" Danielle said in mock surprise.

"I am sure things will go back to normal when the girl leaves," Laurent said.

"And *is* she leaving? Are you sure?"

He looked at her and frowned and she shrugged, indicating Jem's empty chair at the table.

"I am not sure of anything, Danielle."

"Is everything else all right?"

"Yes, of course," he said with forced joviality. "We must invite your Bernard to dinner at Domaine St-Buvard when Maggie and Grace return."

Danielle smiled.

"I hope you will not find Bernard to be a bad influence," she said teasingly. "He is a bit of a jokester."

"I can only ban so many lovers in a single month," Laurent said wryly. "Bernard is safe at least for now."

"That is good to hear."

Laurent reached over and gave Danielle's hand a squeeze. He didn't like letting his worries show, especially not to Danielle who, given half a chance, tended to take the problems of the world on her shoulders. He would stop worrying about Luc and Jem—at least until he could mask his face better when he was around people.

"Ready to go in?" he said as he stacked the dishes and candles onto a large tray that had been leaning next to the table leg. "It is getting too cold to sit out without your sweater."

They moved into the house, and Laurent couldn't help but note how welcoming the glow of the interior of the house looked—especially on a cold spring night. He felt a brief spurt of satisfaction. He'd done well setting up *Dormir*—he'd done well in creating the life he and Maggie shared at Domaine St-Buvard. He might do well to reflect on that more.

He smiled and shook his head.

He really was becoming more American by the hour!

The sound of one of Amelie's inane television shows greeted them as they entered, but the living room was empty except for the three dogs who had abandoned the cold garden for the house an hour earlier.

Laurent frowned when he saw nobody in the room and he got an image of Luc—angry and sulking—bypassing the living room and going straight upstairs to his room.

He moved the dirty dishes to the sink and began filling it with hot water, glancing out the kitchen window into the garden they had just left. The lights he'd set up on poles over the dining patio bobbed gently in the breeze, creating patterns on the terrace. His eye landed on Jem's empty chair, and he fought his natural inclination to be angry about the boy not making it to *Dormir* in time for dinner as ordered.

He plunged his hands into the soapy water and felt the beginning of a small calming effect. The fragrance of the lavender soap wafted up to him as he began to scrub the dishes. He could hear Danielle coming back downstairs from Amelie's bedroom.

"Laurent?"

The tone in her voice sent a razor blade slicing down his spine. He turned from the sink, his hands dripping water onto the floor as she stepped into the kitchen, her face stricken with fear.

"She's nowhere in the house," she said.

42

They stood in stunned silence and watched the plume of smoke spread and dissipate into the sky. Soon, the sounds of sirens filled the evening air. Maggie wracked her brain to try to remember which buildings were situated where in that part of Grasse.

"What do you think is burning?" Grace asked in a hushed voice.

Maggie pulled out her phone and scrolled to the news feature on Twitter. The texts were popping up one after the other.

"It's Florent's factory," she confirmed.

Both Annabelle and Grace turned to look at her.

"This can't be a coincidence," Grace said, turning back to look at the column of smoke.

"No," Maggie said in a quiet voice, dread seeping into every pore. "It can't."

"You think this is deliberate?" Annabelle asked, looking from Grace to Maggie.

Maggie didn't answer. Her mind was abuzz with the implications of what the destruction of the La Nuit Est Belle factory had to mean to the investigation of Vivienne's death. Had it been deliberately burned to eliminate any further clues of wrongdoing by Florent? A chill rippled across her skin.

Did Florent burn his own factory?

Or is this the work of someone else?

Suddenly, Annabelle made a stifled cry and collapsed to her knees. Maggie hurried to her side.

"Annabelle? Are you alright?"

Annabelle gave a visible shudder and shook her head.

"What else didn't I know about her?" she whispered.

Maggie glanced at Grace.

"Stealing trade secrets?" Annabelle said in disbelief. "Our father would have been so ashamed. Our grandfather. They would have killed themselves with the shame of it. She has disgraced the family name."

"Like you said," Grace offered gently. "Maybe it's not what it seems."

Maggie gave her a pointed look. There was no point in pretending something they didn't believe in order to spare feelings. That way rarely led to the truth.

Annabelle shook her head again. But this time she did it with conviction.

"No, I won't be fooled again," she said. "Not even now. She was stealing formulas. She stole formulas." She looked at Maggie. "To sell?"

Maggie shrugged. "I don't know. We're not sure she did it on her own."

Annabelle seemed to think about that and then turned to look out the window at the spreading wisps of smoke in the sky.

"Florent Monet, you think?"

"We did find evidence of his guilt," Maggie said.

"The burnt-up email?"

"Which," Grace interrupted, "to be fair, could be read several different ways. It might not have been an intention to put out a hit on your sister."

"What different ways, Grace?" Maggie said impatiently. "*Something needs to be done about Vivienne.* And then she's murdered? How else are we to interpret that?"

"He could be suggesting that Vivienne deserved a raise or a promotion!" Grace said in exasperation.

"You don't say *something needs to be done* if you're talking about a raise!" Maggie said.

"I agree with Maggie," Annabelle said. "It sounds like an intention to do harm."

"But why put it to paper?" Grace said. "They'd have to be the stupidest killers on the planet to send each other emails about an intended hit!"

"I don't know about you," Maggie said grimly, "but I've not been particularly impressed with Florent's brains." She turned and stared pointedly at the smoke flume.

"You think he burned his own factory?" Grace said.

"And the incriminating email therein?" Maggie retorted. "Why not?"

"But it's his factory!" Grace said. "Surely, he could have just walked in and taken the emails? He didn't have to burn the place down."

"Maybe there was more there that we didn't find," Maggie said. "Maybe he couldn't take the chance that the cops would decide to search the place after all."

"Why in the world would they? Hasn't Landry made it clear he doesn't care who killed who? Why would he bother?"

"I don't know, Grace," Maggie said in frustration. "I just know I don't trust coincidences. That factory didn't burn for no reason. Nobody can convince me it wasn't arson."

The three were quiet for a moment, each with their own thoughts. The fire continued to rage, and Maggie found herself saying a silent prayer that it wouldn't spread to other parts of the historic downtown.

It was Annabelle who broke the silence.

"I was thinking about the fact that Vivienne was covered in rose petals," she said. "It sounds like whoever killed her had a poetic streak in him."

"That has to rule out Jean-Luis, don't you think?" Maggie said. "He doesn't strike me as the poetic type."

"I agree, but we can't eliminate him," Grace said.

"It sounds like you're still working the case," Annabelle said, gently biting her lip.

Maggie glanced at Grace.

"We have to leave Grasse," she said. "But technically, we have until nightfall before we have to be gone."

"I'll track down Jean-Luis," Grace said.

"Are you sure?" Maggie asked, studying her friend's face for any sign of hesitation or consternation.

"Yes, I'm sure. Kindly don't make a big deal of it."

"Okay, it's just that Jean-Luis clearly has anger issues, *and* he was the victim's significant other. In a normal police investigation he would be at the top of the suspect list."

"I know all that."

"Okay, well, the main thing is to find out if he has an alibi. I mean, a confession would be nice, but failing that..." Maggie let her words and their implication hang in the air.

Grace stood up and massaged her lower back, her eyes on the smoke flume through the window.

"I'll try Café Lilou. I heard that was popular with young people. I'd better Google it to get the address."

"I know that place," Annabelle said. "I can write down the address for you if you want."

Grace reached across the table to hand her notebook to Annabelle along with a pen.

"Thanks," she said as Annabelle wrote down the address.

"Okay, good," Maggie said. "That leaves Tremblay, Capuccine and Florent."

"I'll talk to Tremblay," Annabelle said. "I don't know any of them so it might as well be him."

Maggie knew that Mathys was aware of the trade secrets theft, and he hated Vivienne, but was his hatred enough to kill her? She remembered he was in the area on the night of the murder because she saw him after the body was discovered. Plus, as a chemist, he was the most likely person to be able to create the toxic cocktail that killed Vivienne.

"Be careful," Maggie said to her. "If you can get him to admit anything, that's great, but be forewarned. He's really angry at Vivienne."

"*Bon*. It means I won't have to go easy on him," Annabelle said grimly.

Maggie felt a wave of relief to see Annabelle's resolve. After her brief breakdown and grief-stricken realization that she hadn't known her sister as well as she thought, it was a welcome sign of strength from her.

"Okay," Maggie said. "So, I guess I'll go after Florent if I can find him. He's really the only one I've yet to talk to in any depth. And he's the one who wrote the email telling Mathys to get rid of Vivienne."

"Again," Grace reminded her, "you don't know that for certain."

"I don't know what this last-ditch effort will reveal," Maggie said, turning to Annabelle. "So please don't get your hopes up. Grace and I still have to leave."

"For reasons you're not comfortable sharing with me," Annabelle said, not taking her eyes off the smoke through the window.

Maggie glanced at Grace who was looking down at her hands.

"But don't worry," Annabelle said. "I'm not expecting too much."

Maggie sighed. It was pretty clear to everyone that that was a lie.

43

Finding Jean-Luis was easier than Grace had imagined. Grasse wasn't a large village and there were only a few main cafés and bars popular enough to command the lion's share of tourists. Grace went back to *Le Cochon Heureux*, the bar where she'd seen him before.

She allowed herself a brief fluttering of butterflies when she spotted him standing at the bar just inside, clearly visible from the terrace. But her recent interaction with the ME had given her courage. Instead of losing her mojo, she realized that it was entirely possible that Jean-Luis wasn't affected by her charms because she simply wasn't his type. Granted, she'd never met any male who didn't think she was his type, but she was willing to allow the possibility to exist. After all, plenty of women had had to contend with that possibility. It was just her bad luck that in all her forty-seven years, she'd never had to.

Wooden stools lined up along a long glossy mahogany counter, a massive mirror, etched in decorative swirls behind the counter with a pretty blonde bartender stacking highball glasses and taking orders.

Jean-Luis stood at the bar, wearing a black cashmere sport

coat with dark gray slacks and a white shirt. Classic, and completely affected.

Grace could tell he wasn't inebriated, he looked relaxed and easygoing. She reminded herself that he'd just lost his girlfriend to murder. The image of him standing at the bar flirting with the bartender with Vivienne's body not two days cold, stiffened her spine. She advanced toward him.

"Excuse me, Mademoiselle," Grace said to the bartender. "*Un Kir Royale, s'il vous plait.*"

Jean-Luis turned to look at her, giving her a crooked grin as he looked her up and down before turning fully to face her.

"On me," he said to the bartender, his eyes now meeting Grace's.

"You are with one of the tours?" he asked with a flirtatious smile.

Grace realized with a start that did Jean-Luis did not remember her from their earlier encounter. In a flash, her emotions went from relief to annoyance to an undeniable understanding of exactly how to handle him.

"I am, yes," she said to him, cocking her head teasingly as if appraising him too. "I love Grasse, but I had not expected quite so much…excitement."

"If you're looking for excitement," he said smoothly, "you came to the right bar."

Grace laughed. "I was talking about the fragrance factory that blew up earlier today."

"Ah," he said. "I hope you took the tour at La Nuit Est Belle *before* today."

"I did," she said sweetly. "What a loss it will be to Grasse."

He snorted derisively. "If you say so."

"You don't remember me, do you?" she said.

He shrugged but there seemed to be something a little uncomfortable in his gaze now. He narrowed his eyes as if trying to place her.

"Remind me," he said.

"I saw you with Vivienne Curie a few nights ago." Grace reached past him to accept her drink from the bartender. Now when she looked at him, the flirty affect in his face was gone. He was frowning as if trying to remember where he'd seen her before.

"I'm surprised she was on her own that night," Grace said mildly. "She was your girlfriend, wasn't she?"

"I...we'd recently decided to take a break."

"Really? Did the fact that she was stealing secrets from your mother's company have anything to do with that?"

Jean-Luis looked at her with surprise and growing interest.

"How did you know about that? Who are you?"

"Maybe you were helping her steal the secrets?"

His smile faltered for a moment. "I was not. I was appalled when I found out."

But he didn't look appalled. Grace thought he looked mildly perplexed.

"Where were you the night she was killed?" she asked, taking a sip of her drink.

"Watching the parade along with everyone else. How old are you?"

"None of your business. Why didn't you go to the police when you discovered the theft?"

"On my own girlfriend? That's not how we do things around here."

"Oh? Murder a little tidier, is it?"

He laughed, his handsome face open and seemingly completely delighted to talk to her.

"I didn't kill her. I'll admit to *wanting* to at times. Everyone thinks she was this sweet little *fille gentille*, but Vivienne was a force to be reckoned with. Trust me."

"In what way?"

"In every way. Let's just say she had no trouble getting what she wanted."

"I met her. I didn't find her at all the way you're describing her."

"You didn't know her. I've seen her turn down a guy's advances and the poor man ended up withdrawing a bloody stump for his trouble."

"That was not the Vivienne I saw."

"Of course not. You weren't an obnoxious male tourist trying to come onto her after she'd been on her feet all day."

Grace had to admit she could imagine Vivienne's job might be particularly trying in that regard.

"Between me and Vivienne," Jean-Luis said earnestly, "our problem was that she was always trying to be the man."

"I have no idea what that means."

"She wanted to call the shots. I didn't mind it too much—at least not in bed. You're American, right?" He grinned at her. "It's one of the main reasons I like American women. They're not shy, if you get what I'm saying."

"I saw you arguing with her the day she was killed," Grace said.

"Sure. That's what got us juiced. But murder? No way. I loved her." He shrugged. "Sort of."

"What a stirringly romantic proclamation. What about your mother? Did *she* have an issue with you dating the competition?"

He laughed out loud and turned to order two more rounds.

"Are you sure you're not into me?" he said. "Because what's happening here feels an awful lot like how Vivienne and I used to get going."

Grace blushed in spite of herself.

"Now," Jean-Luis said, "if you want to talk to someone who had a serious reason for killing Vivienne, you need to talk to Mathys Tremblay, the nose at La Nuit Est Belle."

"Tremblay? Why?"

"Mostly because he was in love with Vivienne, and she rejected him—and not nicely. She treated him like he was one more obnoxious tourist."

"It's my understanding that Monsieur Tremblay hated Vivienne."

"He probably did after he found out about the stolen formulas," Jean-Luis admitted.

"That makes no sense," Grace said. "As vice president of the company that received the stolen formula, he would've benefited from the theft."

"Yeah, except for one small thing." Jean-Luis drew a lazy line down Grace's bare arm. She shivered and forced herself not to move away from his touch or react in any way that might make him think he was having an effect on her.

"Tremblay was in the process of reverse-creating formulas for all the top scents in Grasse—but particularly *Mon Sang*. It was his life's work."

Grace frowned. "So?"

"So, how do you think he felt when Vivienne just handed over the formula? He was so close to creating a legacy for himself as a master chemist and she essentially ripped that accomplishment away from him."

Grace gave him an unconvinced look. "He'd kill her for that?"

"You don't know much about the fragrance business, do you?" he said, turning to face her and smiling. "It's not always very sweet."

44

Maggie walked down Boulevard Fragonard until it intersected with rue Mirabeau and then went two blocks further to Boulevard Carnot, looking in all the different cafés as she did—each stuffed to overflowing with tourists—before she spotted Florent sitting at an outdoor table in the historic section of town not far from where his factory still smoldered.

As soon as she saw him, she realized that nobody had the motive that Florent did.

It galled her no end that the evidence she and Grace found at the La Nuit Est Belle factory was now destroyed for good. Not only did Florent have motive for killing Vivienne, but he also had opportunity since Maggie had laid eyes on him mere hours before the body was discovered.

As for the burning of his factory, she wasn't sure what that meant. Did he do it himself for insurance reasons? Or to destroy more evidence of his guilt? One way or the other, a confrontation to get him to confess was her best chance.

She walked over to him and was surprised when he looked up at her approach and smiled.

"Monsieur Monet," she said pointing to the empty chair at his table.

He nodded and signaled to the waiter. Maggie sat down.

"I'll make this simple," she said, folding her hands on the table in front of her. "I have some questions about your involvement in Vivienne's death."

He laughed and then shook his head.

"Americans," he said. "It will always amaze me how much of the world you rule in spite of your inability to conduct yourself with basic courtesy."

Ignoring his insults, Maggie plowed ahead. "I know that Vivienne stole the formula for *Mon Sang*," she said. "I have proof of that."

"I...I can't imagine that you do," he stuttered, his voice disbelieving.

"Regardless of what you can or can't imagine," Maggie said, waving away the approaching waiter. "I do have proof. And I have further proof that you hired Tremblay to kill her."

"You can't possibly." Florent looked at her as if unsure she wasn't joking.

Since the truth was that Maggie's physical proof about Florent's involvement had likely gone up in smoke the night before—if it hadn't been destroyed by the police a few hours earlier—she decided to lean heavily on what she'd at least held in her hand and knew to be true.

"I saw the email, Monsieur Monet. The one you sent to Mathys saying Vivienne needed to be gotten rid of."

Now that Maggie thought back, that wasn't the exact wording, but she thought it was close.

"And so, you thought I meant to murder her?" His eyes widened in apparent shock. "That is absurd. I loved Vivienne like a daughter."

Maggie's phone dinged and she glanced at it to see a text message from Grace.

<Had a productive talk with JL. But he's a dead-end. We need to talk to Tremblay. I'm off to find Annabelle to help her question him. See you back at the apt.>

"You cannot come here and accuse me like this, Madame!" Florent said hotly, slamming down the spoon he'd been stirring his coffee with.

"I repeat," Maggie said, putting her phone away. "I have proof you knew that Vivienne had stolen the formula for *Mon Sang*."

"I would never have asked Vivienne to steal it! Why would I do it? Mathys had already successfully reverse formulated it!"

A twinge of doubt fluttered in Maggie's gut. It occurred to her that if what he said was true about the reverse formulation, there went his motive for hiring Vivienne to steal it.

And therefore, his motive for wanting her gone.

But the email!

She decided to dig in.

"I have evidence that you had Vivienne break into the Dix factory," she said, knowing as she spoke that she had nothing of the kind. "Then later, the fact that Tremblay had already given you the formula only made it all the more necessary to erase what Vivienne had done."

"By killing her?" He gave her an incredulous look.

A look that, to Maggie, seemed absolutely authentic.

"She was a living warning to you that at any time she could go to the police," Maggie said. "Or to her boyfriend Jean-Luis Dix—to reveal what you had her do."

"I trusted Vivienne. I loved her like a daughter."

"You might well have done," Maggie said. "Until she blackmailed you."

"I don't know what you're talking about."

But now the look on his face told Maggie she'd gotten a little closer to some version of the truth. She felt an icy finger down her spine as she realized that Vivienne must in fact have tried to blackmail her boss.

"Is that what happened?" Maggie asked. "Vivienne demanded money or she'd tell the world what you had her do?"

"No."

"Well, the emails uncovered on your office computers tell a different story."

Of course, after the factory fire there were no office computers to tell any story anymore. And certainly, no physical paper trail.

"If Vivienne did steal the formula—and I'm not saying she did," Florent said, flustered, "she would know she was untouchable by the law."

"I don't believe that. If Capuccine Dix knew of Vivienne's crime, all she had to do was call her private police dog and have her arrested. She didn't have to kill her. *You're* the only one with that motive."

"You're wrong," Florent said hotly. "Capuccine would never get satisfaction in the courts. Worse, the mere act of bringing it to court would reveal her top-secret fragrance formula to the world."

Maggie had to admit that she'd already suspected as much.

"But to kill Vivienne for the theft? That makes no sense," she prodded.

"It would be a message to anyone else who might be thinking of stealing from her. Besides, what Vivienne did wasn't just theft. After all, who do you think helped her steal the formula?"

When Maggie realized what he was saying, she had to admit he was describing a viscerally powerful motive. If Jean-Luis had helped Vivienne steal from his mother, it would be a betrayal worthy of murder.

"I'm sorry, Madame," Florent said tossing down a few euros on the table. "I understand you want justice for Vivienne, and I hold no malice at your attempt to implicate me to that end. But I cared for her." He stood up. "I would never have hurt her."

He left the table and didn't look back. Maggie watched him go and then got the waiter's attention to order herself a coffee. She needed a minute. She needed to process what he'd said and whether or not she believed it.

Her gut feeling was that Florent did in fact care for Vivienne. But she had met people before who'd been emotionally attached to their victims and killed anyway. No, the problem was that Florent was just too cool and composed during their conversation to have committed cold-blooded murder the day before. Plus, except for the jump drive in Maggie's possession—which Florent didn't know about—the only real proof of what Vivienne had done had gone up in smoke the day before.

She sighed in weariness and discouragement.

So what did it all mean? Was Florent right that Capuccine was the better suspect? If Jean-Luis was involved, then yes, definitely. But Grace had said in her text that she thought Jean-Luis was a dead-end as a suspect. Maggie would need to get a blow by blow of Grace's interview with him to see why she thought so.

That left Tremblay who Grace seemed to think was the better bet. It was true Tremblay would have no trouble getting access to the deadly substance that killed Vivienne. And he had a motive in that she had jumped the gun by stealing the formula.

An idea suddenly buzzed in the back of Maggie's brain and she quickly drank down her coffee.

Maybe it was Tremblay who hired Vivienne to do the stealing? And when she did, he told Florent he'd reverse-engineered the fragrance, thereby making it imperative to keep Vivienne quiet about what she'd done.

Tossing down two euros, Maggie felt suddenly energized. It was as good a theory as any. Plus, Tremblay hated Vivienne. Motive, opportunity and means. The holy trifecta, she thought with satisfaction as she hurried back down the rue Amiral de Grasse toward the Airbnb, anxious to get the details from Grace and Annabelle on what they'd discovered after their conversation with him. And to see what they thought of her theory.

For the first time since she'd begun looking into Vivienne's death, Maggie felt guardedly optimistic.

The light had faded by the time Maggie made it back to the Airbnb. Her excited anticipation turned to disappointment when she saw that there was nobody home. Frowning, she looked at her watch. She'd been gone over three hours.

Shouldn't they be back by now?

A throb of uneasiness skittered across her shoulders as she pulled out Grace's text message again and saw that it had been sent over two hours ago.

She texted her back.

<where are you?>

She went to the kitchen and took down a bottle of wine and a glass and looked at her phone but there was no answer. She texted Annabelle next with the same query before pouring herself a glass of wine, sorry that she'd had that coffee since she was now biting her nails and pacing.

She walked back to the living room and stared out the window where the three of them had stood yesterday, looking at La Nuit Est Belle burn. She took a sip of the wine and then picked up her phone and called Grace, knowing if she was still talking to Tremblay, it would go to voicemail.

It went straight to voicemail.

Her fingers went numb. The call not ringing at all but going straight to voicemail meant Grace's phone was turned off.

Maggie felt her vision blur for a moment.

Grace was like every mother Maggie ever knew. Unless her children were physically with her, she would never turn her phone off. Maggie glanced again out the window at the village as it began to settle into darkness.

Something was wrong.

45

Maggie scoured the apartment to see if she could tell if Grace had come back and gone out again. She tried calling her again and again the call went straight to voicemail as she knew it would. She walked to the window, her fingers nervously twisting her wedding band.

It was dusk now, the shadows lengthening, and nearly nightfall. Maggie punched in Annabelle's number, thinking she and Grace might be together but that call went to voicemail too.

Do I have to actually tell them to keep their phones on? she thought with worried annoyance, as she remembered telling them both that Tremblay was violent and not to be trusted.

She rubbed the back of her neck.

Why did I let them go after him?

The idea flashed briefly into her brain to call the police, but she quickly quashed it. She and Grace were on borrowed time. The last place she could expect help was the Grasse police department.

But she couldn't just stay here and do nothing! She poured her glass of wine down the sink and, keeping her phone in her hand in case one of them called, she left the apartment and walked out onto the street to see if she could spot them in the village.

The temperature had fallen rapidly with the evening and wisps of fog hovered close to the cobblestone streets.

Maggie scanned both sides of one of the streets and peered down every side alley she came to while glancing at her phone in case for some reason she got a call, but it didn't ring. Her agitation and worry compounded by the second and for a moment she had trouble swallowing.

As she came to the end of the street, she spotted Sheila and Bernie, the Canadian couple, standing in front of a restaurant reading the outdoor menu. Maggie hurried over to them.

"Sheila?" Maggie said breathlessly as she ran up to them. "Hello! Do you remember me?"

Sheila was plump with deep set eyes and long blonde hair. She narrowed her eyes at Maggie.

"You're Karen's friend," she said coldly.

Maggie grimaced. She didn't know why Sheila was acting so unfriendly, but undeterred, she smiled hopefully.

"I was wondering if you had seen Grace? She's tall, blonde—"

Sheila snorted unpleasantly.

"You don't have to describe her," she said. "We all know her. She's the American equivalent to Grace Kelly."

Maggie made a point not to mention the fact that Grace Kelly was actually American too.

"Have you seen her today?" Maggie asked.

Sheila looked at Bernie who was still studying the menu. Bernie was powerfully built with a barrel chest and a thick head of white hair. His face was twisted into a squint of intense concentration as he tried to decipher the menu.

"I don't think so. Was she at the Galimard tour?" Sheila asked.

"No. I...I think she was just going to hang in some cafés today in the village."

"Oh, well, Bernie and I have been burning up the tours today, haven't we, Bernie? The only person we saw that we knew was Karen. And trust me, you couldn't miss her. She was in a state."

"Karen? Why?" Maggie was just being polite because if Sheila hadn't seen Grace, she needed to break away and keep looking.

"Well, you know she said some pretty terrible things to that poor little docent Vivienne, don't you? And now you can just imagine—"

Maggie snapped her head around. "What? What are you talking about?"

"You know. The little girl who died on the float?"

"Yes, yes. I mean what mean things did Karen say to her?"

"Oh, Karen feels just awful about it now. I guess she'd stopped Vivienne on the street—the very afternoon the poor girl died—to tell her she'd gotten some bit of information wrong in her presentation—well, you know how Karen is—and things got heated and one thing led to another, and Karen said some things she now greatly regrets. You know. Now that the girl's dead."

"What kinds of things?"

"Oh, I don't know. You know Karen. She's a handful, isn't she Bernie?"

Bernie snorted, never turning from the menu board.

"She's sorry now," Sheila continued blithely. "Well, she would be, wouldn't she? At least for five minutes. Oh, for heaven's sake, Bernie, just pick some place! This restaurant looks fine."

Maggie turned away, stunned. She tried to think when she'd seen Karen since Vivienne's death. She remembered seeing her at the Dix Fleurs tour but hadn't picked up that she was particularly devastated. That would have been the morning after Vivienne was murdered. If what Sheila said was true, Karen had gotten over her guilt fairly quickly.

She needed to confront Karen about her argument with Vivienne the day she died to see just how far the fight had gone. She turned to continue her scouring of the village streets and alleyways.

An hour later, she stood in front of the Grasse police station.

The only option she had left was to report Grace as a missing person. And she had a pretty good idea how that was going to go down.

She sat on a bench outside and punched in the number for the police and asked to speak with Detective Landry. He must have been waiting for her call because she was transferred to his private line almost immediately.

"Madame Dernier," he said smoothly. "I thought I might hear from you."

Nausea swelled in Maggie's stomach at his tone.

"I cannot find my friend Grace Van Sant," Maggie said breathlessly, praying against all odds that he knew where she was, even though that would be nearly as bad as if he didn't.

"And that would be because you did not follow my directions to leave when I asked you nicely," he said sternly.

She sagged back into the bench.

Oh, thank God.

"Detective Landry, please—"

"It is too late for pleading, Madame Dernier," he said. "Madame Van Sant has been detained and is currently being held under suspicion of lying during a police investigation. I would suggest hiring a lawyer for your friend would be the most helpful thing you could do at this point."

46

The waiting room at the Grasse police station was austere and unwelcoming. A glass partition hung between the lines of folding chairs at the reception desk and beyond that the dispatch room filled with its noise and phones and computers.

Maggie waited a full hour before a police constable finally came to the waiting room to usher her into another small interview room where Landry was waiting for her. When she started to speak, he held up a hand to stop her.

"I told you to leave, you didn't. This is the natural consequence of your own obstinance, Madame. Have you called your consulate yet?"

It was the first thing Maggie had done. They assured her they would send someone to Grasse on Grace's behalf first thing in the morning. Or possibly the afternoon. But before the next weekend almost assuredly.

"I have," she said between gritted teeth. "Trust me, you do not want to take on the American consulate, Detective Landry."

Landry waved to the room.

"There is a recorder in this room," he said. "And the French police do not take kindly to its agents being threatened. Not even by our so-called allies."

Maggie let out a long breath. "I apologize," she said, swallowing down some of her anger. "I'm afraid I'm very worried. Would it be possible to allow me talk to her?"

"Are you next of kin?"

"You know I'm not."

"It's not possible, then. Rules, you know."

"Why are you doing this? We were leaving!" Maggie exploded.

"That's strange," Landry said, "because my sources informed me you were out roaming Grasse, both of you, sitting in cafés and not looking at all like you had any intention of leaving."

"Well, now I can't leave!"

"Well, I'm afraid you must, Madame Dernier, and within the hour, too, or I will bring you in as well for deliberately flaunting a direct dictum from a duly authorized agent of the police."

"Why are you doing this?" Maggie said again in sputtering frustration.

"I'm just doing my job," Landry said smugly. "A job you are presently interfering with." He stood up. "You have one hour, Madame Dernier." He held up his watch, which Maggie recognized as a Patek Philippe and tapped its watch face. "Tic toc."

Maggie left the headquarters shaken, her mind flying in a million different directions. Her first instinct was to call Windsor, but he and Grace hadn't remarried so he wasn't next of kin either. All he could do at this point was worry from three thousand miles away. She called the consulate again in Nice and was told to call back during business hours.

Outraged, she put a call in to Laurent, but it went immediately to voice mail.

Wishing she had a door to slam or something to punch, she went to the nearest café, ordered a tall French 75, something she rarely drank because of its potency. She was left with only one other hope. She put the call in to Roger Bedard. He was only ten miles away. If he didn't outrank Landry, he could at least bring pressure on him to release Grace.

Roger had never failed her. Not once when she'd called him in need.

"Hello?" A woman answered Roger's number.

Maggie was taken aback at first, expecting to hear Roger's voice.

"Yes, is this Rochelle?" she said. "My name is Maggie Newberry Dernier. I'm a friend of Roger's."

"I know who you are, Madame Dernier," the voice said, suddenly icy.

"Um, is Roger there? I have a quick question I'm hoping he can help me with."

"Roger is busy at the moment with our six-month-old daughter," Rochelle said coldly.

Maggie felt a moment of disorientation at Rochelle's words. A flush of adrenaline tingled through her body. She'd seen Roger eight months ago for nearly a full five days and never, not at any point had he mentioned that he and his wife were expecting a child.

It really did seem the sort of major life event that friends might mention to one another.

"Oh, I didn't know," Maggie said. "Congratulations to both of you."

"Thank you. As you can imagine, as a result, he has his hands full at the moment and for the foreseeable future. I am afraid I'm going to have to ask you to leave my husband alone, Madame Dernier. He's mine. Mine and our Chérie's. May I assume we have heard the last from you?"

"Sorry to have intruded," Maggie said, her cheeks burning.

Rochelle hung up and Maggie was left holding her phone, feeling abashed and ashamed. She hadn't a leg to stand on, life and death or not, Grace in jail or not. Roger wasn't really a friend and she'd known that for years. He was an extremely useful person who was in love with her. He was someone she'd used when it suited her and called it friendship. There had never been anything two-way about their relationship.

A part of Maggie wanted to write or call him and tell him how sorry she was. Sorry for all the years of taking advantage of him and their friendship. As it was, it was a hell of a finish to their relationship. And she would always owe him for so much that she'd never be able to repay him for.

She vowed that the annual Christmas card would be the only outreach to Roger for as long as she lived. She hoped very much that—unless it was absolutely necessary—she could stick to that promise.

She finished her drink and was surprised that she didn't feel a bit affected by it. She glanced at her watch. Was she really going to just leave? Without Grace? There had to be another way.

Suddenly she remembered Landry hinting that he'd been having her tailed and she wondered if Grace's arrest had to do with the fact that she had been seen talking with Capuccine earlier. If that was true, and Capuccine and Landry were having an affair, then perhaps Capuccine was the real reason Landry wanted them out of town so bad? Maybe that was why he had made good on his threat to arrest Grace.

Appealing to Capuccine might be the only way to get Grace released. As Maggie hurried down the street toward Capuccine's apartment, she was well aware this theory only worked if Capuccine could be reasoned with.

And of course, if she hadn't been the one who'd killed Vivienne.

Robust ivy trailed along the tidy brick walls that encased a courtyard and the front door to the elegant apartment building. The street itself was manicured and pristine. No garbage, no litter, no posters, just elegance and serenity.

Maggie kept to the shadows, reminding herself that if Landry had in fact had her tailed earlier, he likely hadn't stopped. She knew what she was doing was desperate. Coming to Capuccine to beg for her help after accusing her of murder —and implicating her son too—was a last-ditch act of desperation. But Maggie didn't see she had much choice.

Only Capuccine could talk Landry into being reasonable.

Rehearsing her speech, and practicing her most contrite expression, Maggie hurried to stand by the building's security door, under a Juliette balcony, where she waited for someone to come out so she could slip in. Once inside the wrought iron gate Maggie skirted a small courtyard anchored with four large stone planters of climbing roses and peonies. She went through the secondary door to the lobby—a stunning marble floor with a twenty-foot ceiling that soared into a breathtaking atrium. Maggie quickly checked the bank of mailboxes for Capuccine's apartment number.

Second floor.

Praying that Capuccine was home and determined to camp out on her doorstep if she wasn't, Maggie ran up the stairs, telling herself she wouldn't leave until Capuccine promised to help her. What was her option? The worst thing Capuccine could do was call the cops, and if Maggie couldn't get Grace freed, she'd end up in a cell next to her anyway since she also couldn't leave.

She came to the apartment door and took a long breath to steady her nerves. Maggie knew she looked a fright, but she thought that might actually work in her favor. The more distraught she looked, the greater the chance that Capuccine would take pity on her and help her.

That was the plan, anyway.

As she rapped sharply on the door, the door gave way, pushing inward. Maggie hesitated, unsure. She heard a small dog yap from inside which galvanized her, and she pushed the door open.

"Madame Dix?" she called.

The little dog barked again.

Maggie walked inside, the feeling of foreboding pressing in on her like a lead blanket.

Why is the door open?

"Madame Dix?" she called again as she stepped into the living room.

She saw the little dog first. A small Cairn terrier with a lopsided bow in her hair. The animal sat on the couch, twisting its little head in query as Maggie entered the room.

Below her on the carpeted floor lay Capuccine.

Maggie ran to her, and the dog began to bark again with much more agitation. Before Maggie touched her, she saw Capuccine's mouth was open as if frozen in a moment of horror.

A mouth coated with a powdery white substance.

47

The café where Maggie found refuge was a modest one with whitewashed walls and rickety tables whose paint was peeling in various stages. But it gave her a view of the street where Capuccine's apartment was.

It had started to rain again, but Maggie still chose to sit outside on the terrace under the dripping awning. Her hands were shaking as she cupped a glass of whiskey—not even France 75 was going to cut it this time—as she tried to tell herself to stay calm and not to act without thinking. Now, if no other time, she needed to think before she acted.

One thing was sure, calling the police to report what she'd seen would end with her in the cell next to Grace's—if not worse.

Within seconds of bursting free of Capuccine's apartment, Maggie had stepped into one of the many technology boutiques along the main drag and bought a burner phone from which she had quickly made an anonymous call to the police to report Capuccine's death. Then she wiped the phone of her prints, pried out its sim card before dropping it into the gutter in the street, and then the phone itself in the nearest trashcan a block away.

Now as she sat on the terrace of the café she watched as no fewer than three police vans roared down the street to park in front of Capuccine's apartment building. She saw Landry run into the building and a part of her felt sorry for him. She didn't know the extent of his relationship with Capuccine but at the very least he was probably fond of her, perhaps even considered her a friend.

Who would kill her? For what possible reason? Maggie knew it had to be connected to Vivienne's death. The white powder on Capuccine's face told her that. She hadn't seen any rose petals but that didn't mean it wasn't the same killer.

She caught the waiter's attention and ordered another whiskey. She didn't dare go back to the Airbnb tonight. Her mind raced around the same question relentlessly over and over.

Who would have killed Capuccine?

Surely not her own son. She could eliminate Jean-Luis. Then, who? Florent? Mathys? Annabelle?

Maggie hated even thinking of Annabelle as on that list of suspects, but the fact was she was currently missing.

What if, instead of missing, she was actually on the run?

Was Annabelle's absence connected to Capuccine's death? Had she found evidence that Capuccine was culpable and decided to take matters into her own hands? Florent had made a convincing case for why he thought Capuccine had killed Vivienne.

Had Annabelle come to the same conclusion herself?

Except. Then that meant there was a separate killer for Vivienne. And with the white powder, was that likely?

Because if not, then it would mean Annabelle was Vivienne's killer too.

The rain against the window dribbled lines downward, drawing Landry's eyes down, too. One of the crime techs was taking the little dog away. Landry watched as Mignon, cowering in the transport crate, her eyes confused and fearful caught his. He turned away, his glance falling once more on the body as it was being secured in the medical examiner's departmental body bag.

His stomach churned as he watched the ME direct his people in the handling of the body. Landry had been one of the first people on the scene. Whoever had called it in had been very specific. Was that deliberate? Did the caller know how personal this was for him?

He closed his eyes briefly as he remembered seeing Capuccine, her own eyes closed, a scattering of what looked like flour smeared across her face. Her blouse was ripped in half, although her bra was still in place.

He flinched in revulsion at the thought that she had been sexually violated.

Dear God, who would have the nerve to do this? Was there anyone in Grasse who didn't know what she meant to him?

What had she meant to me?

He wasn't in love with her, but he enjoyed her company. His neck corded in fury as he ground his teeth.

Whoever did this would pay.

And pay dearly.

"Chief?"

He turned to look at Docteur Anouilh, the department medical examiner who now stood before him. Anouilh must have addressed him more than once. The look in his eye was impatient and perhaps something else. Something Landry wasn't used to seeing in his subordinates.

Landry cleared his throat. He didn't feel right. He felt weak.

He felt angry and unready to handle what was unfolding. It struck him in horror that a part of him felt...tearful.

"What?" he said gruffly to the ME, an officious little man whom Landry had worked with before and found fairly innocuous, but who he now knew had been speaking to the Americans telling them things he shouldn't.

"I wanted to let you know that I should have my report to you by tomorrow," the ME said.

"Only me?" Landry said, feeling the anger at the crime that had been committed against him now unleashing onto his disloyal underling. "Are you sure you won't be making it available to the press, Docteur Anouilh?"

Anouilh pulled himself up to his height, just a few inches shorter than Landry.

"You can do what you want, Chief," he said sharply. "This is your patch. You can fire me or transfer me, that's your call. But the case you swept under the carpet?—because make no mistake that's exactly what you did..."

Anouilh jammed his thumb in the direction of the gurney with Capuccine's body on it, "...well *that* was nearly an exact repeat."

Landry felt saliva building up in his mouth and his throat thickening.

"What are you saying?" he rasped.

"Did you not even look at Vivienne Curie's body?" Anouilh asked, his lip curling in disgust. "I did a routine autopsy on her, the report is in your inbox, and from what I've seen here tonight, it's the same MO. All except for the ripped blouse."

Anouilh turned to see the forensic techs busy dusting Capuccine's living room, collecting any hairs, fingerprints, footprints, carpet fibers, anything and everything.

"I see you brought forensics in for this one. Now if you only had something to compare the DNA you find."

He turned abruptly and walked away.

Landry stared after the man in shock and disbelief at his blatant insubordination. Only the sounds of the forensics techs conferring quietly as they worked filled the air. He turned away, unable to watch them, unable to be here in this room another moment, his emotions a jumble—out of reach and out of his ability to manage. He feared he might vomit.

What is happening to me?

He walked to the window and looked onto the street. It was such a beautiful avenue, every stone in place, palm trees positioned every half block, the doors of the apartment building opposite gleaming from the polishing attentions of well-paid servants.

Everything was out of whack. Everything was off track. He rubbed his forehead as a migraine began to needle its way into his brainstem. And then it came to him—as sharply and painfully as a slap across the face.

His world had begun to disintegrate the moment Maggie Dernier had come to Grasse.

He clenched his hands and unclenched them as he attempted to get control of himself.

He was tired of being made a fool of. Tired of playing the public relations game. What other police officer was forced to do that?

He watched the street outside where the gurney was now being loaded into the back of the medical transport. Next to it he saw a handful of tourists wander down the street, stopping at a souvenir kiosk before aimlessly meandering further down the street to one of the cafés.

He pulled out his phone, his fury and helplessness ratcheting up until he thought he couldn't breathe. He plugged in the number of the one person he couldn't imagine he'd ever call.

But that was before this. Before Capuccine. Before he so

desperately needed someone to pay for everything that had happened.

He waited for the answering signal on the line. His determination and hatred gelling into one hard lump in his stomach.

He *wasn't* a fool. Not by a longshot.

Dispatch had said that the woman that called in Capuccine's murder had had an American accent.

That was all he needed to know.

48

Everywhere Maggie looked, weathered trees seemed to rise out of the earth to brush the sky. If it hadn't been raining, and the trees dimmed by mist, if it hadn't felt so remote from anything dry and safe and warm, Maggie might have found the scene before her beautiful. As it was, even though the Parc Naturel Départemental de Roquevignon was only a half mile from the center of Grasse, she found the dense area, desolate, creepy and threatening.

Her senses were on hyperalert, and she shivered in her thin cardigan, feeling as if the thick impasse of surrounding trees were engulfing her. The last thing—the very last thing—she had expected was a phone call from August Landry asking to meet someplace away from the police department. But some place this remote and uninhabited? She shook out her hands in nervous agitation.

He didn't suggest in his phone call that he knew it was Maggie who'd called in Capuccine's death. He didn't hint that he was planning to arrest her for not leaving town. He didn't sound like he wanted to trap her.

He sounded distraught.

He sounded for real.

Maggie moved to stand by a boulder that overlooked a narrow dirt road just wide enough for one car. She would be able to see him coming from this point. Would that help?

She shivered again as she looked around and thought how this would be a really good spot to bury a body. Plenty of lavender and May roses to cover up evidence of a freshly dug grave. It might not be as satisfying as seeing her rot in prison for life, but if Landry was unconvinced about whether or not he could make a long prison stint stick for one troublesome American, perhaps this was the next best thing.

Goosebumps marched up and down her bare arms and she rubbed them and tried to regulate her breathing. When she heard a car coming, she slipped behind a nearby ash tree to watch and wait.

The rain was easing and the only sound she heard was the steady crunch of tires on the gravel path as the car drew closer.

A small dark Peugeot pulled up to an ancient tree stump and stopped. The driver's side door swung open, and Landry stepped out, a flashlight in his hand, unmindful of the rain. He swung the beam to the trees where Maggie was semi-hidden.

"Madame Dernier?" he called.

Maggie took in a long breath, said a prayer, and stepped out from behind the tree.

"I'm here."

He flashed the light on her face and began to walk toward her. He stopped no more than twenty-five feet from her.

"It was you, wasn't it?" he asked.

"Pardon?"

"Capuccine's death. You called it in."

Maggie felt a needle of fear drill into her bones.

"The dispatcher said the voice was that of an American woman. Who else but you?"

"Look," she said, feeling her nerves jumping wildly, "I only went to her place to beg her to talk to you about Grace and... and I found her like that. I swear it."

He looked away. "I don't believe you killed her," he said tiredly.

Maggie felt the tension in her shoulders ease.

"But then why..." She lifted a hand to indicate their remote surroundings.

"I need your help."

Maggie forced herself not to gape at his statement. "With what?"

Landry turned away and rubbed a hand across his face. Then he swore and turned back to her.

"It's been too long," he said in frustration. "And this is important. You understand?"

Maggie saw he was angry, but she thought it was mostly at himself. She nodded slowly. It made sense. He meant that it had been too long since he'd done his job. He didn't know how to start.

"You seem to have been able to get certain information from witnesses that my men have not been able to," he said.

"It might help if they tried."

"Fine. I know. The manure flows downward from the chief bull, yes? I admit it. Is that what you want to hear?"

"What I want to hear is that you've released Grace Van Sant from unlawful detention."

"Then we have a deal."

Maggie stared at him in disbelief.

"Will you help me or not?" he asked angrily. "Otherwise I'm happy to keep Madame Van Sant in jail until next Christmas."

"Can you hear yourself?" Maggie said angrily. "Is this how you ask for help? You are the worst!"

His nostrils flared. "Don't bait me! I swear I'll bury her paperwork. She'll never get out. She'll grow old in prison."

Maggie shook her head in disgust.

"You do know she has young children at home who depend on her?" she asked.

That wasn't an exaggeration since Philippe was only ten.

"At her age?"

"Oh, well then," Maggie said, fisting her hands until her nails cut into her palms and forcing herself to turn away. "I'm sorry we couldn't come to an understanding."

He stepped forward and put a hand on her arm. When he did, Maggie felt a charge of electricity. She stopped and looked at him, suddenly very aware of his power, and of the remoteness of where they were. He seemed to read her thoughts. He removed his hand.

"Can we try again?" he said gruffly.

Maggie studied his face. "You and Capuccine were together."

He hesitated and then looked away. "That's irrelevant."

"Seriously? I guess it *has* been a while since you've worked a case."

He sighed. "Yes. Alright. Capuccine and I were special friends."

"Was there anyone who might want to use that information against you?"

He snorted.

"I wasn't being blackmailed, if that's what you're suggesting. My relationship with Capuccine is incidental to her murder!"

"You don't know that."

"Bah! This is useless! I must have been out of my mind." He turned but took only a few steps away.

"Look, I get it," Maggie said. "She was important to you. There's no shame in that."

He looked away, his fists opening and closing as if he wanted to hit something.

"The medical examiner has given his initial assessment that

the manner of Capuccine's death appears to be the same as with Mademoiselle Curie," he said.

"So, they were both poisoned," Maggie said. "With the same substance?"

"He only gave me his preliminary findings. Capuccine's autopsy has not yet been performed."

"But the powdery substance found on Vivienne's body, it was the same with Capuccine?"

"I told you, I don't know yet. But likely."

Maggie looked away, trying to think.

"Vivienne's sister is missing," she said suddenly.

He frowned in confusion. "Who?"

"Annabelle Curie? She contacted you to help find—"

"Oh, yes, yes. I remember. She's missing? Perhaps she went back home."

"And maybe she was beamed up onto a spaceship, but whichever one it was, you need to find out."

He looked frustrated. "That was not our deal! It's not enough that I release your friend?"

"My friend who is innocent in the first place? No, it's not enough! It's only barely enough that you're finally agreeing to do your job. In fact, the bare minimum of your job!"

"*D'accord*," he said. "I will look for the sister *and* release your friend—but only if you help me find Capuccine's killer."

"You're a jerk, you know that?"

"But a jerk with all the power."

"That's probably what makes you a jerk."

He cocked his head and frowned at her.

"I do not know what to think of you," he said.

"I wish I could say the same of you," Maggie said. "But I'm afraid you are all too obvious to me."

He'd reached out to her for help because this was the first time in a very long time when a bribe wouldn't cover the problem. It had been so long since he'd played by the rules that he wasn't sure of how to proceed.

"I need to talk to Grace. She was supposed to have talked to someone tonight. I need to know what she found out."

"I'll set up a phone call."

"And I need any police record on Jean-Luis."

Landry frowned.

"Capuccine's son? Whatever for? You can't think he would hurt his own mother."

"Can we just do this without the comment section lighting up every time I make a request?" Maggie said tartly. "I need to know what I'm dealing with, and *who* I'm dealing with. I also need everything you have on Florent Monet and Mathys Tremblay."

"Wild goose chases."

"Which is largely what thorough detection, is," she said impatiently. "I also need the forensics for both murders and the autopsy results."

"I'll send them to you as soon as I get back to the office. But there was no forensics collected from the float."

Maggie felt a fury build up inside her at the news that no DNA had been collected, although she hadn't really expected otherwise.

"Because Capuccine's clothes were ripped," he said, his voice catching, "we believe it might have been a sexual assault."

Maggie saw the hurt writhing through him as he spoke. As far as she knew, Vivienne hadn't been raped. Landry was saying he didn't know yet that Capuccine wasn't. And it was killing him.

"Anyway," he said, "it means that at least we know her killer was a man."

"We don't know she *was* raped," Maggie said. "She could have been poisoned by anyone. You don't have to be male to rip someone's clothes."

"Who else but a man would bother?"

Maggie forced herself not to respond. Nobody in the business of police investigations today would ask such a ludicrous question.

"I'm not ruling anyone out," was all she said. "In the absence of evidence, like fingerprints or DNA, nobody gets a free pass."

"Fine. I will send them both to you as soon as I get them." He turned and this time he walked nearly all the way back to his car before turning around.

"I don't need to tell you that this arrangement between us is highly confidential?" he said.

Maggie realized that was the real reason why he reached out to her. He couldn't take the risk of his men seeing him needing help. There was literally nowhere else for him to turn except to an expat amateur sleuth with her own reasons for wanting to find out the truth.

"Just start the process of discharging my friend," Maggie said, before turning away and beginning the long walk back into the village.

49

Laurent let all three dogs loose. Kip ran down the driveway and disappeared into the dark night, but the other two milled about the outdoor dining table looking for dropped table scraps. He figured they'd be useless to track her—none of them were hunters—but it was worth a shot.

With no moon, the darkened garden was an amorphous amalgamation of shadowy shapes with the barely visible stone wall around it, and the vineyards beyond. Laurent heard a barking dog in the next village over. A definite scent of decay in the air seemed to mingle with the remnant smell of woodsmoke from the night's grill.

The temperature had dropped significantly since dinner as it had done for the last several nights. His gut churned at the thought of Amelie out in the cold. But there were worse things than the cold.

Laurent thought back to the boar-sighting that Frère Jean had told him about and his stomach tightened in fear. Boars were unpredictable animals but consistent in their viciousness.

Last fall a boar had caught up with a hunter and gored his leg to the tune of forty stitches.

And that man had a gun.

Laurent's mind raced to imagine where the boar might have gone, where Amelie might have gone. He quickened his steps, directing his flashlight beam in a sweeping movement around him, forcing himself not to think and only to notice the rocks, the bushes, the ground itself.

He found his awareness narrowing to the spot in front of him, the sounds of the two dogs at the table, and of Danielle calling Amelie's name behind him, and the feel of the night air against his skin, cold and relentless.

It took all his strength of mind not to think of his little granddaughter out in the cold, alone. He needed to stay strong to do whatever he needed to do to find her.

"Amelie!" he shouted, hearing his voice boom out and echo across the field, the desperation in it evident.

He stopped to listen for her answering cry, but only heard the crunch of his own footsteps on the gravel walkway. Suddenly all he could think of was that agonizing six-hour evening eighteen years ago when Mila had been taken from them.

He remembered the throb of terror throughout every minute of that night, a night he never thought he would ever need to revisit—the heartbreaking sounds of Maggie's tears, the whole village of St-Buvard around them, wanting to help but fearing the worst. And now here he was again. He began to turn back toward the house when he froze, his own words reverberating in his brain.

The whole village around them.

He pulled out his phone and called Frère Jean.

"Amelie is missing," he said tersely into the phone. "I need help."

"We are on our way," the monk said before disconnecting.

Laurent turned back to the house and entered the kitchen where Danielle was pacing the floor, gripping the hem of her apron. Her hand covered her mouth so only her eyes showed, wide with her helplessness and fear.

"Where would she have gone? Why did she leave?" she cried.

Laurent was glad he'd not mentioned the boar sighting to her. He drew her into a firm hug.

"We will find her, Danielle."

"She must be so cold! Why would she go out in the cold?"

"I'm going out to look. Frère Jean is coming with searchers. But I need you to stay here," he said.

"Laurent, no! I can't just sit here and do nothing!"

"You're not doing nothing. If she finds her way home, you need to be here."

Danielle's skin was flushed, and she was breathing heavily. Finally, she nodded.

"Yes, of course, you're right," she said, her voice trembling. "My poor sausage. My poor *petit chou*."

Laurent found Danielle's phone on the counter and put it in her hands.

"Call me as soon as she walks through the door," he said.

She heartened at his words and clutched her phone to her chest.

"Yes, I will," she said. "As soon as she comes home."

He patted her shoulder and then went and dug out more flashlights from under the sink. He looked around.

"Where's Luc?"

"He...he just ran out into the night," Danielle said, her bottom lip trembling with her effort not to weep.

"Okay, good. Frère Jean is bringing help. Why don't you make a big carafe of coffee and maybe some sandwiches for them?"

He knew that keeping her busy was the best way to keep

her calm. She nodded and slipped her phone into her apron pocket.

"Yes," she said. "Yes, I'll do that."

Laurent turned and stepped outside again, the cold temperature instantly hit him. Amelie had only been wearing a cotton cardigan over her t-shirt and jeans. Wherever she was, she was very cold.

He snapped on the beam of his flashlight again and started out toward the garden. He'd need to stay close to see the headlights of the searchers from the monastery.

How far could she have gone?

Out of the corner of his eye he caught movement in the kitchen window and was gratified to see Danielle bustling about. As he turned back toward the dark driveway, and the garden beyond, he thought of the words he'd told her to help awaken her strength.

How he wished he could believe them himself.

50

As Maggie made her way slowly down into the village, she found herself noting that her meeting with Landry was disconcerting on several different levels. First, the man was despicable. He was rotten and corrupt without a doubt to promise that Grace only got her freedom—assuming the consulate didn't prove successful in its efforts—if Maggie uncovered Capuccine's killer for him. But the most unsettling feeling she had was not only she'd just made a deal with the devil, but that in spite of the vulnerability she'd seen in him, he was basically ruthless, used to bending the rules to take advantage of his position in the community.

There might have been a good man lurking inside August Landry once a long time ago, and there had been glimpses of that man tonight, but Maggie needed to remember that he was the kind of man who would sacrifice her—and Grace—to get what he needed.

When she reached the historic section of Grasse, her mind kicking into high gear. There was no doubt in her mind that the answer to who killed Vivienne led directly to the question of who killed Capuccine.

Find one and you'll find the other.

She needed to find Trembley. Annabelle had been hoping to talk to him. Perhaps she'd succeeded, and he attacked her? Or maybe he told her something that had led to Capuccine's door?

In any case, Maggie needed to talk to him herself.

She looked around at the spot where she'd emerged from the serpentine trails and paths that had led her into the hills of the park and recognized she was standing near the front of the Musée de la Parfumerie.

Had it really only been two days since she and Grace had visited here?

She walked past the museum onto boulevard Fragonard and immediately spotted Karen Dixon standing with another couple who Maggie vaguely recollected from the first tour at La Nuit Est Belle with Vivienne. Karen was loaded down with so many bags of perfume bottles that she clinked when she walked.

"Karen! Hold up!" Maggie called as she jogged down the street toward her.

Karen turned and then looked behind Maggie as if expecting to see someone else with her. She turned to tell the other couple she'd catch up with them.

"If you're asking about Grace," Karen said to Maggie, "I haven't seen her. Sheila told me you were looking for her."

"I wanted to know about the fight you had with Vivienne the afternoon she died," Maggie said.

Karen's eyes tightened into a glare.

"I can't believe Sheila told you about that! What a backstabbing witch! You can't trust anybody these days."

"So, you fought with her? Sheila said it was something about how you knew more than Vivienne did about the perfume industry?"

Instantly, Karen's eyes filled with tears.

"It wasn't like that," she said weakly, making Maggie think it was exactly like that.

"I didn't mean to lay into her," Karen said. "I sometimes wish I had a stop button, you know?"

"Did the argument get physical?"

Karen's eyes widened and then snapped with anger.

"No, it didn't. And I resent you suggesting it."

"A lot of bad things can happen without a stop button, Karen. Where were you during the parade?"

Karen's face reddened and she flattened her lips into a sneer.

"Seriously? No, I get it. I'm a pain in the butt so I'm everyone's favorite target. If you must know, I was sitting at a table near the fountain by the main drag watching the parade go by. You ask Sheila. She's got a big mouth, but she and Bernie were both there."

Maggie made a note to do just that. Or better yet, she'd send a text to Landry and have one of his men do it. It would mean more coming from an official source.

"I hate what happened to her," Karen said with a sniff. "It's nearly ruined my whole trip. I can't wait to leave Grasse."

"You're leaving?"

"We're heading to Paris for the *real* Fragonard factory tour. And after that Prague, and then Italy. You know, Gucci Land." She laughed.

Maggie was always amazed when she met people with more money than class—as if somehow being rich came with civility and good taste.

"DJ ain't best pleased about missing out on Germany," Karen said, "but I told him he can go trout fishing in Italy instead. I mean, I hate hiking, but I have enough perfume to cover up a whole fish camp full of mackerel!" Karen turned back toward her waiting friends.

"Good luck finding Grace," she said over her shoulder as she left. "She's definitely your better half."

Then she hurried down the cobblestones—perfume bottles clinking as she went—to catch up with her friends waiting for her by the chalkboard menu of a restaurant at the end of the street.

Maggie watched her go, discouraged and not at all sure of what that interaction had gained her. As she turned back toward the apartment to try to think of her next move, her phone rang. She saw it was from the Grasse police station.

"Hello?"

"Can you believe this?" Grace said with annoyance. "I'm royally pissed, I can tell you."

"Grace, how are you? I hate that this happened to you. I've called the consulate."

"Yes, I called them too. And Capuccine? Oh, my God! What is going on?"

"I know. It's horrible."

"Detective Pain in the Ass has been taking pretty good care of me, all in all," Grace admitted with a long-suffering sigh. "The food hasn't stopped coming and for now he has me in what I think is his private lodging here. Hot showers, television, did I mention the nonstop food service?"

"We'll get you out," Maggie said. "And to that end, tell me more about your conversation with Jean-Luis."

"There's not much to tell, except to say I honestly don't think he's involved in hurting Vivienne. I mean, he's a scamp to be sure, but in my opinion not a murderous one. But back to Capuccine—do you think she was killed by the same killer?"

"I do."

"Well, there you are. Few people are capable of matricide. Certainly not Jean-Luis."

"Okay, well, eliminating one suspect helps," Maggie said. "Nothing else from him?"

"He made it sound as if Vivienne wore the pants in their relationship and they did break up the night she died. That's about it. I looked for Annabelle and Mathys but didn't find either of them."

Maggie sighed. "Okay, Grace. Thanks."

"I have a notebook at the apartment where I jotted down more specifics from my talk with Jean-Luis, but you have the gist of it. I hope Annabelle had more luck with Tremblay."

Maggie didn't have the heart to tell Grace that Annabelle was currently missing.

"I'll get a debrief from her when I see her," Maggie said. "Meanwhile, hang in there, Grace. I'm working on it."

"I know you are, darling. Be careful, okay? I don't suppose Windsor has texted?"

Maggie winced. "No, sorry."

Just then Maggie spotted none other than Mathys Tremblay slinking into the shadows parallel with her on the street and she slowed her steps so he wouldn't see her.

"Listen, Grace," she whispered. "I'll talk to you later. Keep the faith!"

Maggie jammed her phone into her jacket pocket and ran down the uneven cobblestones to the alley she watched Tremblay disappear into. Without pausing, she darted down the alley and immediately slammed into a hard body blocking her way.

She stumbled and desperately flailed with her arms to keep from falling as Tremblay stood watching her, his face twisted into a mask of fury. When she regained her balance, she took a step back and saw he gripped a heavy stone pestle in one hand.

"I think it's about time we put an end to these little surprise run-ins," he said menacingly, as he advanced on her.

51

Maggie made a hurried assessment of her situation and realized that attempting to run would only allow Tremblay to attack her from the rear. Her only real option was to try to talk to him.

"I'm sorry you're upset, Monsieur Tremblay," she said, instinctively holding her hands up in preparation of fending off an attack. "I did not mean to—"

He raised the heavy pestle over his head in a threatening gesture.

"Why are you following me?!" he shouted, spittle flying from his lips, his eyes glazed.

"Please, Monsieur Tremblay," Maggie said, trying hard not to look at the pestle in his hand. "You don't want to do this."

"*You* don't tell me what to do," he snarled as he suddenly lunged at her, dropping the pestle and grabbing her by the shoulders.

He shook her, blasting a spray of alcoholic fumes into her face. Maggie struggled in his grip. This close, she could see his nose was newly broken, and one eye was swollen shut.

And he smelled like smoke.

"I have done nothing to you," Maggie said breathlessly, her heart pounding in triple time until she thought she was having a heart attack

"*Nothing*? You have ruined my life! You have destroyed everything."

Maggie knew most sociopaths tended to blame the world for every bad thing that happened to them. Unfortunately, that awareness did little to comfort her at the moment.

"Florent thinks I burned the factory! So now the police are looking for me!"

"Well, did you burn it?" Maggie asked, squirming desperately in his harsh grip.

He roared in a guttural fury.

"Shut up! *You're* the reason the police are looking for me! You've ruined my life!"

Maggie twisted free and took a step backward. She rubbed her aching arms. Something about the way he looked—lost, angry, self-destructive, perhaps the tiniest bit contrite—made her decide to confront him again.

"If you burned down La Nuit Est Belle," she said, "it seems you've ruined your own life."

He took a menacing step toward her. Suddenly, Maggie felt a blinding fury detonate inside her. Without thinking, she stepped forward to meet him and slapped him hard across the face.

"Stop bullying me!" she said sharply.

He blinked in surprise, as the red imprint of her hand grew on his cheek. His eyes filled with tears and she instantly regretted hitting him.

"Pull yourself together," she said. "You can't accost women on the street and not expect consequences."

A self-pitying look came over his face as he reached up to gingerly touch his swollen eye.

"Who beat you up?" she asked.

"That bastard Dix," he muttered.

"Jean-Luis? Why?"

"Because he killed Vivienne!" he shouted.

"Lower your voice," Maggie said. "That doesn't make sense. Why would killing Vivienne make him want to beat you up? Besides, why do you care who killed Vivienne? You hated her."

"You know nothing."

"Why do you think Jean-Luis killed Vivienne?" Maggie asked more gently.

Tremblay looked at her as if she were the village fool.

"Isn't it obvious? He and Vivienne stole the formula together. How else could she have done it except with him?"

"But why would he do that? And why would doing it make him want to kill her?"

"Any fool can see he did it to get back at his mother."

Maggie frowned. "He hated his mother?"

She had not seen evidence of this when she'd seen the two together.

"Of course! She wanted him to take over the business and he wanted out. He thinks he's an actor or something. He used Vivienne to help deliver the message to his mother."

"But then why kill her?"

"Isn't it obvious?" he repeated.

Maggie gave a helpless shrug.

"Bah! Everyone is blind but me," he said.

It occurred to Maggie that Tremblay blaming Jean-Luis for killing Vivienne was compatible with a sociopath's desire to shift blame to everyone in the world except themselves.

Especially if he himself killed Vivienne.

In spite of what Grace had told her, Maggie hadn't *totally* taken Jean-Luis off her suspects' list. She wanted to see Grace's notebook first and then speak to Jean-Luis herself. Even so, since she believed that whoever killed Vivienne also killed

Capuccine, she found it difficult to see Jean-Luis as their murderer.

It did occur to her that pressing Tremblay for a confession while she was facing him, unarmed, in a deserted alley, was probably not the best idea she ever had. She would have to wait for another more public time to question him about his alibi for both Vivienne and Capuccine's murders.

Tremblay licked his lips and looked briefly confused before glancing at the pestle on the ground at his feet. He frowned as if he couldn't remember why he was holding it.

"What are you doing here?" he asked and looked around as if uncertain of what he was doing in the alley as well.

"I'm looking for Annabelle Curie," Maggie said reasonably as if they had been having a normal conversation. "Have you seen her?"

"Who?"

"Vivienne's sister. She was looking for you to talk to you."

"I saw no one," he said, his shoulders slumping in defeat. Whatever purpose he'd had when he'd accosted her just moments ago had dissolved. His head sagged nearly onto his chest as he turned and shuffled down the alleyway.

Maggie watched him go for a few moments before emerging from the alley to make her way back down the rue Amiral de Grasse toward the Airbnb. She wasn't sure what to do next—or even what her run-in with Tremblay meant—but there was at least the possibility of a clue in Grace's notebook.

Honestly, she didn't have high expectations for what the notebook might tell her, but she couldn't think of anything else to do.

The sun was sinking low behind the surrounding hills by the time she opened the door to their rented apartment. When she did, she saw the folded note under her foot and stopped cold. Carefully, she stepped back outside onto the threshold, her heart pounding at the realization that someone was inside waiting for her.

52

I know you did your best, but you can stop searching for Viv's killer now. I'm at peace with it all.
Thanks for your help.
Love,
Annabelle

Maggie stared at the note in her hand which, when she had stopped and thought about it, she realized must have been slipped under her door rather than having been dropped by someone waiting for her inside waiting.

She sat on one of the dining room chairs and read and re-read the note, perplexed as to why Annabelle wouldn't just tell her in person that she was giving up. She tried to make sense of why Annabelle wanted to pull the plug on the investigation when she knew Vivienne's killer hadn't yet been found.

And why was she suddenly not reachable by phone?

Maggie dug out her phone and put it a call to Annabelle. It went straight to voicemail. She frowned. That had to mean that Annabelle had her phone turned off.

If she had her phone at all.

As Maggie sat and alternatively stared at her phone and Annabelle's note, her phone rang, making her jump. A photograph of Laurent appeared on the screen and she felt a warring stream of guilt and relief.

"Hey," she said, answering the phone.

"Where have you been?" he asked.

"I could ask the same of you," Maggie said, feeling immediately defensive. "Is everybody still alive on your end?"

He snorted. "Of course. When are you coming home?"

Maggie had had a few hours to decide how she was going to tell Laurent—or not—about Grace's situation. Telling him where she was would almost certainly send him racing to Grasse—at least a four-hour drive from St-Buvard or three the way Laurent drove. And to what end?

He could do no more than she was doing. In fact, because of his size and generally gruff affect, would undoubtedly prove a liability to her getting certain delicate suspects to open up. No, activating Laurent at this point was definitely not in order. She would tell him everything when she saw him—when it was all resolved.

"How's Amelie?" she asked.

"She is fine," he said. "Happy, playing with the dogs, learning how to make yoghurt cake with Danielle."

"Oh, that's nice," Maggie said, glancing at her watch. "Listen, Laurent, Grace and I are having such a great time we're going to extend our weekend by a day, okay?"

The pause on the line showed Maggie how surprised Laurent was about this. With good reason too since he'd practically had to talk her into going on the trip in the first place.

"What is going on?" he asked.

"What? Nothing!"

"*Chérie*, I know you. Something is happening and I do not believe it is you wanting to shop an extra day."

"Yes, okay, fine," Maggie said with a tinge of frustration in her voice. "There are a few things going on, but it's all good," she said hurriedly. "I'll tell you all about it when I see you day after tomorrow. Okay?"

She knew very well how furious he would be when he found out was happening in Grasse with Grace, but with a little luck, it would all get sorted out and be nothing more than an amusing story of how she and Grace went to Grasse and Grace was arrested.

After appeasing him and hearing about another antic of Amelie's day, Maggie got off the phone. She sat for a moment and thought about Laurent's tone of voice, and it occurred to her that he might have a few things he was keeping from her as well. He wasn't the only one who could read the truth in what his spouse wasn't saying. She stood up. Whatever it was, she would find out when she got home.

She walked into the bedroom and saw that Grace's bed was made and her clothes neatly packed in her suitcase. Maggie felt a stab of dismay at the thought of Grace being rudely pulled away from this scene of calm and order when she was arrested, but then chased the image from her mind. That wouldn't help anything. She was doing all she could to get Grace free. Fretting about the problem instead of focusing on finding Capuccine's killer was just stupid, not to mention a waste of time.

She found the small lined spiral notebook in the desk in the bedroom and felt a shiver of excitement. She flipped to the page with today's date on it and felt another twinge of sadness at the sight of Grace's familiar handwriting—in peacock blue ink no less, but she pushed past the feeling. Grace must have written the entry just minutes before her arrest, as she waited for Maggie to return.

In her spare and neat handwriting, Grace had bulleted her interview with the ME. As Maggie scanned the points, she confirmed that she already knew all the facts jotted here.

Had Grace had time to put down her thoughts about her

interview with Jean-Luis? Maggie read on with increasing anxiety.

Finally, she saw the passage she was looking for. Grace had written: *JL acts like he loved V. Saw no indication he could kill her or anyone else. None.*

She'd underlined *None* several times.

Maggie read on.

JL said V was a b-buster! Said she was regularly forced to put male tourists in their place—mostly Americans. Said Tremblay was the most likely suspect to have killed her. He was in love with her. T's motive? V jerked the rug out from under him after his attempt to reverse formulate MS.

On the next page line, Maggie saw the address Annabelle had written down for Grace. She went back to the living room where she'd left Annabelle's note and examined it more closely. It was handwritten in the classic French style. Whoever wrote it was almost certainly French. She held Grace's notebook next to the note. They matched.

There was no doubt that Annabelle had written the note.

As excitement and dread mounted inside her in equal measure, Maggie read the note again.

I know you did your best but you can
stop searching for Viv's killer now.
I'm at peace with it all.
Thanks for your help.
Love,
Annabelle

Maggie had never heard Annabelle refer to Vivienne as *Viv*. She went to the next line in the note.

"*I'm at peace with it all*" was not something French people typically say. But it was something Americans say.

Maggie took in a breath and let it out to steady her nerves. Finally, regardless of everything that Maggie and Grace had shared with Annabelle in the last couple of days, they did not really know each other—not as far as the typical French person was concerned—and certainly not well enough for Annabelle to sign off with *Love*.

Maggie sat back on the couch, the implications now clear beyond a shadow of a doubt. Yes, the note was written by Annabelle. There was no question of that.

But they weren't Annabelle's words.

53

Maggie stepped out of the apartment, her heart thudding in her chest. She needed to do something.

Annabelle had been taken against her will.

Should she call Landry? She made a face of disgust as she dismissed the idea.

He has no idea what he's doing. If I can't find her, he certainly can't.

The note had been hand delivered. She stared down the street. Somebody must have seen something. She turned down the street to the building beside hers and went to the front door where she knocked loudly. Within moments a teenage girl answered the door.

"Bonsoir," Maggie said. "I'm hoping you can help me."

She knew that was all wrong. Even young French people didn't love the strictly American habit of eschewing introductions and getting right to the point. But Maggie didn't feel she had the luxury of Franco-American niceties. Every minute that ticked by in a kidnapping put the victim closer to certain death.

"Someone delivered a note to my door today," Maggie said. "I was wondering if you saw anything."

The girl frowned and looked past Maggie in the direction of her Airbnb.

"My mother hates that André rents his house out to tourists."

"I'm sure she does," Maggie said, forcing herself to be patient. "I hope my friend and I have been good neighbors while we've been here. As I was saying, did you see anyone—?"

"The mail carrier comes at noon."

"This didn't come through the post," Maggie said, a headache beginning to form behind her eyes. "It was hand delivered."

The girl shrugged. "I didn't see anything."

"Thank you for your help," Maggie said turning away, intending to go to the next house.

"I bet Madame Agurté saw something but don't bother her," the girl called after her as she pointed to the apartment next door. "She's in a wheelchair."

Maggie waved her thanks and went straight to Madame Agurté's apartment. In her experience, house-bound old ladies saw everything that went on in their neighborhoods.

She knocked on the door. If she truly was in a wheelchair, it would take her a moment to answer the door.

As it happened, it didn't take her long at all.

She must have been watching the street, Maggie thought in excitement.

The door creaked open revealing an old woman in her nineties, her eyes bright. She was sitting in a wheelchair, a wool throw rug over her knees.

"Bonjour, Madame Agurté," Maggie said. "My name is Maggie Dernier and I'm in town for the Jasmine festival."

Maggie knew that the manner in which she could get away with talking to a young teenager was not the case with a French woman of Madame Agurté's age. If she had any hope of the woman helping her, she would need to play by the rules.

Madame Agurté frowned and folded her hands in her lap.

"You are American?" she asked waspishly.

"I am, yes," Maggie said. "I'm staying at André's house two houses down the—"

"I know where Monsieur LeBlanc's house is," Madame Agurté said.

"Great. I'm going door to door because I received a note—a hand-delivered note—and I'm trying to find out if someone saw it being slipped under my door. May I ask if you saw anything like that, Madame Agurté?" Maggie finished breathlessly.

"I might have."

"It's very important that I find the person who delivered the note," Maggie said, tamping down her frustration which was currently threatening to brim over the top of her reserve.

"What do you want with him?"

Maggie nearly groaned when she realized that the old woman was was bored and wanted to talk.

"Nothing bad," Maggie assured her. "I just want to ask him who gave him the note to deliver."

"And he won't get in trouble?"

Maggie felt a pinch of excitement. Madame Agurté knew the person who'd delivered the note!

"Not at all. I promise," Maggie said, nearly hopping from foot to foot in her agitation.

"He's called Pepe," Madame Agurté said. "I see him on the street now and then. Usually, not up to any good. If he's delivering mail now, I'm glad to see he's doing something law-abiding. I would want to encourage that." She narrowed her eyes at Maggie.

"Yes, of course," Maggie said. "I would be delighted to tip him for any helpful information he can give me."

Madame Agurté harrumphed. "Well, you do not need to go

that far. The young man should tell you what he knows without having to be bribed to do so."

"Do you know where I might find him?"

"Do I look like I'm up and about town noticing young men and where they go?" She grabbed the door as if to shut it in Maggie's face before relenting.

"Le Café Bleu," she said. "Or possibly the train station."

Then she shut the door and Maggie whirled around and ran down the street toward the center of town.

Le Café Bleu was full of patrons when Maggie found it a few blocks away. She scanned their faces, cursing the fact that she'd neglected to ask Madame Agurté what Pepé looked like. There were no young men here, just middle-aged tourists and a few young couples.

Suddenly it occurred to her that Pepé likely wasn't a *customer*. If he was getting in trouble and delivering notes for a handful of euros, he probably was around back or even in the kitchen. She made her way through the interior of the café. The sounds of glasses clinking and bowls banging on metal counters with the strong scent of cooking onions and garlic led Maggie in the direction of the restaurant kitchen.

As she passed through the café, she gave its interior tables a cursory look, but she'd already decided she wouldn't find him here. As she squeezed down the narrow aisle, the swinging door to the kitchen gave her a brief glimpse of a man in a dirty chef's jacket chopping a mountain of onions. Except for a waiter lounging by the counter and smoking, there was no one else in the kitchen.

Forcing herself not to get discouraged, Maggie passed the restroom door and arrived at the back exit. She pushed the door open and found herself in a back alleyway. It was a narrow space with one end blocked by two large garbage bins. A light over the backdoor revealed two young men sitting on a wooden bench, both smoking. They looked warily at her as she approached.

"Pepé?" she asked.

One boy shrugged but the other jumped to his feet, his cigarette hanging out of his mouth. His eyes darted around the alley space but there was nowhere for him to go since the line of garbage bins was blocking one exit and Maggie stood in front of the other. She planted her feet firmly and pointed at him.

"Don't run," she said. "I know your name. Run and I'll go straight to the police."

"It wasn't my fault!"

"I'm willing to believe that. Just tell me who gave you the note."

"Some guy," he said. "That's all I know."

"Where did he find you?"

"I don't know. Around."

"How much did he give you to slip the note under my door?"

"Ten euros."

"Hey, *débile*," the other boy said. "You never said you made ten euros! Where's the five you owe me?"

Pepé ignored him.

"Did he give you the note here?" Maggie asked, waving to the alley.

He snorted back a laugh. "*Non.* Not here. At the *Décharger.*"

The *Décharger* was a popular tourist spot. After dark, Maggie had heard that it was also a popular place for miscreants to shoot up.

"How did he know you wouldn't take the money and run?" she asked.

"That's what I want to know," the other boy said.

"He said he'd be watching me," Pepé said with a shrug.

"When I put the note under the door, I walked across the street where he was waiting behind a hedge. He gave me my ten."

Annabelle's kidnapper had been on Maggie's street that afternoon. He'd been standing in the bushes across from her Airbnb.

"And you never saw him before?" she asked.

"*Non*. He is not from around here."

"From somewhere else in France?"

He shrugged.

"How was he dressed?"

This question made both boys laugh.

"I do not look at such things in a man," Pepé said pointedly, looking Maggie up and down.

"Was he tall?" Maggie asked in frustration. "Fat? Blond? Have a big nose? Wear a t-shirt?"

He frowned as if remembering that Maggie could in fact still call the police.

"He was wearing a face mask," he said. "And a baseball cap."

Maggie nearly groaned in discouragement.

"Was he white or black?" she asked.

"White."

It wasn't much and she had no idea where she would go from here with this information, but there seemed nothing more to be learned.

"All right," she said. "Thank you for your help." She pulled a five euro note out of her purse and handed it to him.

His face reflected his surprise and for a moment he looked at the money with suspicion. Then he waved it away.

"I have already been paid, Madame."

"Don't be an idiot!" his friend said. "Take the money!"

"I am sorry if the note caused you…pain," Pepé said stiltedly, looking down at his feet.

In spite of her disappointment, Maggie managed a smile for him.

"Thank you," she said, before stepping forward and tucking the five-euro note in his jeans jacket pocket.

She turned to head down the alley, a sense of heaviness and despair beginning to steal into her body.

"There was one thing, Madame," Pepé said calling after her. "He was American. Does that help?"

54

Maggie walked out of the alley, her hopes elevated by what she'd discovered. It seemed that the man who paid Pepé to slip the note under her door was American or, to be fair, possibly Canadian. Maggie was sure the accent would sound the same to Pepe.

The use of "Viv" in the note made Maggie think of the fact that shortcutting people's names was a uniquely American habit.

What did it mean? Was the dictator of the note one of the male tourists?

As she hurried back to the Airbnb—her brain pinging in every direction at once—she found a fuzzy but insistent thought flitting around the perimeter of her brain but she couldn't quite capture it. She thought it might have been something Grace had said earlier. Maggie wracked her brain to remember.

What was it?

Did it have something to do with Grace's interview with the Medical Examiner or with Jean-Luis? Maggie wondered if

Landry would set up another call with Grace. Then she remembered Grace's notebook.

Was it something I read in the notebook?

Now that she thought back, she remembered that she'd read Grace's notebook earlier, and then gotten sidetracked by needing to compare Annabelle's handwriting sample to the note. Whatever it was that was flitting around her brain, was definitely in that notebook!

Once she reached the Airbnb, she felt her phone vibrate signaling that she'd received a text. She opened the app to see a link had been sent to her from an unknown source. She hesitated only a moment before clicking on the link. When she did, she saw that Landry had sent the two autopsy reports. Maggie sat on the couch and scanned them quickly.

Both women had been asphyxiated by a toxic substance sprayed into their faces. Both showed bruises on their arms and hands that indicated they'd fought for their lives. Maggie read the line that revealed that neither had been sexually assaulted.

At least there was that, she thought. Otherwise, the two killings were nearly identical, proving at least in Maggie's mind, that the killer was one in the same. She wasn't sure how much the information helped her. But she knew that when she finally succeeded in identifying the killer, the information would prove helpful to the prosecution in getting an indictment.

The key phrase there being finally succeeded in identifying the killer.

She found the notebook on the coffee table in the living room where she'd left it. She flipped it open and began to skim the entries that Grace had made on her conversation with Jean-Luis.

JL said V was a b-buster! Said she was regularly forced to put male tourists in their place—mostly Americans. Said Tremblay was the most likely suspect to have killed her. He was in love with her. T's motive? V jerked the rug out from under him after his attempt to reverse formulate MS.

Maggie put the book down and stared. *MS* was clearly short for *Mon Sang,* and, in spite of Jean-Luis and Grace's beliefs that Tremblay had the most motive for killing Vivienne, a picture was forming in Maggie's mind of Vivienne as a frequent target of unwanted attention from male tourists.

Perhaps one in particular?

Maggie stood up, suddenly too antsy to sit still.

If Vivienne had rebuffed a tourist, could he have followed her later to get vengeance?

And could that tourist be an American? That idea matched up with the fact that whoever had forced Annabelle to write the note was likely American. The sickening realization that there was a chance that Vivienne's killer was one of the fragrance factory tourists crept over Maggie before settling firmly in her head as the most obvious thing in the world.

She pulled out her phone and called the police station, asking to speak to Detective Landry.

"If you have Detective Landry's personal number, I suggest—"

"I don't have his personal number," Maggie said. "But he'll want to talk to me."

"Are you calling to report a crime?"

Maggie hung up in frustration. What good was her partnership with Landry if she couldn't get in touch with him when she needed him?

She went to the living room and stared out into the inky evening, racking her brain to remember the other men in the tourist group. It wasn't late, probably only a little past seven. Could she get a list of all the names of the tourists who were at the La Nuit Est Belle Tour on Friday? Would Florent have that?

She glanced at her watch. Annabelle didn't have time for Maggie to do this by the book. There was no time to be looking at manifests or tourist guest books. Besides, did it even help to figure out *who* took Annabelle when *where* was the most vital question?

Maggie suddenly remembered Karen saying that she and DJ were leaving today which reminded her: *DJ had hung around with a few of the male tourists.* He might have an idea of any of them who were perhaps a little aggressive, perhaps a little disrespectful to the women?

She grabbed a cardigan and the keys to the rental car and stuffed them in her tote bag before heading out the door.

Any lead at all was better than what she had right now.

55

The woods surrounding *Dormir* were densely packed, full of natural divots and unseen debris. Luc vaulted over the stone wall that contained Danielle's *potager*, landing solidly on the other side into a patch of yellow broom. Normally he enjoyed their sweet smell. He wondered if he'd ever be able to smell them after tonight where they didn't nauseate him.

He swung around at the unexpected sound of heavy breathing to see Philippe's dog Kip leap effortlessly over the wall and land beside him. He had no idea if the animal was any good at tracking but even if it was, Luc didn't have a piece of Amelie's clothing to get him started. But he was grateful for the company. He told himself that if the dog just helped in being able to see better than Luc that would be worth something. Plus, Luc wasn't sure that Amelie would come to him if he called, but she would definitely come to Kip.

"Amelie, where are you?" he shouted into the darkness.

Only the sound of the rustling of the wind in the nearby trees came back to him. There was no moon and visibility was nearly nil. Luc realized that Amelie could be right next to him, and he'd never see her. He pulled out his phone and texted Jem.

<Amelie is missing! Come home NOW!>

He knew that sounded a little dramatic and it was definitely tinged with his anger at Jem. But Luc knew that Laurent would find Jem's absence hard to forgive. He also knew, although he didn't know the details, that Jem was in trouble totally unrelated to the rude but sexy American girl he'd brought home.

In his own way, Luc felt he was covering for Jem. He scanned the field against the horizon, looking like a black shapeless mass beneath the perimeter's tree line.

This is hopeless.

"Amelie!" he shouted again. "Come home! You're not in trouble!"

His phone dinged, indicating an incoming text.

<im here>

Luc looked up and saw the wobble of headlights driving on the main road, heading for the drive at *Dormir*. He ran down the driveway with Kip barking at his heels.

Luc stopped in front of the car and waved for it to stop.

"Just pull over and park here," Luc said when Jem stopped the car and rolled down his window.

Jem got out of the car, his cellphone in his hand, looking shaken. Luc suddenly realized that he didn't envy Jem. Regardless of what had happened in the hotel room in Aix Jem had not been here when the family needed him.

And nothing, not a smart-mouthed girl with a great figure nor anything else mattered more than that.

"Does Dad have any idea where she might have gone?" Jem asked.

"I don't know," Luc said. "But she was talking at dinner about wanting to pick the apples in the southeast orchard."

Jem nodded grimly. "Let's go."

The two hurried through the brambles. A gust of wind

swept the fallen leaves which swirled before them. For a moment the fog that had begun cleared enough to allow them to see the tree line looming to the east.

Luc could hear traffic from the main road and he stiffened. It wasn't that busy of a road. But a child in the dark could still be run over.

Twice, he slipped on the slick leaves underfoot and tripped on the fallen branches and roots hidden beneath.

"Would she have gone this far?" Jem asked as they both stopped to get their bearings. "It's a long way from the main house.

"You know how she is."

Jem had only known Amelie a very little bit—he'd been overseas for most of the time she'd been living at Domaine St-Buvard—and had only spent a short time with her over the Christmas holidays. But even he knew she was headstrong and stubborn. And determined.

They scoured the orchard from where they stood. At this distance from the main house, they could hear people at *Dormir* as they searched the garden and grounds. Luc realized that Laurent had called for help.

That right there shows how afraid he must be.

Some of the people were banging on pots and pans. They were all shouting Amelie's name.

"There's no way she can't hear us," Jem said. "Let's try some place else."

"I think she does hear us," Luc said.

Jem turned to him and frowned. "She hears us and doesn't answer? What sense does that make?"

"Plenty if she thinks she'll be punished when she's found."

"Dad has never raised a hand to her."

"He can be pretty gruff."

Jem had to admit that was definitely true.

"But surely she knows him well enough by now to know he'd never hurt her."

"How well do we know *her*, really? Do we have any idea of what her life was like before?"

Jem looked around the orchard.

"So you think she could be here but deliberately not answering?"

"I'd bet my life on it," Luc said.

Jem turned to look at his foster brother—who was actually his uncle. Sometimes he forgot Luc's own shaky start in life. He got so used to him being the big brother on hand for all the major milestones—for dealing with Laurent—for forging a life in the US and steering the sometimes choppy waters of being an expat—always a stranger in a strange land like himself—that he forgot that Luc's beginning was not unlike Amelie's.

Except it had gone on a lot longer before he'd finally found his people.

"I've got an idea." Luc said. He knelt by the dog at his side and raised his voice.

"Kip, you are a bad dog for not finding, Amelie!"

The dog twisted his head to look at him in confusion. He whined.

"Yeah, Kip," Jem said, realizing what Luc was doing. "We're going to throw you in the well for being such a bad dog!"

"No, you don't!" a little voice chirped up twenty yards away. "You leave him alone!"

Luc let go of Kip's collar and followed him as the animal raced into the thicket. When they arrived right behind him, they peeled back the branches in the ground thicket to find Amelie, her face stained with tears and her foot caught in the roots, her shoe missing and her arms wrapped around Kip's neck.

"Don't you hurt him! I'll tell *Opa*! He'll throw *you* in the well!" Amelie said, between gulping tears.

"Sorry, sweetie," Jem said as he reached in to pull her out of her hidden den of brambles and wildflowers. "We're not going to hurt Kip. He's a hero for finding you." He gathered her into his arms as Luc gently inspected her foot.

"Ankle's swollen," he said.

"Wasn't my fault," Amelie said softly.

Jem kissed her face.

"Better not let *Opa* hear you say that," he said. "He's got a thing about taking responsibility for your actions. Might as well learn it now." He turned to Luc. "Speaking of which, I'm sorry, man."

Luc shook his head. "Yeah, me too. I don't know what came over me."

Jem laughed. "Probably the same thing that came over me."

"I'm sorry," Amelie said, sniffling. "I knew I shouldn't have left."

"You know Dad's not going to spank you, right?" Jem said.

She nodded as they made their way slowly down the trail toward the house.

"But he'll yell," she said.

"Oh, yeah," Luc said. "He's definitely going to yell. And you will find out, little sis, that that is not the end of the world."

"I wish you hadn't said that," Jem said.

"What are you talking about?" Luc frowned.

"Nothing. Just that it reminds me that I've got to have a talk with him about something. And there's going to be a whole lot of yelling."

Luc snorted and then started laughing.

"What's so funny?"

Luc shook his head. "Nothing. It's just, you know…you and me both." He patted Amelie's back again. "And you haven't heard yelling, little sis, until then."

56

Maggie vaguely remembered Karen saying she was staying at the *Sunflower*, an expensive and popular lodging for those tourists who were fluent in French—a group Maggie knew did not include the Dixons. She jogged down the uneven sidewalk, catching her foot once and nearly falling before reminding herself that breaking a kneecap wouldn't help Annabelle or Grace.

Frantic that Karen had already left Grasse, Maggie nearly groaned in relief as she entered the *Sunflower* lobby and saw Karen at the front desk loudly haranguing the concierge.

"Well, we want to leave *tomorrow* instead of today," Karen was saying. "Don't tell me you gave our room away because I'm not buying it."

"Karen?" Maggie said breathlessly as she ran up to her.

Karen turned and made a face when she saw her.

"Can I help?" Maggie asked.

Karen jerked a thumb at the concierge.

"I know he speaks English as good as I do," she said, her face screwed into a visage of petulance.

"Please, allow me to interpret," Maggie said, turning to the concierge with a smile. The man's face was a mask of granite. And dislike.

Some people just didn't have enough sense to know what business they should be in, Maggie thought.

"Monsieur and Madame Dixon were checking out today," he said flatly.

"I know what he's saying," Karen said loudly. "I can see it in his ugly face. And I ain't buying it."

Maggie turned to Karen.

"You told him you would check out today but now you want to stay longer?"

"One measly night! That's all! You tell him I'll have my embassy down his neck! I know he hasn't rented our room yet."

Maggie turned back to the concierge.

"Would fifty euros help you find your new guests a different room tonight?" Maggie said to him in flawless French.

The concierge hesitated and glanced at Karen and then her Gucci bag.

"One hundred euros," Maggie said. "Add it to the final bill and list it as gratuity. Take it out in cash before they check out."

He then turned to Karen and smiled the coldest, ugliest smile Maggie had ever seen.

"*Bon*," he said almost pleasantly.

Maggie and Karen walked away from the desk.

"Thanks, I guess," Karen said. "Although I was handling it. And now I'm late for meeting Sheila at the Chez Monsieur café."

Maggie looked around the lobby. "Where's hubby?"

Karen shrugged.

"He's sore because now we only have time for him to get a little bit of fishing in when we go to Italy and he's bitching that this whole trip has been about me." She looked at Maggie and raised an eyebrow. "I know he looks like a pushover but trust me, he gets his way plenty."

"I just need to ask him something," Maggie said. "Is he in your room?"

"Seriously?" Karen stopped walking and grinned at Maggie. "He *said* you were into him but I told him he was nuts! You got good taste! I'll give you that!"

Maggie stopped walking and felt a chill ripple through her.

"He said that?" she asked slowly.

Suddenly, the thought of interviewing DJ to find out what he knew about the other men in the tour seemed much less the point than it had been just seconds before. All at once, she got an image of DJ in the crowd as Vivienne gave her docent spiel. Only now when Maggie remembered his face, instead of seeing what she had assumed was embarrassment over Karen's public impropriety—now she saw something different.

Something predatory.

"Karen, when you watched the parade two nights ago, you said Sheila and her husband Bernie joined you?"

"Yeah, so?"

"Was DJ there too?"

"Oh my God. Now *he's* on your doo-doo list? For your information, missy, he was napping back in the hotel room. He had a dodgy tummy. But I'll be sure and let him know you think he's a murder suspect. You really are the living end, lady."

"Where is he now?"

"He went out to check out the woods around here to do a little hunting."

Maggie felt a sudden wave of sickening dizziness.

"Are you saying he has a gun?" she asked.

"Pretty hard to go hunting without one." Karen snorted laughter and turned to see if anyone else had heard her joke.

"He got a gun through customs?" Maggie asked in disbelief.

"Yeah, well, he had to show he had a reservation to shoot red deer in Austria so of course he had to check it."

Maggie's skin tingled ominously.

He's armed.

"I'm pretty sure it's not hunting season now," Maggie said.

"Yeah, that's what our stick-up-the-butt desk clerk told him too. DJ said he just wanted to check out the area."

"Did he tell you which area exactly he wanted to check out?"

"Why are you getting so freaked out? I have no idea—oh, wait, he mentioned he didn't want to stop for gas because of the price gouging the French do and he only had a half tank."

So, a quarter tank from here, and it can't be south because there's the Mediterranean. And due east is Nice. That leaves north or west.

Maggie felt a thread of panic needle into her. That was not a very significant narrowing down.

"When was the last time you saw him?" she asked.

"At lunch."

That means he's had Annabelle for at least six hours.

Karen saw Sheila at the street corner and waved to her.

"What is he driving?" Maggie asked, raising her voice.

"Our rental car. Look, why all the questions?" Karen asked, narrowing her eyes.

"What kind of car?" Maggie asked impatiently. "Do you have its documents?"

"It's a blue Renault. Now if you don't mind, I've got a date with a friend. A real friend. I thought you were nice but maybe that was only Grace who was nice. I think DJ was right when he said you were stuck up."

Karen turned to walk away, and Maggie hurried down the street, opening up a browser on her phone to see if there was any mention of any area around Grasse possibly being good for hunting. She couldn't find anything. She ran back to Karen and DJ's hotel and found the concierge who she knew she had built up a cache of credit with.

"If someone was looking for a place to hunt in the area," she asked, "where would you suggest?"

He frowned and looked at her outfit which was clearly not appropriate for hunting.

"I have already told Monsieur Dixon where the most likely place to go would be. Although I also told him it is not hunting season."

Maggie felt her insides seize.

DJ isn't really interested in hunting.

"Where did you tell him to go?" she asked.

The man gave Maggie a guarded look and then pulled a small, laminated map out on the counter and took a pen from his breast pocket.

"There is an area northwest, off the D2085. You will need to take the D4, the access road," he said. Maggie glanced at the area on the map. It appeared to be a huge section with no houses or neighborhoods. She thanked him and took the map before hurrying to where she'd parked her car. She quickly plugged the coordinates that the concierge had given her into her GPS. Then she tried to call Landry again.

As she maneuvered out of the parking lot, her call connected and was answered by the Grasse Police Department dispatcher.

"Bonjour," she said breathlessly to him. "My name is Maggie Dernier and I have information I need to get to Commandant Landry. Please tell him that—"

Before she could complete her statement, the line disconnected.

57

Amelie was in her room upstairs fast asleep by the time Danielle and Laurent had finished feeding the twenty searchers from the monastery. Danielle had long since gone to bed, happy, and relieved but emotionally and physically drained.

When Laurent had spotted Luc and Jem coming down the driveway with little Amelie in their arms, he tried to remember ever seeing a more joyous sight. Luc had texted him that they'd found her, but the bliss of seeing it had brought tears to his eyes.

In spite of her trepidation over the kind of serious trouble she was in, Amelie had immediately reached for her *Opa* and Laurent held her tightly, murmuring words of comfort and reassurance to her as he brought her into the warmth of the *Dormir* kitchen.

He knew he should scold her, and he promised himself he'd have an unpleasant chore or two waiting for her tomorrow. But tonight he just needed her to feel his relief and gratitude.

The kitchen sink was stacked with dirty bowls, utensils and plates from the left-over *coq au vin* and sandwiches that they'd fed the searchers. He'd opened a couple of bottles of wine in celebration before the people from the monastery had left. Laurent wiped up the breadcrumbs from the *baguettes* and brought the dirty glasses to the sink from the kitchen table. He filled the sink with hot soapy water and allowed the peace of the moment and of the aftermath of the night to fill him.

"Need a hand?" Luc said as he came into the kitchen and picked up a hand towel.

For several moments they just washed and dried in companionable silence. Laurent knew Luc would talk when he was ready.

"I met this girl in Napa," he said finally. "I've been seeing her awhile."

"Oh?"

"I'm not sure why but I needed to step away for a bit and get my feelings sorted out."

Laurent said nothing.

"I met her when I was doing the marketing for Beaumont Wine tours earlier this year. I guess we've been seeing each other on and off for the past year. I knew she was special, and I've been thinking lately, I don't know, that I might want to marry her."

Laurent glanced at him as he continued to rinse the dish in his hands.

"Then what was all that with Jem's girl?" he asked.

"First of all, she's not his girl. And secondly, I told you, I was working some things out."

"Are you sure now?"

"I think so."

"Is that good enough do you think?"

"It might be as good as I can do. I just got off the phone with her and invited her to come over this summer to meet everyone. And to help with the harvest. She's a viticulturist."

Laurent's eyes widened. A viticulturist was someone skilled

in applying the growing processes of grapevines in order to create the kind of quality desired in wine production.

"Yeah, I thought that would get your attention," Luc said wryly.

"*Oui*, for me, it is a plus," Laurent said. "But I'm not sure that matters as I will not be the one married to her. Is that Jem lurking in the hallway?"

"Yeah, he's got something to tell you too. We drew straws and I got to go first."

Laurent dried his hands and pulled Luc into a hearty embrace.

"I look forward to meeting your girl, my son," he said. "Maggie will be ecstatic."

"Thanks, Dad," Luc said, grinning widely.

Jem stepped into the kitchen. "Oh, great," he said dejectedly.

"I take it you don't have an engagement to announce?" Laurent said, releasing Luc and clapping him on the shoulder.

"Not even close," Jem said morosely.

"I'll leave you to it," Luc said, smiling sadly at Jem as he made his way out of the kitchen.

Laurent turned to look at Jem and felt a wave of wistfulness as he thought of how much the boy always wanted to please him—or at least to not displease him. Like most fathers, Laurent's main wish for Jem was for him to be safe and to be happy.

He had a feeling he was not going to be granted either tonight.

"All right, *mon vieux*," he said. "Let's hear it."

58

Annabelle's world was reduced to a nauseating milieu of darkness and pain.

The agony in her arm rocketed up into her brain—already swamped with terror—making coherent thought impossible.

When the man had grabbed her, she had felt her arm break in his hands. She was so shocked at the time, she only remembered crying out—she couldn't help it! After that there was nothing to remember except the moment she woke up in the carpeted trunk of a moving car.

Every bump in the road sent a shock of agony shivering through her. She willed herself to black out again, anything to suppress the pain in her arm—along with the certain knowledge of what was going to happen to her next.

She moaned loudly. She knew he couldn't hear her. He had the radio on, the volume up loud. She wept and screamed through her gag which tasted of gasoline. Wherever they were, there was nobody to hear her.

Her stomach lurched as she felt him turn off the main road.

She braced herself for the pain of riding over broken ground. She knew the secondary roads in the country were unpaved.

The first jolt sent a tsunami of agony curdling her guts. Desperately, she tried to turn over so that she was laying on her other arm and the harsh movement of the car wouldn't jostle her so much. The pain was unrelenting, but she stayed conscious. Her head ached and she suddenly remembered he'd hit her on the head.

She began to pray. She had no Rosary, but she didn't need one. Squeezing her eyes shut tight she begged God to give her the rest and peace that the repetition of the Rosary usually gave her. She needed it now if she ever had.

She murmured the words to the *Apostles' Creed*, trying to focus on each word instead of the constant, relentless pain that each jolt in the road sent through her body. She touched a bolt on the spare tire next to her and pretended it was a bead and said the *Our Father*, gasping behind her gag on every word.

By the time she'd spoken the three Hail Mary's, she thought the pain was less. Not much, but enough. It was no longer the all-consuming fire in which each bump in the road had engulfed her just seconds before.

Glory be to the Father, and to the Son, and to the Holy Spirit. As it was in the beginning, is now, and ever shall be, world without end.

She felt the car begin to slow and her eyes filled with tears as she felt the car make a sharp turn, jerking her forward onto her hands.

Her arm erupted again in nauseating pain at the motion and she tried desperately to catch her breath. Huffing against the pain, she whispered the words, "*Joyful mysteries.*"

And fainted.

59

Landry bit his lip as a line of sweat dribbled down his forehead. He gripped his cellphone so tightly he was sure it would snap in his hand. He looked at the clock on the wall as his supervisor, Commissaire Milo Deschamps railed at him on the phone.

"*Two* unexplained deaths in two days?" the man shouted. "How is it I am just hearing of this from a reporter calling my office?"

"I...I am not sure where your source—" Landry began.

"Your medical examiner called a reporter in Nice!" the man shouted. "A reporter who then wrote a story and called my office to confirm details. *Two* deaths? What's going on over there? Are you on top of it or not?"

"Yes, sir, the paperwork got clogged on the first death—"

"Is it or is it not a suspicious death?"

"Well, yes, we believe—"

"My assistant said he saw that the case was closed! Twelve hours after the body was discovered? Without an arrest?"

"Incorrect, sir," Landry said, now starting to sweat even more heavily. "We have made an arrest and—"

"You have a suspect in custody?"

Landry nearly groaned. He couldn't lie. It was too easy to check. Deschamps probably had the information in front of him on his computer right now as they were speaking.

"Well, no, not for the murder, sir, but in connection with it. And again, in my defense, the paperwork got mislaid—"

"How can paperwork get mislaid when everything is online?" Deschamps shouted. "Are you a total idiot, Landry?"

"Yes sir. No, sir!"

"I don't know what's going on over there, but I want copies of both autopsies sent to me before I hang up this phone. Do you hear me?"

"Yes, sir. At once, sir."

"And I want you in Nice tomorrow morning in my office to give me a full report *in person* on why I am hearing about this debacle from a damn reporter!"

"It's Anouilh, sir," Landry said. "He's a loose cannon and he—"

"Enough! The autopsies immediately and you in my office at eight o'clock tomorrow!"

The phone call ended abruptly. Landry sat without moving, still holding the phone to his head as if frozen. The air seemed to have been sucked out of his office.

He tried to put together a coherent thought about what had just happened and how he might fix it. Deschamps hadn't been open to hearing any excuses—or explanations.

He finally put his phone down and stared at his trembling fingers.

Who was he kidding? The truth was there for anyone to see. He'd been too arrogant, too sure that his people would cover for him.

His people. He thought of Anouilh and felt a surge of loathing well up in his chest.

The job was one thing—but if his men were interviewed by Internal Affairs, he'd end up in jail for gross misconduct if not corruption.

He ran a hand over his face.

That damn Anouilh!

How could he not have seen this coming? The man owed him no loyalty. He was new, barely respectful. He never went with the rest of them when they went out for drinks at the end of a shift. Landry hadn't taken the time to groom him and now, unless he solved these two murders before tomorrow morning —impossible!—*and* threw one of his loyal subordinates under the bus for the purported paperwork snafu—he would be out of a job—or worse, in jail.

He felt his muscles quiver with the fury that was building up inside him. He stood up and shook out his hands to dissipate the feeling and then sat back down, turning to his computer where he called up one of his tracking apps. Within seconds, the phone was ringing again.

"Commandant?" his sergeant said on the line. "The American Consulate is on the line. Do you want to speak to them?"

His heart began to race and he felt a tightness in his chest at his sergeant's words.

"No," he said. "Say I will call them back." He hung up and put a call in to Maggie Dernier. He had to have *something* to tell Deschamps tomorrow. Anything she'd found out would at least look like he'd been actively working the case.

The call went straight to voice mail.

Where was she? Had she made a fool of him too?

He felt a prickling on the back of his neck as he tried to focus on his next step. He ran a hand over his face. He called his assistant back.

"Get the American woman—Grace Van Sant—prepared for transport," he said.

"Yes, Commandant. To where?"

Landry licked his lips as if to stop himself from saying what he knew he was going to say. But he couldn't have this woman threaten everything he'd built in Grasse. He needed her to disappear. Sooner rather than later.

And if her friend wasn't going to help him, all deals were off.

"To Clairvaux," he said.

Clairvaux Prison was far enough away in north central France.

"She can await trial there. And Thierry?"

"Yes, Commandant?"

"If the US Consultant calls back, you are not to tell them where she is."

"Understood, Commandant."

As Landry hung up, he realized that it was his assistant he'd have to betray. He was young, he'd find other jobs. He could think of it as his last service to his superior. Landry rubbed a shaking hand over his face when he realized that he needed to have a conversation with his men to try to get in front of what was happening. As he gathered up his keys and cellphone, he flashed back to the memory of the last time they'd all gone out for drinks.

Had they been as deferential as before? Or hadn't there been a few instances of disrespect?

He felt an uncomfortable heat flush through him.

If I tell them to lie to Internal Affairs, might they just as easily grass me out instead?

Landry wiped the sweat from his forehead again. If he couldn't trust those *bâtards* to lie for him, he was finished. It was one thing to obey orders without questioning him, but could they be trusted to lie to Internal Affairs?

His stomach churned and a new sheen of sweat developed on his top lip as he realized the painful truth.

Was there another way to handle this? He glanced again at his computer screen. And groaned.

But, at this point, what did he have to lose?

60

Maggie sped out of town on the D2085, the hills surrounding Grasse seemed to spill down all around her in a crazy stair-step fashion of greens and browns against a gun metal gray sky that promised more rain. Forcing herself to be mindful that getting pulled over for speeding would *not* be helpful, she slowed down and began to visualize the pieces of the whole terrible picture of what had happened to Annabelle—and Vivienne—slowly fall into place.

How could I not have seen it? All the other husbands skipped the tours and hung out at the cafés and bars. Only DJ went on all the tours with Karen.

Maggie chided herself for thinking DJ was just an exceptionally dutiful husband.

Instead of the predatory monster he really was.

She hadn't gone thirty kilometers when she saw two men standing in front of the gas pumps of a rural gas station. They were talking intensely to each other and something about them made Maggie pull into the gas station. When she did, they looked at her curiously but did not approach.

Maggie walked over to them.

"Did either of you happen to see a blue Renault go by today?" she asked, knowing it was hardly likely.

To her amazement, they looked at her with shock. At first, she thought it was because they hadn't expected her French to be so good—she was obviously not French. But when they started talking, it became clear that it was because a blue Renault had indeed driven by recently and made quite an impression.

Both men erupted in a volley of indignant debate as they described the rude American who pulled in to get a bottle of water and who spoke no French but who expected the two of them to be fluent in his language.

Between the invective and the colorful exchanges, Maggie pieced together that DJ had come by nearly an hour earlier. He was traveling alone as far as they could see, meaning that Annabelle, at best, was in the trunk—if not stashed somewhere in the countryside.

The two men indicated that the rude American had driven west, prompting Maggie to believe that DJ was following the concierge's directions. She dug out her phone and opened up a map and showed it to the men, asking if there was anything in this area—a cabin or blind nearby.

They both insisted there was no public access to any cabin or hunting blind, and she emphasized to them that a private cabin would be ideal for the man's purposes. They looked horrified at the thought that the rude man might be heading toward someone's private property—and it wasn't even hunting season! They pointed out two separate places on her map marked as hunting lodges. DJ would have no problem finding them.

"And the caves," one of the men said. "The Germans built a warren of tunnels and caves during the war."

Maggie frowned. "Does anyone know about these caves?"

He shrugged. "Not really. But they are everywhere."

"No," his friend said, shaking his head. "The caves are marked now on most maps. Something about war remembrance."

"That makes no sense," the other man said.

"Well, maybe it's to prevent someone from accidentally falling into one."

His friend snorted in derision. "How does one fall into a cave?"

Maggie was about to rip her hair out.

"But whichever hunting estate you go to, you will have to walk from the car park," the other man said.

"How far from the parking lot?" she asked, knowing they would think she was concerned about the amount of hiking necessary but in reality, she was thinking of DJ having to carry or prod along a possibly injured hostage. For his purpose, the shorter the walk the better.

They both shrugged and looked at each other as if about to launch into long—and differing—opinions about the length of any walk from any parking lot in the woods.

Finally, after thanking them, Maggie got back in her car. It had been worth the stop, she decided. At least she now had a better timeline of events. As she accelerated past the posted speed limit, her phone lit up and she saw that it was Danielle calling her. She hit *Decline*. If there was a problem with Amelie, Laurent was there to handle it. Maggie couldn't explain what she was doing, and Danielle couldn't help her.

Squinting at the map on her phone, she saw the first turn off to one of the hunting blinds was coming up. She turned down the dirt road, her car bumping violently over the holes in the unpaved roadway. As she turned a final corner, she saw the parking lot ahead, fringed with trees.

A vacant parking lot.

Maggie's stomach clenched in disappointment. She turned the car around as quickly as she could, spraying dirt and gravel in an arc behind her as she raced back to the main road. It was another twenty kilometers before she saw the next turn off. She double-checked her map to make sure it was really a navigable possibility before turning off the main road.

It was even worse than the last but that encouraged her. DJ wouldn't opt for a popular or well-used park. The good news about that, was that it was not hunting season meant thereby lessening the chances of other people being nearby.

Of course, from Annabelle's point of view, that was also the bad news.

Maggie bumped the car down the rugged, unpaved road, her anxiety ratcheting up as she realized how much time she was wasting—especially if she had to turn around and bump her slow way back to the main road. She felt a thin line of sweat dribble down from her forehead.

A hand-painted wooden sign, broken and hanging by one hinge, indicated the parking area was ahead.

Maggie was so antsy about the time she was wasting that she was already prepared to do a quick turnaround in the area when she spotted the lone blue Renault in the dirt lot.

61

The house was finally quiet, all three children asleep in their beds—or at least if the boys weren't asleep, they were in their rooms watching their various screens.

It was well after midnight but after all the drama of the evening, Laurent was finding it impossible to go to sleep. It was just as well. He went to the kitchen to pour himself a glass of marc.

His conversation with Luc had been a surprise but generally a reassuring one and if he truly *was* about to bring a wife home, then a happy one. Jem, on the other hand...

When the phone rang Laurent was glad for the opportunity to stop his train of thought. He picked up.

"*Allo?*"

"Hey, Laurent," Windsor said. "It's me. How's everything?"

"Windsor? It's good."

This was unusual, Windsor calling him.

"Look, I'm calling because I can't get in touch with Grace and I was wondering if you'd heard from her recently?"

Laurent glanced at his watch. It was a little after one in the morning, so it would be around seven o'clock in the evening in Atlanta.

Windsor couldn't get ahold of Grace? Could she and Maggie really be having so much fun that Grace wasn't answering her phone?

"I am sure they are both fine, Windsor," Laurent said, but he felt a stab of uneasiness in his gut.

It was true he had spoken to Maggie a few hours earlier but even then he'd registered that something was not all that it seemed—or how Maggie would have him believe. She had gone out of her way to sound normal and composed, which of course only confirmed to him that she wasn't either. He knew he'd get the full story when she came home but now if Grace wasn't reachable? What did that mean?

"Philippe was hoping to talk to Grace," Windsor said. "And also Amelie, although I told him she might be in bed. It's after nine o'clock there, right?"

Laurent snorted. Windsor had never been able to get the time difference right between France and Georgia.

"Yes, Amelie is asleep," Laurent said. "And how are you? Your trip is going as hoped? How is your daughter?"

Not for the life of him could Laurent remember the child's name. Maggie told him it was the name of a midwestern city but that was no help for him in remembering it.

"She's good," Windsor said. "But it's hard connecting with her. She's mad at me. I've been gone so long, so she treats me like a stranger. And she and Philippe don't get along. She makes fun of his accent. Did Grace tell you we're staying with Susie?"

"Ah, *oui*?"

That was a surprise, but none of Laurent's business.

"So you haven't heard from the girls at all?" Windsor said. "I mean it's really unusual for Grace not to be answering her phone, you know? And she's been texting me pretty steadily until today."

There it was again. That bud of doubt that had been pulsing on and off ever since Laurent talked with Maggie. Should he be worried?

For all the things Maggie *hadn't* said when they'd spoken, Laurent had a hundred experiences in their shared past where those things had been revealed to be deadly treacherous. It was completely like her not to tell him something for fear he'd barge in and upset the delicate balance of whatever scheme she was in the middle of concocting.

Laurent glanced at the kitchen clock. He couldn't leave Danielle and Amelie in the middle of the night but if he left in the morning it might be too late. It occurred to him that he could reach out to Bedard who was nearer to Grasse.

On the other hand, if he left right now he could—

"Laurent?"

He turned to see Danielle enter the kitchen in a floor length floral robe.

"It's Windsor," he said. "He can't reach Grace."

"Tell her hi from us," Windsor said on the phone. "Has Grace called her?"

Danielle went to the kitchen sink and pulled down a mug from the cabinet that she filled with water and a tea bag before setting it in the microwave.

"I haven't heard from her," Danielle said. "But I'm sure she's fine. She just needs some time to herself."

"She's been texting me regularly all weekend," Windsor said. "And now, all of a sudden she's radio dark? I think something's wrong."

"I'm asking you not to leave tonight, Laurent," Danielle said abruptly.

Laurent looked at her in surprise.

"Amelie needs you more than Maggie or Grace do," Danielle said firmly.

Laurent glanced upward in the direction of Amelie's bedroom. As he imagined Amelie asleep safe and sound in her bed he felt a sudden certainty that of course Danielle was right. He knew that. Whatever Maggie was up to—and there was no doubt that *something* was going on—it was just possible that now was the time for him to trust that she knew what she was doing.

He took in a long breath as if to settle it within himself.

"Do not worry, Windsor," he said into the phone. "I talked with Maggie earlier and she and Grace are both fine. There is nothing to worry about. Okay?"

"Are you sure?"

Laurent glanced at Danielle who looked as tenaciously determined as he'd ever seen her.

"I am sure," he said, feeling not at all sure.

But he was determined in any case that whatever Maggie was up to, he would finally allow her to handle it on her own.

62

Maggie stopped inside the parking lot, her heart pounding at what she was seeing. She shut off the engine and allowed the eerie silence of the impinging woods engulf her.

She felt a breathlessness descend upon her as she pulled out her phone and saw that the battery was flickering. It was just as well. Who would she call? Especially since Landry wasn't taking her calls.

Quietly, she leaned over and opened the glove box and pulled out her Taser. It was illegal to own in France and she'd been careful not to brandish it about since she'd gotten it. But it had come in handy too many times for her to consider giving it up.

She set her phone to the record function and stepped out of her car, careful not to slam the door in the overwhelming country silence. Walking softly to the blue Renault, Maggie was well aware she was bringing a shock wand to a gun fight.

Praying that Annabelle was in the car and alive, Maggie crept up to the car and peered inside. The front seat was empty with nothing to indicate that DJ had been traveling with a hostage. There were no food wrappers, plastic ties, duct tape or water bottles.

Maggie glanced at the rear of the car and her stomach tightened. It was too quiet. If Annabelle was in there, she was likely not alive. Maggie swallowed hard and then jogged back to her car where she went into the glove box, looking for any kind of tool and found a set of screwdrivers. She grabbed a flathead screwdriver and hurried back to DJ's rental car.

Praying as she inserted the screwdriver into the trunk lock that she would not find Annabelle, Maggie jammed the tool into the lock and moved it firmly from side to side until it finally sprung the lock. She stepped back, her heart in her throat and her hands shaking as she slowly opened the trunk.

It was empty.

She let out the breath she had been holding without realizing it, then dug out her phone and put on the flashlight function. She raked the trunk with its beam looking for anything that might indicate someone had been held here.

And then she saw it.

Stuck on the tire jack was a handful of red hair strands. Maggie felt a flutter of horror deep in her gut. She turned and looked around. There was a path leading from the parking lot into the woods. Would DJ have taken the obvious path? She turned to look in the direction of the woods. They were dark and dense. The new spring growth made them look impenetrable.

She shivered at the thought of plunging into the interior without a path to follow and felt her desperation edging up into her throat. Overhead, the light was steadily leaching from the sky. Clouds had gathered and now loomed, bunched and ominous. She wasn't much of a tracker when conditions were optimal. She'd never find them in an evening rain.

Ticking off all the reasons why she wasn't going to find them triggered a shot of adrenaline through her system.

Maggie forced herself to breathe deeply for a few moments to calm herself and find the courage she needed for whatever came next.

First, she pointed the beam of her cell phone flashlight on the ground by the car trunk and saw scrape marks—dramatic evidence of something being dragged through the leaves and the dirt.

Her stomach lurched in nausea as she envisioned Annabelle being pulled into the woods. She turned and followed the marks of the shuffled steps—not in the direction of any known path.

So be it, she thought determinedly. *The hard way it is.*

She wondered why she ever thought it would be any other way.

She shined her light on the trail and followed it, being as mindful as she could of her surroundings and the noise she was making.

She needed to take DJ by surprise. He had a gun.

She needed every advantage she could get.

The smell of something organic and foul, flooded Annabelle's nostrils.

She opened her eyes and strained to see in the dim light. Slowly, she realized she was entombed, surrounded by uneven stone walls, some of them pierced by tree roots. She had an impulsive urge to scream but she bit her lip to suppress it. Making herself small was the answer. Not calling attention to herself.

Something skittered overhead and a cloying and fetid odor cascaded over her in sickening waves.

A cave.

She shifted and felt cold hardness beneath her. She was

leaning against a large rock. Horrible things slithered in caves. Terrible biting things.

The pain in her arm was gone. She thanked God for the reprieve, grateful for what she knew must be shock. She blinked hard several times to clear her vision and focus on the man standing at the mouth of the cave, backlit by the fading light.

A rifle in his hands.

She didn't remember getting here. She didn't remember walking. She remembered the trunk and then nothing. The gag had loosened, and she twisted her head to get it from her face. But it wouldn't fall.

The American turned to her.

"Finally awake, are ya?" he said, walking over to her. He stood staring down at her, a baseball cap jammed on his head, his legs planted in a wide, aggressive stance.

She stared at him in terror. There was no other reason for her to be here but that he was going to kill her. Tears filled her eyes.

"Cry, and I won't take the gag off," he said. But he leaned over and tugged it down anyway.

Annabelle sucked in a gulp of air, desperate for it, especially in the cave, but the movement ignited the pain in her arm. She moaned against it.

"You know this is all your own fault, right?" he said.

"Please," she said, her mouth so dry she could barely speak. "Please...water?"

He laughed.

"Wouldn't be much point, now would it? Man, what a load of trouble you got me into."

He held up his phone.

"No service out here so I can't even tell the Old Lady I'll be later for dinner. That's on you, too."

"Please, water," Annabelle said. "I am so thirsty."

"Why did you have to ask me all those questions?" he said with a frown. "Do I look like a depraved murderer to you?"

She shook her head. "I am sorry."

"Damn straight," he said. "You oughta be."

He set the rifle against the wall six feet from her. Annabelle's eyes followed his movements. She knew how to use a rifle. Her father had taught her during boar hunting season.

But her hands were tied in front of her and one arm was broken.

She wasn't going to be able to use a rifle. That rifle was going to be used on her.

"Why is every woman over here so uptight? I haven't met a single one who's at all as advertised. You know what I mean? You know you Frenchies have a reputation for being sex kittens, right? That's BS is what that is."

Annabelle licked her lips. She closed her eyes and began to pray, her lips moving silently.

"Hey, hey!" he said. "Stop that! That's creeping me out!"

He knelt and grabbed her by the front of her blouse. The pain in her arm exploded throughout every part of her body and she cried out.

"You're making me hurt you!" he shouted. "Your sister did the same thing and look what happened to her!"

Annabelle felt her surroundings beginning to spin and her nausea clawed up her throat. In spite of the pain it caused her, she tried to inch away from him. He leaned in closer.

"We're going to have some fun, you and me," he said in a harsh whisper. "You feel me?"

He laughed, his breath blasting a mixture of onions and garlic into her face, as she closed her eyes to shut out the horror, the inevitability, of what was coming.

63

The forest that Maggie stepped into was so dense with only one or two rough footpaths of mostly mud and pine needles that were barely discernable as trails at all. The smell of pine and rotted wood filled her nostrils as she walked, pushing branches and bushes out of her face as she did. The canopy of trees overhead had eliminated most of the light and she finally had to use the flashlight function on her cellphone to see even three feet ahead.

Could DJ really have carried Annabelle this far? Maggie had quickly lost the track of the few footprints she'd found and was now depending strictly on broken bush branches along the path to tell her that people had recently come this way. She was mindful of walking as quickly as she could and yet still as quietly as possible. But branches snapped back on her unexpectedly, twigs crunched loudly underfoot in the silent forest.

She touched the Taser tucked in her back waist band for comfort and thought of Landry—who *should* be doing this—and who she would do everything in her power to get fired once this was all over. If she lived to do it.

Would she find Annabelle? Would it be too late? His car

was in the lot so DJ must be here too somewhere. Unless he abandoned the car? But no, that didn't make sense. He needed to go back to Grasse to accompany Karen out of town as if nothing had happened.

Suddenly it seemed as if the compressed woodland path had evolved into a more defined trail. Granted, not much of one. But here the long grasses were somewhat tamped down. Her stomach gurgled in anxiety.

He brought her this way.

She was on the right track. She wiped her palms against her cotton slacks and felt the fear and anxiety build in her chest as she inched forward, afraid to walk too quickly. Afraid her urgency to find Annabelle in time would doom them both.

It would be dark in another thirty minutes and Maggie cursed the fact that time was not on her side.

Suddenly she saw a small clearing just beyond the last shards of branches and leaves. She stopped and looked around but there was no structure, no cabin, no hunting blind, nothing man built that she could see.

But ahead of her was definitely a clearing. As she studied the perimeter of the space, she finally saw it.

The opening of a cave.

Maggie pushed past the final fronds of tree branches and stepped into the clearing, feeling suddenly vulnerable and exposed. There was no dead campfire to indicate anyone had used this cave in the seventy years since it had been created. Past the cave mouth, she saw the hazy green line of a distant tree ridge against the sky's fading light.

Mindful of where she put her feet to avoid snapping any twigs, Maggie crept up to the cave entrance and stood beside it, her back against the stone wall, her knees shaking, and the light fading from the sky.

"Trust me, you're gonna understand me real good before we're done."

The voice was taunting, cruel. And American.

Maggie's heart was pounding out of her chest. Was he talking to Annabelle? Himself? Did he have an accomplice? Maggie hadn't even considered that possibility.

"It's not my fault," DJ said loudly. "You can see that, can't you? I mean, give me a break. You can ask anyone who knows me. I'm a great guy. I frigging love women. I mean, give me a break. You see who I'm married to? If that's not love, I don't know the meaning of the word, you know?"

Maggie pulled out her Taser and took in a steadying breath and let it out slowly. She couldn't hear anything from Annabelle, but neither did she hear another man's voice, which was reassuring.

Who is DJ talking to?

A terrible image developed in Maggie's head of DJ talking to Annabelle's corpse and she angrily shook the vision out of her head.

"Now don't be like that," DJ continued. "I did my best by you. I patched you up as well as I could, didn't I? Why do women always cry? I mean, it's not my fault we're where we are. If anybody has a reason to cry, it's me. Why'd you have to ask me all that stuff? It's not *my* fault you're where you are."

Maggie held her Taser in both hands, trying to gauge exactly where DJ's voice was coming from inside the cave. In her mind, she saw herself enter the cave, locate DJ—he would be taken by surprise so she would have a few seconds to line him up in her sights—and shoot fifty thousand volts into him.

Then what? She had a second charge in her back pocket. She could shoot him again after that, but depending on how badly hurt Annabelle was, she'd never make it back to the parking lot with her before DJ recovered.

She leaned in closer to the cave to listen to DJ's monologue, waiting for her moment, when a chip of rock by her shoulder crumbled and hit the ground loudly.

DJ stopped talking.

Cursing to herself about the loss of the element of surprise, Maggie ran into the cave entrance, her eyes desperately trying to pick DJ out in the murky light. Her foot hit a soft bundle on the floor and she stumbled. She fought to stay on her feet. But with nothing to hold onto except the gun in her hands, she fell, hitting the ground hard and landing on her forearms. The sudden impact of the fall sending her Taser flying out of her hands.

Desperately, Maggie clawed her way to a sitting position, her jaw clenched tightly. She'd bitten her lip and tasted the salt now as blood dribbled down her chin.

The darkness of the cave seeming to swallow her up, her eyes went everywhere at once, looking for her weapon, trying to see DJ, looking for the thing she'd tripped over.

Annabelle.

Maggie struggled to her feet and felt for the wall behind her to steady herself. Her eyes began to make out the forms around her until a picture developed.

DJ was standing over Annabelle on the ground.

And he was holding Maggie's Taser.

64

Maggie stared in horror as DJ tilted his head as if trying to place who she was.

"Karen sent me to find you," Maggie blurted out, hoping that the fact that she knew Karen might trigger something in DJ's mind that let him know that whatever he was contemplating, he was not going to be able to get away with it. Out of the corner of her eye, she saw the bolt-action rifle propped up against the cave wall.

Annabelle wasn't moving but Maggie thought she saw her blink, so she was at least alive. She lay against the cave wall, her hands tied in front of her.

"Oh, yeah," he said, pointing at Maggie. "I remember you. In the jail cell. And nice try, but there's no way Karen would send anyone after me. She knows better."

Suddenly, the shroud of her prior assumption fell away and Maggie saw what she should've seen before—that just because Karen was obnoxious and publicly said the wrong thing, didn't mean she wasn't being abused behind closed doors. From what Maggie had read, women who were mistreated usually did a masterful job of keeping their abuse hidden.

"Do you mind telling me what's going on?" Maggie asked, attempting to lend an air of normalcy to the situation just in case DJ could be convinced that things hadn't gone too far.

Although, from the looks of Annabelle, Maggie had to admit that things looked like they'd gone pretty far.

"You two friends or something?" DJ asked, nudging Annabelle with his boot.

Annabelle moaned. Maggie didn't know whether to be relieved or sorry that she was conscious for all this.

"Look, DJ," Maggie said reasonably. "Annabelle is hurt. I need to get her to a hospital."

He brayed with laughter.

"You got to be kidding," he said, shaking his head and grinning. "Would I have her trussed up in an effing *cave* if going to a hospital was an option? Think about it."

"Okay, so what's the plan? Kill her and then kill me? You don't think *four* murders won't get the authorities on your trail?"

"I'll be long gone from France by then."

"When it comes to capital crimes the European Union doesn't recognize borders," Maggie said evenly. "Interpol will share your face with every police department across two *hundred* countries. You might make it out of France, but you won't make it out of Europe."

"Says you," DJ said, hefting the Taser. "I was thinking about getting one of these. Might have to switch to one after today."

"I told no fewer than four people where I was going," Maggie said. "I even stopped and talked to the two men at the gas station that you did and told them I was looking for you. People will be coming after me."

"You're stalling," he said. "I would too, in your shoes. But you're lying and I'm in no hurry."

Annabelle groaned again. Maggie turned to her, but DJ aimed the Taser at her chest.

"Do you mind if I check on her, please?" Maggie said.

"I do mind. She got what she deserved. And now *I'm* the one in trouble for killing two women—which I never did!"

"Oh?" Maggie said lightly, trying to smile in order to disarm him, "Well, then you have nothing to worry about."

"Are you kidding? The way they hate Americans over here? I'll be lynched without trial."

"Our embassy would never allow that. If you're innocent, you're fine."

"I am totally innocent. Those two women got themselves killed, is what happened."

"They were both poisoned by a toxic mixture sprayed into their faces," Maggie said. "The coroner has ruled it wasn't suicide in either case."

"I didn't say suicide, did I? I said they got themselves killed."

"You're saying they deserved what happened to them."

"Well, it wasn't my fault. That's all I know."

"I'll bet you know more than that," Maggie said.

DJ looked at the Taser in his hand for a moment, aimed it at Maggie and then giggled.

"Well, actually I just might at that," he said. "I was at a bar our first night here hanging with one of the 'noses' after Karen pulled an early night. This guy was bragging about how chemists were the original inventors. He was so wasted he'd never remember talking to me if you asked him later. But he gave me an idea. So later when Viv wouldn't play nice, I did a little Yankee recon at the perfume lab, if you know what I mean."

DJ stood, crossing his ankles and leaning against the wall of the cave as if he were in his own living room.

Maggie remembered reading that psychopaths lacked remorse and took pleasure in inflicting pain. On the other hand, sociopaths were antisocial and liked to break the rules. She had no idea which one DJ was except he had to be at least one. She held her tongue in hopes that would encourage him to continue talking. In her experience, the extra time could only help her.

"I slipped into the guy's lab, and I found the very bottle he was talking about. I mean it was right there on the shelf, labeled and everything! Plus, there was nobody around! What rubes! Everyone was taking those famous two-hour lunches, you know? What losers! Anyway, I put it in my pocket thinking it would be just like Rohypnol, you know? I use it back home, no problem. It would just make her a little sleepy. So that night I pull little Vivvie behind the float for a little slap and tickle, you get me? And when she fought me, I sprayed it in her face. Nothing happened so I blasted her again and then holy crap! She started seizing and jerking and then just collapsed. You can't blame me for that!"

Maggie stared at him, trying not to let her revulsion show in her face.

"What about Capuccine?" she said. "Did you not mean to kill her too?"

He glowered at her.

"That was totally not my fault! She saw me coming out of the lab the day I took the stuff. I didn't give a rat's patootie at the time. But when the French girl died, I knew I couldn't have the old broad running around telling people what she saw."

"That makes it premeditated," Maggie said.

He shrugged. "Whatever you want to call it. It was her own fault."

Looking past DJ's shoulder Maggie could see that it was totally dark out now. If there was a chance that she could get Annabelle outside, they might be able to hide. She looked at Annabelle who was still not moving. Maggie felt a wave of despair.

There's no way I'm going to get her outside.

Her only chance was to stall for time, keep him talking, engage him until a miracle happened—or an opportunity she could take advantage of. It wasn't a safety net by any means but it was all she had.

"Can I ask, why the flower petals?" she asked.

"Are you serious? To make it look like someone else did it, what do you think? Pretty smart, huh?" He laughed. "You can ask anyone who knows me. Poetic, I ain't."

Maggie stared at him and let the implication of what he was saying sink in. Neither killing had had anything to do with stolen formulas. Nothing at all. They only had to do with the fact that this piece of work had made a play for Vivienne, and when she'd repulsed him, he had just tried again in his usual brutish way. She felt like throwing up.

"People know where I am," she said again, taking a step toward the cave entrance.

"I told you, I know that's BS," he said, aiming the Taser at her. "Don't go any further."

"The police know."

"The police don't care."

Suddenly Maggie felt a stab of panic as she realized that doing nothing was going to get her and Annabelle killed. Waiting to do this on DJ's timeline was going to end up with two bodies buried in shallow graves in the woods.

But she wasn't ready. She didn't know what the next step was or what a miracle would look like. She only knew that she couldn't let DJ decide what happened next.

"Oh, my God!" she shouted, looking over his shoulder. "They're here!"

The minute he turned, she launched herself at him, trying to grab for his hand, determined to sink her teeth into anything she could reach.

She never even got close.

He swirled around and elbowed her hard in the face. She tumbled to the ground, her face aflame with pain, stars spinning inside her head and clouding her vision. Gasping, she tried to sit up as she watched DJ walk over to her and aim the Taser at her chest.

And pull the trigger.

65

The pain was like nothing Maggie had ever felt before. Every muscle in her body locked into a series of inflexible, excruciating contractions as she rocked helplessly in its throes. Her body was frozen, her brain rattled in mind-numbing pain. She was so encompassed by the pain that when it finally ebbed, she was surprised to find herself laying on the ground, trembling with only the terrible memory of the jolt of electricity as it had coursed her body. That memory was enough to make her sit up and vomit down the front of her blouse.

DJ was talking, angrily. He was pacing and cursing.

"You're as bad as the others!" he shouted. "You made me do that! I didn't want to. You made me!"

Maggie flexed her fingers and limbs. Only seconds ago they had been vibrating, her legs quivering involuntarily. Now they almost felt normal.

"Look at you," DJ said as he walked over to her. "You've got sick all down the front of you."

He reached into her jacket, patting her pockets until he found what he was looking for.

The second Taser charge.

Maggie felt a thickening in her throat as hopelessness swept over her. She couldn't endure being shocked again. She *couldn't*. The very thought of it made her break out in a sweat. But once he loaded the Taser up, she knew he would use it on her again.

"Think you'll mind your manners now?" he said. "Think you'll know I'm not kidding around?"

"Can...we talk?" she gasped.

"*Now* you want to talk?" he said, jerking her hands together and pulling out a roll of duct tape. "Like hell."

Maggie knew that as soon as he bound her hands, it was over. The thought triggered a sudden explosion of desperation. Without thinking, she arched her back and swung her head forward as hard as she could, connecting her forehead with the soft cartilage of his nose.

As he twisted away, howling in fury and pain, she brought both hands up and grabbed his ears, drawing his face down to hers. She sank her teeth into his cheek, closing her eyes, and holding on with all her might.

He stood up with a roar, easily batting her away. She fell on one knee and instantly tried to crawl toward where she remembered seeing the rifle. She blinked sweat or blood out of her eyes and saw it still leaning against the wall.

DJ wrenched her to her feet by her waist, screaming obscenities, as he twisted her around to face him. Blood was pouring out of the raging wound on his cheek. His face was near hers, his eyes glistening with insane fury.

"I'll teach you! I'll teach you!" he screamed.

Suddenly, he took a step back and backhanded her. The blow exploded in her face, the force of it flinging her across the clearing, slamming her against the cave wall. She hit her head against it and slid to the ground.

Groaning, barely holding onto consciousness, her head throbbed in a vibrating agony. All at once, she felt the cave floor beneath her begin to crumble. She reached out in desperation to grab something to try to catch herself. Her hands flailed wildly to reach anything to keep from falling, but her hands met only air.

Rocks rattled down on top of her as she fell and then landed on a small ledge a few feet down from the cave floor.

"Where are you, you stupid cow?" DJ shouted. "You can't escape!"

Relief mixed with fear as Maggie got shakily to her feet. Her fingers throbbed with the fingernails she'd lost on the fall from the cave floor, her naked forearms scratched from the sharp stoneface of the cliff. She looked around in the dim light. She was on a small ledge, no bigger than a foot wide.

"Are you dead?" DJ shouted to her in the cave. "Did you just make my job a whole lot easier by killing yourself?"

Maggie tried to determine what direction—other than up—his voice was coming from. He'd loaded the Taser. He could easily reach her. Her legs began to shake until they could no longer hold her. She grabbed for a hanging nearby vine for support and dislodged a piece of stone that fell a very long way down before making a splash. Horrified, she slid to a kneeling position, and pressed her face into the cliff wall.

"Madame Dernier? Where are you?"

Maggie felt a fluttering of confusion at hearing the words. Why DJ would address her by her French name? And then the realization hit her.

Landry!

She snatched at a nearby tree root and pulled herself to her feet, her heart pounding in hope as her mind raced.

"I'm here!" she called out, realizing that her voice was only a whisper.

"Identify yourself!" Landry demanded. "Who are you and what are you doing here?"

Maggie pulled herself up to a foothold in the cliff wall a half foot from the edge. What she saw made her gasp. Detective Landry and DJ were facing each other. DJ aimed the Taser at Landry.

"I don't speak French," DJ said with a sneer. "And I can dig three holes as easy as one."

Maggie watched in horror as DJ shot Landry full in the chest from less than a foot away.

She cried out as Landry staggered and then dropped to his knees, his flashlight dropped from his hand and rolled off the cliff. Somewhere in the back of her mind, she heard it hit the ledge below her and then fall into the water.

"Where is that stupid gun?" DJ muttered as he tossed aside the now useless Taser.

Landry convulsed on the ground, helpless, as DJ went to the wall of the cave where the rifle was.

Maggie followed his movements, her own eyes searching desperately for the gun. Her mind raced as she tried to think. Should she hide? He could easily use a flashlight to see her clinging to the side of the cliff. Worse, he could easily reach down and grab her. With shaking hands, she lowered herself back down onto the ledge. It was no safer against a bullet but at least he couldn't reach her.

DJ cursed loudly and now Maggie began to hear things crashing around above her.

Her heart hammered in her chest.

He can't find the gun!

Hope surged inside her. She must have knocked the gun from its place when he slapped her over the cliff!

Fiercely, she shoved the sound of Landry's moaning and DJ's cursing to the back of her mind as she looked around the ledge, hoping against hope that the rifle might have fallen into the ravine with her. But there was nothing.

She listened to DJ continue to swear, now louder and angrier. The gun must have gone over the cliff. She grabbed another tree root and found the same toehold to pull herself up in order to peer over the lip of the cliff. Landry was lying twenty feet away. He wasn't convulsing but he was clearly impaired. One foot twitched spasmodically.

"Guess we're going to have to do this the hard way after all," DJ said.

He walked over to the detective on the ground and suddenly straddled his chest. Maggie shuddered as she watched in mounting horror as DJ grabbed Landry around the throat and began to strangle him.

66

The image of DJ sitting on Landry's chest throttling him to death would be one that would stay with her forever.

Maggie squeezed her eyes shut to blot out the terrible picture. Only the sounds of DJ's grunts filled the cave.

If there was ever a time to escape—if that was even possible—it was now while DJ was focused on killing the detective. Hating herself for using Landry's last moments as her desperate chance to escape, Maggie reached for another root higher up and searched frantically for another foothold. She didn't know how much longer a man could hold out who was being strangled by someone who outweighed him by fifty pounds.

She found another toehold and pulled herself up another six inches, her shoulders now clear of the cliff edge. She reached out again for something—anything—to help anchor herself and her hand hit the hard buttstock of the rifle, teetering at the cliff's rim.

A flair of agonizing despair shot through Maggie as her hand closed over the rifle stock. She couldn't pull herself up and hold the gun at the same time. She pulled it close to her chest and slid back down the cliff. When her foot touched onto the ledge again, she steadied herself against the cliff wall and screamed.

"Let him go! I've got the gun!"

Her words echoed throughout the cave. No one responded. Could he not hear her?

With fingers twitching and slick with sweat, she fumbled for the safety lock, turned and pressed her back against the stone wall of the ledge. She pointed the gun barrel straight up into the cave ceiling and fired.

The roar of the gunshot echoed around the cave. A thundering shower of rocks fell from the ceiling, raining down all around her, peppering her head in painful missiles. The noise was all-consuming, blotting out any possibility of hearing what was happening up above.

When the sound of the barrage subsided, Maggie became aware of movement up above.

Footsteps.

She ran her fingers over the rifle. Her heart was thundering in her chest. She gripped the rifle tightly, sweat squeezing out between her fingers. She wasn't familiar with this kind of rifle. She was afraid to open it up to check for more bullets. She glanced up at the cliff top. If DJ came for her and lay on his stomach, he could easily reach her. Or he could throw rocks at her until she fell, or lasso her with his rope—

She gulped down terrified breaths and felt her legs go weak.

Was there another bullet in the chamber? She glanced at the darkness below the ledge. A fall from here would be to the death.

Her legs began to tremble and she knew she couldn't stand much longer. All she could do was pray there was one more bullet in the chamber.

The rifle felt like it weighed twice what it had. She inhaled and when she exhaled, she lifted the gun, her arms trembling with the effort. She aimed it to a point over the cliff lip where she thought he would appear.

Even with the sound of her blood pounding in her ears, she could hear him coming, walking toward the ledge, the gravel crunching under his boots.

She whimpered in fear and anticipation.

If she was out of ammunition, he only had to lean down and grab the gun from her hands, then reload. She was trapped, nowhere to hide, nowhere to run.

She stood there, her arms shaking, the sweat pouring off her face, praying, and waiting for him. And when he appeared, she closed her eyes, making a final desperate request to God, and pulled the trigger.

67

Nothing happened.

Terror raced through her as Maggie pulled the trigger again and again. Each time she heard the deadly tell-tale click of an empty chamber. Panic crawled up her throat as she stared up at the figure standing over her from above.

"Are you trying to murder me too?" Landry yelped as he jumped back from the ledge. "Put the gun down!"

Maggie's arms sagged and the gun clattered to the ground and then over the ledge and into the abyss below.

She crumpled to her shaking knees and bowed her head. Thank God there'd been no more bullets. She would've shot Landry by accident!

Relief and exhaustion vied for dominance over her as she knelt on the ledge, shaking and spent. The last time she'd seen him, Landry had appeared practically dead. She couldn't imagine he was on his feet. Where was DJ?

"Are you hurt?" Landry called down to her.

Maggie shook her head.

"I asked you, are you—"

"No!" she said, loudly. "I'm sorry. I...I thought you were him."

"Get ready. I'm tossing down a rope. Don't shoot me with it."

It took Landry a few minutes to pull Maggie to the lip of the ledge where she lay quivering and exhausted. Even so, she had to stop herself from immediately asking him where DJ was. And by the time she did, she could see for herself.

DJ lay on his back, his hands cuffed in front of him. He wasn't moving.

"What...? How did you...?"

The last time Maggie saw DJ he was strangling the life out of a virtually senseless Landry.

How in the world...?

"Ricochet bullet," Landry said, winding up the rope. "Lucky you didn't shoot all four of us."

Maggie crawled over to where Annabelle lay, her eyes wide and alert. She pulled the young woman to a sitting position and started to untie her, but Annabelle cried out in pain.

"My arm," she gasped.

It looked broken but at least she was alive. Maggie looked around the cave and realized how dangerous it had been for all of them for her to fire the rifle into the air. She cringed at the thought of how truly horrendous it could all have turned out.

"How are you, Mademoiselle?" Landry asked Annabelle as he pulled out his phone. Before she could answer, he swore. "I can't get cell service in here." He turned to Maggie. "Are you okay while I step outside?"

"We're fine," Maggie said, astonished to realize it was true.

She turned back to Annabelle whose face was white with pain and shock.

"I can't believe you came," Annabelle said, her voice thick with tears. "He was going to kill me. How did you know it was him?"

"Long story," Maggie said. She glanced at DJ and saw him move.

"Listen, when Landry returns," Maggie said, "I'll go to my car. I've got some ibuprofen there."

"No, Maggie, don't leave me. Please." Annabelle winced in pain.

"Okay. I'm sure he's calling an ambulance for you. Just hang on."

Annabelle nodded and closed her eyes.

Maggie couldn't help asking, "How in the world did you end up with DJ?"

Annabelle opened her eyes and licked her dry lips.

"I ran into him as soon as I left your apartment," she said. "He said I looked familiar and then he said he knew someone who knew what happened to Vivienne."

It was a basic ruse and one anybody not emotionally embroiled in finding answers would ever have fallen for. But Annabelle was desperate. Plus—and unlike her sister—Annabelle had had a fairly high opinion of Americans before until her encounter with DJ.

"I can't believe how stupid I was," she moaned. "I actually got in his car. I remembered him, you know? He was the husband of the loud-mouthed woman in the La Nuit Est Belle tour. I thought he was harmless."

Maggie glanced at DJ. He was moaning. Landry had at least tied a sweater around his shoulder to staunch the blood flow.

"Do you think he'll die?" Annabelle asked.

"Probably not," Maggie said, before turning back to her. "Do you care?"

"Of course," Annabelle murmured, closing her eyes again.

"Well, that's to your credit," Maggie said. "You've kept your humanity and under the circumstances, a lot of people wouldn't have."

"He attacked me because I started asking him questions," Annabelle said. "I don't know how you and Grace do it."

"Well, we get attacked a lot too," Maggie admitted.

"I asked him—'*How did you know my sister? When did you see her last? Where were you the night she was killed?*'" She laughed. "No wonder he hit me on the head and stuffed me in his trunk!"

"I am so sorry that happened to you, Annabelle," Maggie said, squeezing the girl's hand. "But because of you we got Vivienne's killer."

Landry hurried through the cave entrance holding a lighted lantern, stopping first where DJ lay and roughly turning him over, to squawks of agony from the man.

"Maggie?" he called.

Surprised that he would call her by her first name, Maggie hurried over to him. He handed her a packet of pills and the lantern.

"Give Mademoiselle Curie these," he said. "They're stronger than Paracetamol."

Maggie took the pills from him but hesitated. At worst, Annabelle had a broken arm or dislocated shoulder. DJ had a bullet in him.

"Do you have enough?" she asked.

"For him?" Landry asked with a snort. "No. I can stop the bleeding and keep him alive until *l'auxiliaire médicaux* arrive. But pain relief is not a part of the concierge service."

Maggie couldn't help but smile. Before she turned back to Annabelle, Landry spoke again.

"Tell her the paramedics will set her arm when they come. I don't want to make it worse. Here. Give this to her, too." He handed Maggie a bottle of water.

"Detective Landry," Maggie said. "You figured it out on your own."

He snorted. "Is that supposed to be a compliment? *You* found Capuccine's killer. All I did was follow you."

Maggie was impressed. Not every man would be willing to admit that.

"But you did follow me," she said. "Without backup. That took guts."

"Please do not make me sorry I pulled you out of the *crevasse*, Madame Dernier. Go help Mademoiselle Curie."

Maggie went back to Annabelle with the meds, the lantern and the water which Annabelle swallowed gratefully. Maggie pulled off her jacket and folded it to put under Annabelle's head to try to make her more comfortable. Annabelle closed her eyes and Maggie watched her shoulders relax.

Once he was finished binding DJ's wound, Landry came over.

"How is she?" he said softly.

"She's going to be okay," Maggie said. "Thanks to you."

She saw his face tense as if trying not to be pleased at her praise. She imagined it had to feel pretty good to do the right thing after so many years of not bothering.

"How did you find us?" she asked.

"Basic detective work," he said evasively.

Maggie knew that couldn't possibly be the truth. They were out in the middle of nowhere. Nor could she imagine him following the same elusive breadcrumbs that she had. But for the moment, she was so grateful he was here that she'd didn't care how he'd found them.

"My men will be here soon," he said, sitting next to her. "I've called for two ambulances. I didn't think Mademoiselle Curie should have to share one with the man who killed her sister."

Maggie gave him a sharp look.

"It's true, is it not?" he asked. "And also Capuccine?"

Maggie nodded. "He said Capuccine saw him steal the poison that he used to kill Vivienne."

"Ah."

"I might have his confession on the recording app of my phone, if it's retrievable. I think it fell over the cliff."

"Never mind. We'll get another confession out of him during his interrogation."

Maggie didn't want to think of all the implications of what that might entail. She was feeling positively affectionate toward Landry and didn't want to spoil the mood.

He settled down next to Annabelle and ran a hand over his face. It was then that Maggie saw how harried he looked. The stress of the last few days had played out on his face.

"My men discovered a few things in the investigation of the fire at La Nuit Est Belle," he said.

"Like what?"

"Florent Monet accused his nose Mathys Tremblay of starting the fire and our arson specialists confirmed it was him."

Maggie had suspected as much.

"I think he is mentally distressed," she said.

Landry snorted. "Is that a defense?"

"Do you at least know why?"

"Not yet," he said.

"I guess this means Florent will get a sizable insurance payout," she said.

"Now that he's not a suspect in his factory's demolition?" He nodded. "I know him a little. We were once friends."

That surprised Maggie but not more than the fact that Landry was sharing the fact with her now.

"I think he might use the money to correct a few mistakes he made years ago when he started out."

"Sounds like a good idea," Maggie said.

"You are not very subtle, Madame," he said with an arched eyebrow.

"Sorry. It's just that I'm really very grateful that you came tonight. No matter *how* you knew where I was."

"Just doing my job," he said ironically, glancing at her as if expecting her to laugh.

"I know," Maggie said solemnly. "But still. Thanks."

He nodded, looking altogether, Maggie thought, extremely pleased with himself indeed.

68

The next morning, the sun was struggling to peek from behind the tall line of buildings facing the terrace café where Maggie and Grace had chosen to meet Annabelle for breakfast.

Annabelle was at the table waiting for them, her arm in a cast and sling. They all gingerly hugged in greeting.

The night before had been a dizzying blur of lights, ambulances, stretchers and police field interrogations. Maggie was allowed to ride to the hospital with Annabelle and from there accepted another ride from one of Landry's uniforms back to the Airbnb where Grace was waiting for her. They had silently greeted each other with a long hug before both falling into bed, too exhausted to process what had happened then.

Now as Maggie looked across the breakfast table at Annabelle, she thought the young woman should still be in the hospital. Her eyes looked haunted, but the young woman insisted she felt fine.

"I just can't believe how things turned out," she said, looking at them both with glassy eyes as she shifted uncomfortably in her sling.

"It turned out well," Maggie agreed. "But it might not have if DJ hadn't been desperate enough or stupid enough to kidnap you."

"Why in the world did he?" Grace asked as she buttered a piece of croissant. "Why not just leave Grasse while he was still free?"

Maggie nodded at Annabelle.

"Turns out, when he bumped into Annabelle, he was going for one last conquest, but when Annabelle started asking difficult questions about Vivienne, he panicked."

"I think the most bizarre aspect of this whole thing is how we never in a million years thought of DJ as the killer," Grace said. "I would've suspected Karen first."

The women were quiet for a moment thinking of Karen. Maggie had shared with them what she'd suspected about DJ's abuse of his wife.

"I feel sorry for her now," Grace said. "I thought she was just one more annoying tourist not bothering to learn basic French phrases and speaking too loudly. I wish I'd known what she was living with."

They ate in silence for a moment. The village street before them had slowly begun to come to life with the sun finally making a dramatic showing of shining onto the cobblestones and shop facades. The street's boutique and souvenir proprietors, clearly expecting a fine day, set out their postcard display racks, produce bins and fragrance products.

"How did Landry even find you?" Grace asked.

"I wondered about that," Maggie said, "until I checked the wheel well of my car and found the tracker he'd put there."

Maggie's rental car had been delivered to the apartment that morning. In all the excitement, the tracker was still in place.

"He was tracking you?" Annabelle asked with surprise.

"He should've dropped an air tag in my purse," Maggie said.

"I don't know why he put it on the car since I barely used it this trip."

"Probably wanted to make sure he knew when you left town," Grace said.

"Or maybe he just wasn't thinking," Maggie said. "I'm surprised he had the initiative to have me tracked in the first place. If you remember, he'd already hinted to me that he was having me followed. My guess is he heard from his dispatcher that I'd called, then he saw I was out in the middle of the countryside and decided to check it out."

"Without backup? Pretty brave."

"I know. A part of me thinks that something must have happened to prompt him to come after me without his men, but I don't suppose we'll ever know."

"He probably came alone because he didn't want to make a fool of himself to his men by driving out into the middle of nowhere for no good reason," Grace said.

"There's that, too," Maggie admitted.

"In any case," Annabelle said, "he did come, and he saved us."

"Seems to me *I* was the one who shot DJ and saved *him*," Maggie said with a laugh.

"*Accidentally* shot DJ," Grace pointed out, and then shivered. "It could've gone wrong in so many ways."

"Tell me about it."

"Do you have a report on DJ?"

"He had surgery last night. He's expected to make a full recovery."

"In prison, one presumes?"

"That's the plan," Maggie said as she spread strawberry jam on her croissant.

"So have we changed our opinion of Detective Landry?" Grace asked.

"No reason why we should," Maggie said. "We'll likely never see him again."

Maggie had spoken very little to Landry after his men showed up at the cave last night. But in the few exchanges she'd had with him during that time she'd noticed a definite change in his affect. Gone was the bullying, the arrogant posturing, the easy threats.

She didn't think it was so much the result of having had fifty thousand volts drilled into his chest from less than a foot away as it was a different kind of eye-opening. Maggie only had a hunch to support that but some of her best work were hunches. There had been good buried deep inside the man and when push came to shove, it had found its way to the surface. She really thought it was as simple as that.

One of Landry's men had found Maggie's phone—it hadn't gone over the cliff after all but only accidentally kicked to the perimeter of the cave. As Maggie had followed Annabelle's stretcher out of the cave, she'd called the number Landry had given her to hear that Grace had been released and was on her way back to the Airbnb in Grasse.

Landry had kept his promise. And while Maggie knew he was no Roger Bedard, he *had* stepped up when he was needed.

"You know, I didn't think much of it at the time," Grace said. "But I could swear DJ winked at me at some point during that first tour."

"That hardly makes him a psychopath," Maggie said teasingly. "It's more astonishing that you didn't think anything of it. You're so used to having that effect on men, so you didn't even register it."

"I *used* to be used to having that effect," Grace said, but Maggie could tell her confidence—while perhaps not back to her pre-Windsor days—had recovered since Jean-Luis's initial rejection of her two days ago.

"Jean-Luis tweeted this morning that he is going to sell Dix

Fleurs," Annabelle said. "It will likely be absorbed into one of the larger perfumeries." She paused. "His mother would be horrified."

"About a lot of things, I have no doubt," Grace said.

"Did I tell you that Monsieur Monet called me to ask if I would be interested in Vivienne's old job?" Annabelle asked.

Maggie's eyes widened in surprise. She was glad to hear that the two of them were going to get a chance to go forward after the terrible events of the last weekend.

"Does that sound like something you might like to do?" Grace asked.

Annabelle shrugged and then winced in pain.

"I don't know," she said. "I'm going to think about it. But honestly, I think I'm happiest on the farm. He also suggested it might help support the farm if I were to grow flowers for him."

"Now that's more like it!" Grace said. "I love the idea of that."

"Me, too," Annabelle said, a tear tracing down her cheek. "I wish Vivienne could have seen how it all turned out. I mean, it won't alter the change that's coming but maybe that's not all bad."

Maggie leaned across the table and patted her hand.

"I know she would have been so proud of what you've done for the family name," she said.

Annabelle sniffed as she fought unsuccessfully to stop the tears.

"I think so too," she said.

69

Maggie came home to Domaine St-Buvard to big hugs from Amelie as well as Jemmy and Luc. It had been a long time since Jemmy had thrown his arms around anyone. After what Laurent had told Maggie on the drive home, she was much less shocked than she might have been.

As for Luc, Maggie's relationship with him had always been a tad formal, no matter how much she wanted to get closer to him. He actually held her hand while Amelie held the other, as Jemmy and Laurent emptied the car of luggage, and walked with her back into the house.

Laurent had waited until they dropped Grace off at *Dormir* before telling her that Amelie had been naughty while she was gone, Luc wanted to bring a girl home for them to meet, and Jem was in a little bit of trouble.

Maggie stiffened at his words.

"What kind of trouble?" she'd asked, nervously fingering a gold necklace around her throat.

"He lost his job," Laurent said as he drove toward St-Buvard and their *mas*.

"Oh, Laurent. I was afraid it was something like that. But why come home? Is he thinking of looking for a job in France?"

"*Non*. He is here because he is unsure of what to do next."

"What do you mean?" Maggie felt a sliver of fear. "Why did he lose his job? I thought he loved it."

"He was fired after being arrested for driving under the influence."

The words sliced into Maggie's heart, and she gasped.

"Now, *chérie*, you must not fall apart when you see him, yes?"

"Oh, Laurent." Tears welled up in Maggie's eyes as she imagined her precious son spending a night in jail. "Why didn't he call us?"

"Shame," Laurent said. "He called Ben instead."

Maggie didn't love that but had to admit it made sense for Jem to call his uncle if he was in trouble. Ben was a lawyer in Atlanta. Maggie knew that the two of them occasionally got together. If Ben had stepped up to help Jem when he needed it, she wouldn't hold that against her brother. She had too many other things to hold against him.

"Does he have to go to court?" Maggie said.

"*Non*. He has lost his license for four months and will take a driving class when he gets back."

"Is that all? Then why did he lose his job?"

Laurent made a face.

"The daughter of his boss was with him in the car at the time."

Maggie forced herself to focus on the fact that Jem had learned an important lesson and that nobody had gotten hurt in the process. She didn't love that her brother hadn't picked up the phone to tell her what was going on. But she imagined that Jem had begged him not to.

Maggie took several long moments staring out the car window as they drove home.

"Do you think he has a drinking problem?" she asked finally.

Laurent shrugged.

"He swears not. He said he's never done anything like that before."

"I guess it's just as well that he never took to the winemaking business," Maggie said, looking out the window, her heart heavy in her chest.

"Jem is not in the business because he's uninterested," Laurent reminded her.

"Hasn't he been driving since he's been home?"

"We've had words about that. He's not driving on any continent now."

They drove in silence for a moment.

"He's worried what you'll say to him," Laurent said.

"Well, if he survived telling *you*, I'm sure he's not that worried about what I'll say." She turned to look at him. "Were you very hard on him?"

"*Oui*," Laurent said and left it that.

The next night, Maggie stood in the garden, surveying the long wooden farm table at Domaine St-Buvard. It had been set for an elegant dinner for the whole family, Grace and Danielle too, complete with crystal goblets, silverware, matching dishware set on a vintage linen tablecloth that Maggie had found years ago in a *brocante* in Marseilles.

Luc and Jem were both scheduled to fly back to the States the next morning. Luc to propose to his girl, and Jem to return to Atlanta to begin his job search—and to take the DUI class necessary to get his license back at the end of his four-month suspension.

Maggie's late-night discussion with him the night before

had been uncomfortable for both of them. He was ashamed, and it broke her heart to see him so. It reminded her of when he was a small boy. But she also felt sure he'd never drive intoxicated again and she was relieved he could learn that lesson now—with no harm done beyond the fine and an inconvenient period of time taking MARTA wherever he needed to go. She shook off a remnant shimmer of sadness that filtered through her. Tonight was not a night for rueful musings.

Tonight was a night for laughter and closeness, for connecting with family and enjoying being alive. Tonight was not for thinking about the fact that Mila was not here, or that Jemmy had some work to do, or that Grace had a painful decision to make that would impact more than just herself. Tonight was a time to focus on enjoying each other *now*, and trying not to wish for more.

From where she stood examining the table in the garden, there was an uninterrupted view of the vineyard, past the stone wall that enclosed Laurent's *potager*. It wasn't yet dark and seeing the long rows of vines as they snaked up the hillside in perfect order felt reassuring and comforting to Maggie.

She turned to look at Laurent who had materialized in the frame of the double doors leading into the house. He had prepared *haricots verts* from his garden, and potatoes Anna. He would also make his famous cognac Dijon cream sauce for the tiny grilled lamb chops.

Maggie had worried it would be too cold to eat outdoors—something they did almost every meal in the summer—but when Laurent got the braziers going at the two corners of their terrace, it was perfectly comfortable. Besides, she thought, she didn't have the heart to tell Amelie—who had set the table herself with the help of Luc and Jemmy—that it was too cold to eat outside.

"It looks lovely," she said to Laurent as he examined the table with a frown.

"Perhaps a few more candles," he said, turning to amend the situation immediately.

Maggie smiled. She was so glad to be home and surrounded by family once more. She reached for the glass of Aperol she'd been sipping.

Their little dog Nougat ran to where she stood and barked sharply once, letting her know that their guests had arrived. Maggie gave the beautiful table one last look before turning to go through the house to welcome her dearest friends.

The night was a relaxing and merry one, filled with laughter, dogs barking, and good food. After the main meal had been enjoyed, the boys cleared the table, and Laurent took Amelie upstairs to put her to bed so that Maggie could spend some time alone with Danielle and Grace.

Maggie was sorry not to be the one to put Amelie to bed, but she had many more nights ahead of her for that special pleasure. As she turned to her two friends, she caught sight of Jem and Luc through the French doors in the kitchen cleaning up and preparing the coffee. The scene was reassuring and so normal.

"So is next month good for the dinner with Bernard?" Danielle asked almost shyly.

"Of course," Maggie said. "Are you sure you don't want to have it at *Dormir*? After all, that's your territory. He'll see you in your natural habitat."

Danielle shook her head.

"I thought so at one time," she said, "but I think Domaine St-Buvard feels like neutral ground, you understand?"

Grace reached out and took Danielle's hand. Danielle didn't have to say it in words but as much as *Dormir* would always be home to her, it had once been her home with Eduard. Nobody could blame her if she didn't want to start her exciting new relationship off with the specter of her angry first husband in the background.

"I really like Bernard," Grace said to her. "We all do."

Danielle smiled, pleased and then cleared her throat to change the subject.

"So tell me more about your adventure in Grasse. It sounds like more than you bargained for."

"That's the truth," Grace said, shaking her head. "I still can't believe it all happened."

Getting the final details on the Grasse case had involved a few phone calls with Detective Landry earlier that day. Maggie found out that DJ Dixon was awaiting trial in a detention center near Nice, and that his request for extradition to the US had been denied.

"Did I tell you that Karen texted me that she has no hard feelings?" Maggie said.

Grace snorted. "You did her a favor!"

"She also said she's filing for divorce as soon as she was back home."

"Well, I'm glad to hear it," Grace said. "I can't believe how he treated her."

Maggie nodded although, truthfully none of them ever saw evidence of how he treated her. They'd only seen an obnoxious woman and her supposedly long-suffering husband.

"I was thinking that maybe I should call her," Maggie said.

"I wouldn't," Grace said.

"Really?" Maggie frowned.

"I'm sure she has a support system at home. You, my darling, would only remind her of what has to be a terrible time in her life."

"I suppose so."

"She might even think you were calling her to gloat," Danielle said.

"You're right," Maggie said with a sigh. "In the end, we're really mostly strangers."

"Except for the fact that you shot her husband," Grace added.

Maggie made a face. "Thanks, Grace."

"I was wondering if you ever found out why Monsieur Tremblay burned down the fragrance factory?" Danielle asked.

"Nervous breakdown, basically," Maggie said. "And possibly guilt."

"Guilt? About what?" Grace asked. "Wait! Was *he* the chemist who told DJ about the poison?"

"He was," Maggie said. "But he was too drunk to remember his conversation with DJ. I think his guilt was because he'd threatened Vivienne when she revealed that she'd stolen the *Mon Sang* formula. I think he felt that *he'd* caused her death because a part of him wished it."

"Well, I hope he gets the help he needs," Grace said.

"But why would a lethal poison even be in a perfume laboratory?" Danielle asked.

"It's not lethal in proper doses," Maggie said. "It's just a concoction meant to mix with other chemicals."

"That might be another reason he felt guilty," Danielle said shrewdly.

"How so?"

"He was clearly well aware of the substance's deadlier properties."

"Good point, Danielle," Grace said. She turned to Maggie. "If he was bragging about having invented the French version of Rohypnol, he was hardly innocent himself."

"I know. I guess I just feel sorry for him."

"Good thing you're not the prosecuting attorney," Grace said dryly.

A few minutes later, Jem and Luc brought out a tray with

coffee cups and a French press, the scent of the just-brewed coffee drifting deliciously into the cool night air. Behind them, Laurent came with Amelie in his arms and Maggie nearly laughed out loud. She could just imagine Amelie's stubbornness at refusing to miss out on all the fun. He handed the child to her, and Amelie immediately put her head on Maggie's shoulder and closed her eyes.

After a wonderful *bichon au citron* that Laurent had found at a new *patisserie* in Aix that morning, the boys once more cleared the table and Laurent took the now sleeping Amelie back up to her room.

"You've got a good life here, darling," Grace said as they watched Laurent carry the child into the house.

Maggie looked at her.

"You do too," she said, glancing at Danielle who was studying her empty coffee cup. "What's going on?"

Grace sighed.

"Windsor has decided to stay in Atlanta," she said. "He's renting a place there this week."

Maggie was torn between indignation and anger at Windsor for hurting Grace like this, and the creeping feeling that it was likely for the best.

"How's that going to work?" she said.

"I honestly don't know," Grace said. "I'm pretty sure it has nothing to do with anything except his wanting to be a part of Peoria's life."

"'Pretty sure'?" Maggie asked softly.

Grace shrugged and looked away.

"And that little unpleasantness that happened two years ago?" Maggie asked. "The one where he dodged a murder charge? You don't think that's at all pertinent?"

Grace winced.

"It might be," she admitted. "I wouldn't blame him if he looked at France with mixed feelings."

"Except *you're* here. And Phillippe and Zouzou."

"Zouzou's grown. She has a relationship with Windsor on her own which is mostly virtual anyway. She doesn't need him like Peoria does. As for Philippe, he's asked to live with his grandfather."

"What? No! What about school? And Kip? And his friends? What did you tell him?"

"I told him no. I have full custody of him. This isn't summer camp. He lives with me and Danielle and will do so until he leaves for college if I let him go then."

Maggie leaned over and took Grace's hand.

"I can't believe Windsor wants to leave. What about you and him?"

"That *is* the question, isn't it?"

Maggie scooted her chair over to Grace's and put an arm around her and Danielle did the same from her side.

"We're here for you," she murmured. "You know that."

"I do," she said, leaning her head on Maggie's.

Later, after Grace and Danielle had left, Laurent joined Maggie outside where he began feeding fat wood into the firepit. It was a cold night even for spring and the fire felt good. Maggie sat in one of the two Adirondack chairs and pulled a thick cashmere rug over her knees.

"Where are the boys?" she asked.

"Luc's upstairs talking on the phone to Charlotte. Jem is in his room."

There was a moment of silence.

"Is everything okay, Laurent?" she asked, regarding him.

He turned to look at her. "Of course." He took his seat next to hers and reached out for her hand. "Mila called," he said.

Maggie sat upright. "She did? When?" She looked around but she'd left her phone in the house.

"Ten minutes ago. I answered your phone when I came downstairs from putting Amelie down."

"What did she say? Is everything okay?"

"Everything is fine, *chérie*. Why don't you call her back later?"

Maggie eased back into her chair. It was six hours earlier in Atlanta. She smiled at the thought of talking with her daughter later before she went upstairs to bed.

"She said she's coming home for spring break after all," Laurent said casually, leaning over to jab a stick into the fire.

Maggie felt a surge of happiness at his words. "She is?"

Mila had thought she might go with a friend to the Florida Keys over spring break.

"I knew that would make you happy," Laurent said, turning to her. "Any interest now in telling me what really happened in Grasse?"

"Oh, Laurent, I already told you the main bits."

"Did you?"

She squeezed his hand and laughed.

"As much as you ever tell *me* about what you get up to," she said. "And aren't I all in one piece?"

He grunted and turned to look back into the fire.

"It all seems to be falling into place," she said. "I mean, except for Jemmy."

"*He* will fall into place, too, *chérie*," Laurent said. "It's just a bump in the road."

She thought about that for a moment.

"It's just that, nights like this with all of us together—and the promise of Mila coming home soon too—it just makes me feel that as long as we can keep them coming back and keep them knowing that we're always here for them no matter what life throws at them, everything will be okay."

"*Je sais, chérie*," Laurent said, leaning over and kissing her. *I know.*

And just like that, with the flames of the open grill crackling, its fragrant smoke drifting into the star-filled sky, all the problems of tomorrow were firmly pushed away into the land of the unknowable future.

Because tonight, right at this moment looking around at her world, Maggie knew that everything was exactly as it should be.

To follow more of Maggie's sleuthing and adventures, look for the release of *Murder in Monaco, Book 23 of the Maggie Newberry Mysteries!*

RECIPE FOR GRILLED PORK CHOPS WITH LAVENDER, THYME AND ROSEMARY

Cooking with flowers is always so very French, n'est-ce pas? Here's an aromatic and floral approach to pork chops that Laurent likes to do when he has the grill super hot and he's feeling a tad playful.

You'll need:

4 rib chops
2 tsp fresh thyme leaves, chopped
1 tsp fresh rosemary leaf, chopped
½ tsp dried lavender
1 tsp fresh ground black pepper
1 tsp kosher salt
3 garlic cloves, minced
Fresh juice of 1 lemon
2 TB extra virgin olive oil

1. Combine thyme, rosemary, lavender, pepper, salt, garlic, lemon juice, and olive oil. Put mixture into a large sealed plastic bag with the pork chops, making sure that chops are thoroughly covered by the mixture.

2. Let pork chops sit in mixture 1 to 2 hours at room temperature.

3. Place pork chops on hot barbecue grill with cover down and cook 4 to 5 minutes on each side until done.

4. Remove chops and serve.

ABOUT THE AUTHOR

USA TODAY Bestselling Author Susan Kiernan-Lewis is the author of *The Maggie Newberry Mysteries,* the post-apocalyptic thriller series *The Irish End Games, The Mia Kazmaroff Mysteries, The Stranded in Provence Mysteries,* and *The Claire Baskerville Mysteries.*

Visit www.susankiernanlewis.com or follow Author Susan Kiernan-Lewis on Facebook.

Printed in Great Britain
by Amazon